BAD GIRLS HAVE MORE FUN

Other Ellora's Cave Anthologies Available from Pocket Books

ON SANTA'S NAUGHTY LIST
by Shelby Reed, Lacey Alexander, & Melani Blazer

ASKING FOR IT
by Kit Tunstall, Joanna Wylde, & Elisa Adams

A HOT MAN IS THE BEST REVENGE
by Shiloh Walker, Beverly Havlir, & Delilah Devlin

NAUGHTY NIGHTS
by Charlene Teglia, Tawny Taylor, & Dawn Ryder

MIDNIGHT TREAT
by Sally Painter, Margaret L. Carter, & Shelley Munro

ROYAL BONDAGE
by Samantha Winston, Delilah Devlin, & Marianne LaCroix

MAGICAL SEDUCTION
by Cathryn Fox, Mandy M. Roth, & Anya Bast

GOOD GIRL SEEKS BAD RIDER
by Vonna Harper, Lena Matthews, & Ruth D. Kerce

ROAD TRIP TO PASSION
by Sahara Kelly, Lani Aames, & Vonna Harper

OVERTIME, UNDER HIM
by N. J. Walters, Susie Charles, & Jan Springer

GETTING WHAT SHE WANTS
by Diana Hunter, S. L. Carpenter, & Chris Tanglen

INSATIABLE
by Sherri L. King, Elizabeth Jewell, & S. L. Carpenter

HIS FANTASIES, HER DREAMS
by Sherri L. King, S. L. Carpenter, & Trista Ann Michaels

MASTER OF SECRET DESIRES
by S. L. Carpenter, Elizabeth Jewell, & Tawny Taylor

BEDTIME, PLAYTIME
by Jaid Black, Sherri L. King, & Ruth D. Kerce

HURTS SO GOOD
by Gail Faulkner, Lisa Renee Jones, & Sahara Kelly

LOVER FROM ANOTHER WORLD
by Rachel Carrington, Elizabeth Jewell, & Shiloh Walker

FEVER-HOT DREAMS
by Sherri L. King, Jaci Burton, & Samantha Winston

TAMING HIM
by Kimberly Dean, Summer Devon, & Michelle M. Pillow

ALL SHE WANTS
by Jaid Black, Dominique Adair, & Shiloh Walker

BAD GIRLS HAVE MORE FUN

Arianna Hart

Ann Vremont

Jan Springer

POCKET BOOKS

New York   London   Toronto   Sydney

Pocket Books
A Division of Simon & Schuster, Inc.
1230 Avenue of the Americas
New York, NY 10020

First Pocket Books trade paperback edition December 2008

POCKET and colophon are registered trademarks of Simon & Schuster, Inc.

For information about special discounts for bulk purchases, please contact Simon & Schuster Special Sales at 1-800-456-6798 or business@simonandschuster.com

Designed by Jamie Kerner Scott

Manufactured in the United States of America

10 9 8 7 6 5 4 3 2 1

Library of Congress Cataloging-in-Publication Data is available.

ISBN-13: 978-1-4165-7769-0
ISBN-10:   1-4165-7769-6

CONTENTS

CONVINCE ME

ARIANNA HART

This book is dedicated to my husband, who had to convince me to go on that first date with him. I'm so glad we decided to be more than "just friends."

I'd also like to thank all the people who work and volunteer to help abused women in shelters across the country. Leaving an abusive relationship is a near-impossible thing to do. Thank you all so much for providing places for women and their children to go to when they find the strength to make that decision.

Although the shelter in this story is fictitious, if you are interested in finding out more about battered women's shelters in your area, look in the yellow pages of your phone book under Domestic Violence or contact your local police department.

ONE

SAREENA'S EYES PRACTICALLY GLAZED over as the mayor droned on and on. She loved raising money for the battered women's shelter, but these charity dinners were beyond boring. The only thing that kept this one from being a total yawn fest was her seat assignment.

Eye candy at twelve o'clock sharp.

Officer Brogan Donahue had a polite smile on his face but it didn't reach those gorgeous blue eyes of his. They'd been working together on fund-raisers for months now and she hadn't wrangled so much as an invitation for a cup of coffee. He was unfailingly pleasant but distant.

That had to change.

They'd worked side by side remodeling the shelter and she'd flirted outrageously with him. A few times—usually when she was covered in paint or drywall dust—he'd let down his guard and flirted back. She'd thought she'd finally made some progress with him, only to have him slam those damn walls up as soon as they went their separate ways.

Every time she saw him she had to start from scratch, breaking down the barriers he placed between them. Boy, was he stubborn. But then again, so was she. If it was the last thing she did, she'd get him to take her out on a date.

A shiver of sexual hunger raced through her as she thought about how she'd like that date to end if she ever got the chance.

Better get those thoughts out of your head right now, girlie. Sareena glanced down to make sure her nipples weren't poking out under her emerald green silk sheath. She had to speak next and didn't need to put on a show for half of New York City's wealthiest citizens. With her luck there'd be a close-up of her "high beams" in the society section tomorrow morning. Or worse, a picture of her with a wet spot because she decided to forgo underwear tonight to avoid panty lines in the tight dress.

Being an heiress had its drawbacks.

"And now, it gives me great pleasure to introduce the woman of the hour, Ms. Sareena Wilton."

Sareena approached the podium as the polite applause died. After the mayor's never-ending speech the audience was probably more than ready to listen to someone who didn't say "as you well know" every other sentence.

"Thank you, Mr. Mayor. Good evening everyone. I hope you enjoyed your dinner and the entertainment provided by the Williams Jazz Ensemble. I promise I won't keep you much longer." It was already eleven-thirty and she really didn't want to be hanging around with the socialites come midnight. Then again, having a huge black cat stroll through the lobby of a five-star hotel would liven things up a little.

Now *that* would make the papers for sure.

"Domestic violence is one of the most vile of all societal ills. It doesn't discriminate by race, color or economics. Many women are at risk from murder by the very men who vowed to love and protect them. The city's shelters are in desperate need of provisions to help these women and their children find better, safer lives. Your contributions this evening will help make that possible. Mr. Stevenson, I'm thrilled to be able to present this check for twenty-five thousand dollars to the Phelps House of Brooklyn."

She paused and waited for the director of the Phelps House to make his way to the raised platform.

"Fucking bitch!"

Sareena's ultra-sensitive hearing picked up a disturbance in the lobby, even over the enthusiastic applause. The double doors in the back of the ballroom crashed open.

"I want my wife back!"

A burly man pushed his way through the crowd and charged toward the podium. "It's my God-given right to show her who's boss!"

No one moved to stop the raging lunatic as he knocked over anything in his path. Murder was in his eyes and it was directed at her. Fear sent adrenaline shooting through her bloodstream. Her hackles rose at the threat and her muscles bunched in preparation to change.

Not now!

She fought the pull of the moon and her survival instincts and managed to stay calm and upright at the podium. Barely.

The enraged man had made it halfway through the room before security caught up to him. Sareena relaxed slightly as they grabbed his arms and fought him to the floor. A flash of copper-bright hair snagged her attention and she realized Brogan had jumped into the fray as well. Her heart leapt into her throat as she watched him dodge a kick before he tackled the bull of a man.

"I don't care how much money you have! I'm gonna kill you! You have no right to keep a man from his wife. No right!"

The man continued to scream threats even as security dragged him out of the ballroom. Cameras flashed in her face and Sareena remembered she was still at the podium.

"Well, that wasn't part of tonight's festivities." A nervous twitter ran through the crowd. "As you can see, your continued support is desperately needed to prevent men such as him from continuing their abuse. Thank you all for your participation. Should you have any questions or wish to help further, Mr. Stevenson will be on hand to take additional donations. Thank you and good night."

Sareena's muscles trembled with the effort to hold back the change as she smiled brightly for the still snapping cameras. It was all she could do to walk calmly to the manager's office and not snarl at the microphones being shoved into her face.

"My secretary will have a statement for you all tomorrow. Right now I need to talk to the police. I'm sure you understand," she said as she walked through the mob of reporters surrounding her.

The media was a necessary evil. She needed them on her side to win additional support for the shelters, but right now she wanted them out of her face.

Brogan watched with a combination of lust and awe as Sareena Wilton crossed the lobby toward him. Not a sable hair was out of place and her long stride didn't show even the slightest of hitches.

Un-fucking-believable.

Some wife-beating motherfucker just threatened to kill her and she waltzed across the hotel in shoes that cost more than a car like nothing happened. Did nothing faze her? He'd seen her deal with snot-nosed kids, hysterical women and now an enraged man. Nothing disturbed the calm façade she presented to the world. He wondered what it would take for Sareena to lose her cool—for him to make her lose her cool.

Don't go there, Donahue. She ain't for you.

But damn, sometimes it was hard to remember that. He'd been attracted to her the first time he saw her playing peek-a-boo with a toddler at the shelter. She didn't look anything like the Wilton heiress with her hair in a ponytail and dressed in faded jeans and a denim work shirt.

Thank God he'd figured out who she was before he'd asked her out on a date. Wouldn't that have been a fucking joke? She'd have laughed her ass off at the idea of a cop asking her to the movies. Christ, didn't her family own a production company or something?

Not that he'd researched her or anything.

Her sultry fragrance reached him a second before she did and his cock twitched in his rented tux. Just because his head knew he didn't belong in the same room as her didn't mean his body agreed.

"Thank you, Brogan, for your timely intervention. I'd hate to think of what that man would have done if you hadn't stepped in."

"The hotel's security had him pretty much under control by the time I got there. I just made sure he wouldn't get up."

"Well, it was a lot more than any other man in there did, and don't think I didn't notice."

"I'm a cop, it's what I'm trained for." *And those other idiots wouldn't know how to stop a cab, forget a pissed-off bastard like that.*

A commotion in the foyer snapped the spell ensnaring Brogan's senses.

"I'll get you, bitch! You can't escape me!"

Security struggled to control the attacker and keep him away from Sareena. The man's eyes blazed with either extreme fury or insanity. It took two security guards and another cop to wrestle him out the door and away from Sareena.

"Ms. Wilton, do you want to press charges?" A beat cop stood off to the side as they finally hauled the handcuffed attacker out.

Brogan looked at Sareena to see if she was upset by the situation but she only glanced at her watch nervously.

"Is it something I can do tomorrow? I'm still a little shaken up now."

"Of course. Stop by the precinct house in the morning and we'll take care of it."

Brogan didn't think she looked shaken up at all. In fact, she looked more irritated than scared. His instinct said something was up, but he couldn't put a finger on what it was. Shouldn't she be a little more upset by all this? At least nervous for Christ's sake? She had amazing control over her emotions and once again he couldn't help but wonder what it would take to break that control.

Any other thoughts were sucked out of his brain along with the blood supply when Sareena pressed against him. That tempting perfume infused his senses as her silk-covered chest brushed his arm. Images of peeling that scrap of fabric off her inch by inch flashed in his brain as she reached up to give him a quick peck on the cheek.

"Thanks again, my hero. I'll have to come up with a suitable reward for your bravery."

Her smile reminded him of a cat with a bowl full of cream—hungry and looking forward to every taste.

He could think of several ways she could reward him but somehow he didn't think she'd go for them. Despite her flirting, he knew she didn't have any intention of following up on the promise her eyes made.

"Just doing my job."

"I think tonight you went above and beyond the call of duty."

She shot him another sultry glance from those mysterious cat eyes before she walked out of the hotel and into her waiting limo.

He shoved his hands in his pockets to hide his growing erection. Sareena Wilton might not be the typical trust fund party girl, but she was still way out of his league. The only thing they had in common was the volunteer work they did for the shelter. He was blue-collar all the way and she was diamonds and limos.

She'd flirted with him every time they'd worked together but he didn't take it seriously. With any other socialite he'd think they'd want to try slumming or use him as a boy toy or something. Sareena was different. She worked damn hard for the shelter, not only raising money with gigs like this but also cleaning and hauling supplies to the building.

Hell, she'd even helped paint and drywall. No, she definitely wasn't a pampered princess. She put her heart and soul into the shelter, not just her money. He respected that, even if he didn't really understand it.

There had to be a story there somewhere but she'd never

mentioned it and he was too polite to ask. Hell, polite had nothing to do with it. He didn't want her asking him why he worked so hard for the shelter, so he'd kept his mouth shut.

A disturbance on the sidewalk caught his attention and Brogan ran for the door. He hit the cement reaching for his gun, which wasn't holstered in his tux.

"Stop him!"

The squeal of brakes and a crunch of metal meeting metal echoed against the building. Two taxis were smashed together and several other cars were haphazardly scattered along the street.

"What the fuck happened?" Brogan asked the uniformed officer who dabbed at a cut on his mouth.

"Just as I was loading him into the back of the cruiser the bastard slammed his head into my face and took off."

"Didn't you have him cuffed?"

"Hell yeah, whatdaya think, I'm a rookie or something? His hands were cuffed behind his back. Shit, they still are. He took off across the street, scrambled over the cab and disappeared with the cuffs on tight."

"Why didn't you chase after him?"

"I was still picking myself up off the ground when he caused the two-car accident out there. Murphy was helping me get the bastard in the car. He almost got flattened by the cab when he ran after him."

"Well, call it in."

"No shit, Columbo."

Horns blared from all directions as the congestion spread up the block. Brogan didn't mind helping out but he was not directing traffic in a rented tux all night long. Good thing Sareena's limo pulled out before that bastard escaped.

Oh shit, Sareena!

This guy was after her in the first place. Brogan would bet his last dollar the jerk was heading uptown to finish what he started. Fuck. He cursed the tell-all book by a fading pop star that dished many of the city's celebrities' addresses. Including Sareena's. The guy shouldn't be able to get into her place but he shouldn't have been able to get away from two cops while handcuffed either.

He yanked his phone out and called dispatch to send a unit to cruise by her Central Park condo. But with this traffic snarl, if there wasn't a car in the neighborhood they'd never get there in time. His conscience prodded him. Did he take the chance that a patrol car would get there before the sick bastard that was after her? Not when he could walk there in five minutes.

His feet were moving before he even finished the thought. If he remembered correctly, she lived on Fifty-Seventh Street along Fifth and Sixth Avenue. He didn't know exactly which building was hers, but he could scope it out and keep his eyes peeled for an asshole wearing handcuffs.

Damn, he wished he had his gun with him. Central Park was freaking creepy at night. It always took him by surprise that there were so many trees in the middle of the city. When he was a kid he'd hide in there and pretend he was a jungle explorer. Right now he could almost believe there was a jungle hidden in the darkness out there.

The dress shoes pinched his toes something fierce. They weren't meant for walking five city blocks. Brogan leaned against a bench and considered taking the shoes off and going the rest of the way in his socks.

Probably not a good idea. If he had to take the assailant down he'd rather have a little protection, no matter how uncomfortable. He straightened as a limo ghosted by his spot on the bench. That couldn't be Sareena's limo, could it? She had to have made better time than that. He took a quick glance at his watch. It was midnight already.

Sure enough, Sareena stepped out of the back of the long black car with the help of the uniformed chauffer. He walked her to the front of the building where a doorman waited for her, then drove off.

Good, she'd be safe once she was in her building. These places were guarded better than Fort Knox.

He felt a little stupid for walking all the way here with some half-assed idea of protecting her. She had all the protection money could buy. Now he'd have to schlep all the way back to midtown just to get a cab. The chances of finding one on this street were slim to none.

With one last look at Sareena's sexy bod, Brogan prepared to head home.

A flash of movement caught his eye as he turned. Something rustled behind the decorative shrubbery. Before he could call out a warning, a man jumped out and attacked the doorman, knocking him to the ground with a sickening thud.

The wife beater had found Sareena!

Somehow he'd freed one hand from the cuffs and found a knife—a knife he now held to Sareena's throat.

Brogan sprinted forward, cursing the slippery shoes that

slowed him down. He was still a hundred yards away when a roar rent the night air.

He couldn't believe his eyes. A huge black cat stood where Sareena had been seconds before. The attacker couldn't believe it either but he wasn't as stunned. He took off across the street for Central Park. The cat—a jaguar or something—leapt after him with a growl. Where the hell had it come from? He swore a blue streak as he raced for the fence, intent on following the cat and the attacker, but a cry of distress stopped him.

"Sareena?" Brogan changed direction and ran back toward the building.

"Help me, please." The doorman lay on the sidewalk, blood dripping down his face from a gash on his temple.

Brogan growled in frustration. He wanted to go after the jaguar and the wife beater to make sure Sareena was safe, but he couldn't leave the doorman in this condition. He bit back another swear before yanking his cell phone out of his pocket yet again.

"Just hold on a little longer. Help is on the way." He searched the sidewalk for something he could use as a bandage to apply pressure to the wound but didn't see anything.

Except for a pile of glimmering green silk lying on the sidewalk next to a pair of skyscraper heels.

TWO

ES! POWER SURGED THROUGH her muscles as she jumped over the fence into Central Park. The Conservatory was *her* territory. It was about time the wife-beating bastard felt what it was like to run for his life.

Sareena lifted her nose and sifted through the scents coloring the air. Her ears perked up to listen for the smallest movement from her prey.

What was that? Over to the left, off the path. There. The foolish man had stripped off his shirt and hung it in a tree to try to distract her. Maybe if she was a regular jaguar that might work, but she retained her human thought processes and knew a decoy when she saw one.

She slunk into the trees, the soft loam cushioning her steps. The glow from the streetlights didn't reach this deep into the woods and she knew her black coat made her invisible to the human's weak eyesight.

He'd never know what hit him.

The part of her that was pure jungle cat let out a roar of triumph when she found her target. The chase was on. The man took off through the trees in a blind panic. His ragged breathing was as loud as thunder to her sensitive hearing and she could smell his sweat and his fear.

Good. Let him fear. He liked to pick on those weaker than him, now he was the weakling. And she'd make him pay dearly.

Her muscles bunched and stretched as she raced through the forest after her prey. It felt good to be free, to run through the night, to hunt. The knife wound on her neck stung a little but she ignored it. It was infinitely more satisfying to feel the wind on her coat and the dirt under her claws.

The wife beater had managed to trap himself against the fence on the far side of the Conservatory. He cried in fear as she slunk toward him. He wasn't issuing threats now.

"N-nice kitty."

Fat chance, asshole.

She prowled closer, her belly low to the ground, prepared to pounce on him if he jumped to the side. The feline part of her urged her to let him go just so she could chase him down again but she forced it back. She needed to deal with him quickly, not play with him all night. No matter how sweet his fear smelled or how much fun it would be to toy with him, it was time to be done with this.

He held the knife in front of him. Ha! As if that puny blade could stop her.

Inching closer, she allowed her fangs to show as a growl rumbled low in her chest.

"Fuck!"

He darted to the side and she was on him in a second. Her

roar echoed through the trees as she knocked him down and rolled with him. Sharp claws dug into his soft belly and she clamped her powerful jaws over his head.

Some last bit of sanity stopped her from instinctively crushing his skull like a wayward doe. Since she wasn't about to eat this piece of filth she couldn't kill him without bringing undue notice from the authorities. The police already wanted him. If they found him dead from a jaguar attack near her condo there'd be too many questions she couldn't answer.

It was almost painful to release him. Every cat instinct she possessed cried out for her to finish the kill. With a growl of frustration she sheathed her claws and released her prey. Her tail lashed with fury but she backed off.

Blood dripped down the man's torso but his entrails were still inside his abdomen, so she hadn't fatally wounded him. Too bad. The bastard didn't deserve to live.

He didn't look so damn dangerous now, cowering in fear and curled up into the fetal position. Maybe he'd remember what this felt like, to be afraid for his life, the next time he wanted to strike a woman.

Anger churned in her gut and she sprang away from him before she did something she'd regret.

No, she wouldn't regret killing him but it would cause problems for her she didn't need. She'd expend the fire in her blood on something else tonight.

Brogan called an ambulance to take care of the doorman and alerted dispatch *again* about the maniac on the loose. It pissed him off to no end that he couldn't go after the guy but he couldn't let the doorman bleed to death either.

While he waited for the rig and squad car to arrive, he picked up the green dress lying on the ground. Sareena's perfume wafted up from the delicate silk, leaving no doubt that it was indeed hers.

If this was her dress, where was Sareena? And what was she wearing?

A black fur pelt?

No fucking way. There was no way she had turned into a cat right in front of his eyes. Shit like that didn't happen in real life. And it especially didn't happen to millionaire heiresses whose lives were examined in the newspapers daily.

Sure, he'd heard the urban myths of alligators in the sewer system and escaped lions and shit like that, but that was just crap made up on the Internet. If someone actually turned into a big freaking cat, that would be all over the news. Or at least in the tabloids. Especially if it was about someone as famous as Sareena.

There had to be some sort of logical explanation for how she escaped from the wife beater and why her dress was left behind.

And he was going to camp out on her front doorstep until he got it.

The wail of sirens bounced off the buildings, alerting him to either the ambulance's or the police car's imminent arrival. Brogan suddenly remembered he still held Sareena's dress. He scooped up her shoes and wrapped them in the length of silk and stuck the bundle under a nearby bush. If she complained about the condition of her dress she could send him the cleaning bill.

The ambulance beat the police unit by a minute. Brogan stayed out of the way as the EMTs packed up their patient and got his information from the building supervisor. He gave the beat cop as much information about the suspect as he could. How hard would it be to identify a guy wearing half a handcuff anyway? Then again, this was New York.

He watched the cop go in pursuit and moved off to the side. Brogan's brain spun and he needed to pull his thoughts together. This whole night was unreal. First the attack at the banquet, then seeing a big black jungle cat appear before his eyes on Fifth Avenue. The only thing that could make it more surreal would be seeing . . .

Sareena emerging buck naked from the shadow of the building.

Brogan blinked his eyes to make sure it was really her creeping around the corner of the building.

Probably looking for a side entrance.

She moved damn silently. If he hadn't been standing off to the side he'd have never noticed her. With as much stealth as he could muster in dress shoes, Brogan retrieved her clothes and followed her.

When she reached an unmarked door on the side of the building, he stepped behind her and slammed his hand against the door before she could open it.

"Looking for these?"

"Brogan! I didn't know you were there."

"Obviously. Aren't you a little underdressed?"

She stood straight and proud and made no attempt to hide her nakedness. Even barefoot and windblown, she still had the carriage and demeanor of a queen. Brogan couldn't stop himself from visually exploring every creamy hill and valley. His cock tightened painfully and his blood caught fire.

Her skin was smooth and golden, every flawless inch of it was mouthwateringly perfect. He wanted to run his fingers over her body and see if it felt as silky as she looked. The tight curls between her luscious thighs begged for his touch and her dusky nipples pebbled in the cool night air. He could stare at her for hours, finding something new to admire with every glance, but she spoke and brought him back to reality.

"I'm perfectly dressed . . . for some activities." Her eyes glowed with heat, sparking a new blaze in his veins. "But I thank you for returning my dress. It's one of my favorites." She held out her hand imperiously.

"I don't think so. You have some explaining to do."

"Oh really?" She arched a brow. "I don't believe I owe you any explanations for my actions. Unless you're going to arrest me for indecent exposure."

"If you're not going to give me the answers I'm looking for, maybe I'll do some digging. And if that digging takes me to the newspapers and tabloids, oh well."

"You're blackmailing me?"

"I prefer to call it bargaining. You tell me what the hell is going on, and what happened to that bastard who attacked you, and maybe I'll keep my mouth shut."

Sareena tapped her foot while she eyed him up speculatively "Fine. But it'll take a while to fill you in on everything. Let me find the secret key I leave out here and we can continue this discussion in the comfort of my condo."

Brogan held back a groan as she bent over and searched the ground. Her sweet ass gleamed in the light of the full moon. It was all he could do to keep his hands to himself and not caress those luscious globes. He'd be lucky if he could find a working brain cell by the time she got around to explaining herself.

"Here it is." She held up a rusty key triumphantly and unlocked the door. "Unfortunately, I don't keep the key to my private elevator here so we'll have to take the stairs."

"I think I can handle it." His apartment was on the third floor and there were no elevators in the building. He was used to stairs.

As he followed her through the dimly lit stairway, he admired the curves of her backside. She was more muscular than he'd thought. Although, he'd never had much of a chance to examine her legs and ass this closely before. She'd always seemed trim and fit to him but now he realized she was all tightly coiled muscles and sinews.

Except for the most important areas. Those were nicely plump and soft.

Get your head out of your pants and pay attention. Brogan needed to focus on what she said, not on her body. He couldn't let his dick distract him from finding out what the hell happened tonight.

The memory of that bastard holding a knife to Sareena's throat deflated his erection. He pulled his eyes from her shapely legs and examined her throat for any sign of injury. It was hard to see anything in the murky light of the stairwell but he thought he detected a glimmer of blood marring her smooth skin.

"Hey, are you okay? Did he hurt you?"

"Nothing a shower won't cure."

When they reached the fifth floor she entered a code on the door and yanked it open. Brogan stepped in front of her before she could walk through.

"Hold on a second. Let me check to make sure the coast is

clear. Don't think you want your neighbors seeing you like this."

"Aren't you sweet? But don't worry. I own the entire floor."

She brushed by him and all he could do was follow. The door opened into a mudroom type area with a washer and dryer against one wall and coat hooks against the other. Brogan imagined this was probably the servants' entrance.

"You can leave my dress over there. Lana will take care of it on Monday."

"Sure. Who's Lana?"

"My housekeeper. She was my nanny when I was a child and I couldn't stand to let her go once I grew up. She refused to retire so I hired her as my housekeeper."

"And does she know about your penchant for running around naked?"

"Of course. If you'll excuse me, I'd like to take a shower before we get down to business discussions. Make yourself at home. I won't be long."

She strode through the little mudroom into a gleaming kitchen filled with stainless-steel appliances and shining chrome. Brogan trailed in her wake until he came to the enormous living room. He gasped and almost stumbled as he took the two steps into the sunken room.

"If you're hungry there should be something in the fridge. Help yourself to anything behind the bar," she called over her shoulder as she disappeared down a long hallway.

Brogan barely heard her, he was still trying to take in his surroundings. This one room was easily twice the size of his apartment. The freaking place had a cathedral ceiling complete with crystal chandelier. Enormous bay windows looked out over Central Park and a floor-to-ceiling entertainment center took up one whole wall.

So this was how the other half lived?

He kicked off his shoes so he wouldn't trail any dirt onto the thick white rug and crossed to the oak bar next to the entertainment center. A U-shaped leather couch that could seat his entire softball team took up a good section of the room. The image of Sareena's black hair spread over her naked body on the white cushions flashed into his brain.

Damn, he needed a beer. She probably didn't carry anything as pedestrian as that but he really needed something to cool the fire raging in his blood. If ever he thought the two of them could get together, seeing how she lived trashed that notion in a hurry.

She might flirt with him when she saw him but he knew now it meant less than nothing. What could she see in him? Christ, his mother was a cleaning lady and his father . . . best not to even think about what his father was.

Miracle of miracles, she had beer. It was even domestic. Hallelujah. He twisted off the top and downed half of it in one gulp. This was some place. The track lighting was dimmed but the full moon shone in through the huge windows and made the room glow.

The soft leather couch looked inviting but Brogan was afraid to sit on it. He probably had something on his pants from the wrestling match in the banquet room and would end up staining the white cushions.

"You don't have to sit here in the dark," Sareena said as she walked into the room.

Her hair was still damp and gleamed darkly against her white silk robe. She flicked on the overhead lights then crossed the room. Brogan smelled her perfume as she passed him and got a bottled water from the bar's refrigerator.

The shiny fabric of her robe clung to her curves and showed a hint of leg with every step she took. All the moisture in his mouth dried up as he watched her breasts shift freely under the scanty covering.

"Please sit. You might as well get comfortable while you interrogate me." She curled up in the corner of the couch and tucked her legs beneath her.

"You seem pretty relaxed after everything that's happened tonight." He joined her on the couch, sitting gingerly on the edge. This thing probably cost as much as his truck.

"I'm not prone to excess displays of emotion."

No shit. "So why is this asshole after you?"

"I don't even know who he is but I can hazard a guess. When he grabbed me by my front door he said, 'Tell me where my wife is or you'll take her place.' I can only believe he blames me for hiding his wife in one of the shelters."

"I figured that much out. But why blame you?"

"Maybe because I'm the most visual target?"

That made sense. The people who worked at battered women's shelters tended to keep a low profile to protect their clients.

"I'll buy that. Now tell me how you got away from him and why you were naked?"

"I don't suppose you'll believe I know an ancient form of martial arts?"

"I was there. I saw him with a knife to your throat one second and then you were gone the next." He didn't mention the part about seeing the big cat there. That was just too freaky.

"What else did you see?"

"Who's asking the questions here? Tell me what's going on, Sareena."

"How come the first time you don't call me Ms. Wilton has to be when you're angry?"

"Just answer the question."

"Why don't I show you instead? You won't believe me otherwise."

She uncurled from the sofa and let the robe slip from her shoulders. Brogan's cock stirred to life yet again.

"Not that I don't appreciate the show but this isn't telling me anything other than you have a beautiful body."

She smiled slyly and closed her eyes. Her muscles shifted and writhed beneath her skin and he swore he saw her bones move. Seconds later, a gigantic black jaguar stood where Sareena had just been.

"What the fuck?" Brogan jumped to his feet, knocking his half-empty beer bottle over. "Sareena?"

The jungle cat gave a sinuous stretch then padded lazily across to him. It nudged its head against his leg as if waiting to be petted.

"Is that really you in there?"

Emerald green eyes flashed at him as the cat let out a deep purr.

"Holy Mother of God! That is you." Brogan collapsed on the couch, stunned.

He'd seen the cat before but didn't believe his eyes. Now

there was no denying it. Sareena Wilton had turned into a jaguar right in front of him.

"Shit. What are you, some sort of werewolf—err, werecat?"

Sareena rubbed against his knee before hopping onto the couch. Ropey muscles rippled under the glossy coat and moments later Sareena—the woman—sat next to him.

"I'm a *jaguatium*, a shapeshifter."

"Are there more of you?" His hands shook as he straightened his fallen beer. It was almost impossible to keep his eyes on her face and not on her naked body but he tried damn hard.

"Lots. There are clans scattered all over the world. My family is in the United States mostly, and all of us can shift. Some better than others."

"I didn't realize there were degrees to this sort of thing." Was he really having this conversation?

"Oh yes. Some shifters can only change when the moon is full and once changed can't turn back until daybreak. Others can shift at any time but the effort is extraordinary. Some can barely change at all. Everyone is different."

"And you?"

"I can shift at any time and can go back and forth at will. Although it's easier on nights like tonight when the moon is full. If I change too often it takes a lot out of me though."

"So you can control when you turn?"

"Pretty much."

"Pretty much? You mean sometimes you *can't* control it?" Brogan's muscles tensed in nervous reaction.

Sareena sighed and moved off the couch. She picked up her robe and slipped it back on. "During the full moon it's more difficult for me to keep my cat in check, which is why I usually avoid staying out past midnight during that time."

"I can't believe this. If I didn't just see it, I *wouldn't* believe it. You're a millionaire fucking heiress and you turn into a cat."

"Believe it." She got another beer from behind the bar and handed it to him.

Brogan drank half of it without even realizing it. A few strands of short black hair lay on the white carpet and he couldn't seem to take his eyes off them.

"So are you going to keep my secret? Or are you going to go to the tabloids?"

Anger shook him out of his daze. "What do I look like to you? Some sleazeoid gold digger?"

"It doesn't matter what I *think*. I need to know you won't betray me. If it were made public that I'm a *jaguatium* scientists would want to study me. They'd capture my people and lock us in cages. Or worse yet, put us on display like some freak show."

"How many of you are there?"

"I don't have an exact number. My clan is spread out between the States and Europe. We're not like werewolves who run in packs. We mostly go our own ways except for the occasional family gathering or business meeting. There are more *jaguatium* in Asia and I'm sure there are some other shifters here that I don't know about. We don't exactly broadcast our presence."

"Are they all wealthy like you?"

Sareena gathered some paper towels and blotted up the spilt beer. "Lana's going to have a fit if this stains. It's bad enough I had to change in here and there'll be cat hair over everything. If she smells beer on the rug she'll kill me."

"Isn't she your housekeeper?"

"Only in the sense that I pay her. She's more like my mother than an employee. But to answer your previous question, no, we're not all wealthy. Although it helps. Money buys silence and loyalty. Very few not of the blood know about us."

"Who else knows you're a shapeshifter?"

"Only Lana, her husband Sanders and now you."

"Don't forget the guy who attacked you."

Guarding a secret this big was an enormous responsibility. It implied a level of trust that he wasn't sure they had yet. What if he screwed up?

"Isn't it dangerous for you to be in the public eye so much? I mean, whenever you go out there's cameras following you. Aren't you afraid someone will catch you in the act?"

"There's always that worry but I take precautions. Tonight, for instance, I had another limo waiting for me on a side street. The car I got into at the hotel went off to a club in the Village while my real ride circled around before coming here."

"Pretty slick." So that was why he beat her back here.

"I'm very careful when it's a matter of life and death."

"Then why do the work for the shelters? That puts you in the public eye even more. I mean, every time you do a function like tonight, during a full moon, isn't that a risk?"

"Some risks are worth taking. Protecting abused women is important to me and I'm willing to chance my safety in order to help them." Her eyes glittered with emotion.

Oh yeah, there was a story here.

"What happened to the bastard who attacked you? Did you kill him?"

"Unfortunately, no. I thought it might look a tad suspicious if the police found him with a crushed skull and his intestines hanging out."

"So he could come back to attack you. Or worse, he could go to the tabloids and tell them how you turned into a jaguar."

"Perhaps, but would anyone believe him? It would be one thing if a respected officer of the law came forward and said that Sareena Wilton was a shapeshifter. It's a totally different story if the man who attacked me in full view of several reporters claimed I became a cat."

"So why do you believe I won't say anything?"

Her fingers toyed with the edge of her robe where it made a V between her breasts. The blood roared in his ears in its rush to reach his cock as her long legs stretched out along the cushions just inches from him. Sweat dripped down his back and the collar of his fancy shirt felt way too tight.

"I guess I'll just have to convince you it's in your best interests to keep quiet."

THREE

AREENA'S NIPPLES TIGHTENED AS Brogan's eyes zeroed in on her drifting hands. She'd wanted him in
her bed for a long time but he'd been too aware of
their different income brackets. Maybe now that he had some
leverage over her he'd be willing to overlook the disparity in their
bank accounts.

The thought of him having leverage over her in bed made
cream flood her pussy and her body heat. Shifting always made
her hot and needy but smelling Brogan's arousal pushed her further than usual. How wonderful would it be to actually make
love to someone and not have to worry about revealing her
secret?

No, how wonderful would it be to finally make love with Brogan? His honest face and boy-next-door good looks had captured
her attention from the start but it was that hint of danger about
him that hooked her but good. He might look like Opie but a serious bad boy lurked behind those beautiful blue eyes.

It was that hint of bad boy that she was hoping to bring out
now. Granted, she wanted to make sure he wouldn't tell the world

about her, but she knew she didn't have to ply him with sex to ensure his silence.

But oh how she wanted to.

Brogan polished off the rest of his beer and toyed with the empty bottle. He looked flushed and slightly nervous and couldn't keep his eyes off her chest.

Good.

"I can't thank you enough for taking care of that man during the banquet. If he had managed to attack me I don't know if I could have kept myself from changing. The survival instinct is strong, especially during the full moon."

"I didn't do much, security already had him by the time I got there." He loosened his bow tie and unbuttoned his collar.

"I still think you deserve the reward I promised you earlier." She slid across the couch to him and unfastened his shirt the rest of the way.

His chest had only a sprinkling of light hair across his muscular pecs. Her pussy lips swelled as she scented his increased arousal. A glance down showed his cock pushing at the fabric of his pants. Her heart beat faster and her breathing hitched.

A shiver of anticipation raced down her spine as his masculine scent drifted through her sensitive nostrils. Finally, she could explore his body like she'd wanted to for months. Every time he'd helped out at the shelter she'd wanted to see what he hid under his jeans and tight T-shirt. She'd seen his muscles ripple as he'd swung a hammer and wanted to feel them bunch and move against her. Now she could.

Her fingers trembled with lust as she trailed her fingers down his torso.

"You don't need to do this to keep me quiet," he said as she reached for the snap of his pants.

"I know. But I want to."

Oh God how she wanted to.

Sareena knelt between his legs and worked his zipper down. When his cock sprung out of his boxers she let out a purr of anticipation. He was thick and hard, waiting for her touch.

"I've wanted to do this since the first day I saw you."

Her hand shook as she grasped his cock. It felt like silk over steel. The texture was soft and smooth but his shaft was oh so very hard. He was so hot and full it made her mouth water. Licking her lips, she blew a stream of warm air over his pulsing tip. His groan was music to her ears but she was far from done with him. She wrapped her lips around the head of his cock and drew the tip into her mouth. He tasted salty and wonderful.

"Holy shit," he gasped as she drew him the rest of the way in.

His hands clawed at the couch as she cupped his balls and slid her tongue along his length. She loved the taste as she pulled him deeper into her mouth.

Fire raced through her as she continued to make love to his cock. Her breasts grew heavy with need and the feel of the silk sliding over them made her nipples tingle. His tortured breathing grew more labored and she knew he fought to hold back his orgasm.

Not for long. She'd wanted to touch him like this forever. She'd dreamed for months of sucking his cock and stroking him.

The reality was so much better than her fantasies.

She hummed in pleasure as she felt his balls tighten in preparation.

"I'm going to come." He threaded his fingers in her hair and tugged, as if to pull her off before he exploded in her mouth.

No way. Sareena sucked harder, wanting to taste his essence.

A harsh shout tore through him as he arched off the couch in pleasure. She lapped up every drop of fluid, loving the weak quivers each touch set off. Her heart beat faster as she watched him collapse against the cushions. His shirt was undone but still on and his cock lay slightly erect.

"That was . . . indescribable." He looked at her lazily through half-closed eyes.

"My pleasure." She stood and crossed to the fridge, feeling his eyes on her every step of the way. "Do you want another beer?"

"No thanks. I'll take a water if you're getting one."

Sareena grabbed two bottles of water and headed back to the couch. He'd made no move to cover himself and she shivered with desire at his rumpled appearance. Her pulse raced at the thought of exploring his muscles and feeling them over her. She took a big gulp of water to cool down. He didn't need to be attacked ten seconds after he'd come.

Screw it.

Slipping off the robe, she tossed it to the side before straddling his lap. "I know you need some recovery time but I've waited so long to get you here, I just can't keep my hands off you." She pushed his shirt and jacket off and ran her nails down his bare chest.

"I know that feeling."

He cupped her breasts and tweaked her nipples with his thumbs. Searing heat spread from his fingers to her core.

"What took you so long? I made it pretty clear I was interested in you."

"I didn't know if you were serious or playing games. We don't exactly travel in the same circles."

He placed nibbling kisses along the column of her throat. Shivers of lust made her tremble.

"I don't mind playing games but my attraction to you has always been a hundred percent serious." She could feel his cock stirring under her pussy and need raced through her. Her hips rocked against him in mute supplication.

"How far is it to your bedroom?" His hands drifted over her ribs and across her torso.

When his fingers reached her ass and squeezed, she thought she'd die if she had to wait any longer. "Too far."

She rolled off his lap and pulled him on top of her. The couch was as wide as a twin bed and twice as long. She thanked the stars she'd gone against Lana's advice and bought it.

Brogan pushed his pants off and slid between her thighs. "Do you have any protection?" he asked as he nuzzled her breast.

"Somewhere. I don't have many occasions to use it so it's not handy." She gasped as he drew her nipple between his lips and sucked hard.

"Good thing I have a spare in my wallet."

"I always knew you were a Boy Scout."

"Honey, nothing could prepare me for tonight."

A brief flash of worry tried to fight its way through the fog of her desire. Would he regret this in the morning?

Brogan took a sip of water then drew her nipple into his mouth. The coolness flooded her burning tip and sent bolts of need straight to her pussy. She rocked her hips against him to ease the ache but the contact only made it worse. Sunbursts of desire grew in her core, scorching every cell in her body.

Morning was a long way off. She'd worry about regrets later.

As he swallowed, he tugged her nipple harder and she whimpered in need. Brogan trailed his fingers lightly across her heaving chest and down her stomach. Fire trailed in his wake as he slowly drew closer to where she wanted him. Too slowly. She was going to die if he didn't reach her clit soon.

Sweat dripped down her face as she bit her tongue to keep from begging. At last he slipped his hand through her curls and caressed her slick lips with one finger. It felt good but not good enough. She shifted her hips to get him where she wanted but he only laughed. It took eons before he drifted lower. He teased her swollen nub, shooting hot sparks across her body.

"You have the softest skin. It's like satin under me." His tongue speared her belly button and swirled around a bit before he moved on. "I can't wait to feel your softest spots surrounding me, squeezing me."

Sareena's inner muscles clenched as he slipped a finger into her. He slowly drew the digit in and out, teasing her with a preview of what was to come. Tingles rushed through her bloodstream like champagne, fizzing faster and faster as she felt his face brush against her thigh.

Please God, let him hurry. She couldn't hold on much longer.

Her legs trembled as he nuzzled the crease of her pelvis. She felt his hot breath against her pussy and whimpered when he moved away from it to fondle the back of her bent knee. Sareena's head whipped side to side against the leather cushions.

Her body burned with need yet Brogan took his time nipping and licking every inch of her skin. Every inch—except for the ones she really wanted.

"Do you know how often I dreamed of feeling these long, gorgeous legs around me?"

"Do you know how often I wanted them around you? You've proved to be a most elusive prey."

"All good things are worth waiting for." Blazing blue eyes stared up at her before he lowered his head.

His lips captured her desperate clit and sucked it into the warm cavern of his mouth. Sareena practically shot off the couch as his tongue stroked her over-sensitized nubbin. A scream tore from her as the wave of her orgasm crested.

Spasms rocked her body but Brogan didn't stop the exquisite torture. He stroked her G-spot slowly while licking her clit.

"Stop. I can't take it anymore." Sareena's hips bucked as another delicious quiver shook her to the core.

"But I don't want to stop. I want to bring you over again and again. I want to take you in so many different ways you'll come just thinking about it. If I have my way, you'll be spasming into next week."

His sexy tenor rumbled through her. Sareena felt another orgasm build just from the vibrations of his voice next to her pussy.

She wanted to come back with a snappy retort but her brain had ceased functioning. Her entire focus was on Brogan's lips and tongue on her pussy, his finger inside her channel and his body between her legs. The force of her pleasure grew until she couldn't take it anymore and shuddered to completion.

Vaguely she realized he'd grabbed the condom but she was

still too busy shooting to the stars to pay attention to his actions. At least until he knelt between her spread legs and pulled her hips snug to his. She could feel the blunt tip of his cock probing her moist entrance and licked her lips in anticipation.

"Look at me, Sareena. I want to see those beautiful cat eyes of yours when I make you mine."

It was a Herculean effort to raise her eyelids but she managed it. Brogan's blue eyes stared at her with an intensity that stunned her. His muscled chest gleamed with sweat and his pulse throbbed visibly in his neck.

Slowly, he pushed his way into her creamy pussy. His steely hardness stretched and filled her. Sareena raised her hips higher to get more of him in.

With a groan he slid in to the hilt. Brogan lay still for a moment, letting her get used to his size. Sareena felt him along every cell of her channel. Her inner muscles wrapped around his cock and pulled him even deeper.

There was something so very right about having Brogan in her home and in her body. She wanted to keep him there forever and almost sobbed when he began to pull out.

"Easy, sweetheart. I'm not going far." He drew back slightly then slammed in again. Every glide of his cock spiraled her higher.

Sareena, so used to being in control, could only lay back and revel in the sensations rolling over her. The sheer pleasure of Brogan's skin touching hers had reduced her brain to mush.

"Look at us," he ordered when her eyes closed again.

Sareena glanced down to where their bodies joined. Brogan's light skin rubbed against her darker tones as his cock disappeared and withdrew from her pussy. The scent of their lovemaking drifted through her nostrils, musky and hot.

She was drowning in sensations. The taste of him remained on her lips, his scent filled her mind, his touch drove her to madness and the sounds of their bodies straining to attain the highest pleasure was too much for her to resist. Sareena pulled him on top of her and dug her nails into his back as yet another tidal wave of pleasure swamped her.

Brogan's heart raced and his cock quivered with aftershocks. He'd felt that orgasm down to his toes and back up again. It was like every atom of his body had come and was now basking in the afterglow. Sareena lay soft and still beneath him. Too still. If he couldn't feel her pulse pounding as hard as his own he'd think she was dead.

He lifted his upper body off her to keep from crushing her. "You okay, sweetheart?" Her cheeks were flushed and sweat had made the hair along her face curl.

"I'm not sure. When I can feel my extremities again I'll let you know."

"Then I won't bother to ask if it was good for you."

"If it got any better I wouldn't be able to walk."

Brogan slid out of her warm body with a shudder of pleasure. As quickly and unobtrusively as he could, he disposed of the condom in a tissue then returned to the couch. Sareena's beautiful hair and golden-toned complexion were a stark contrast to the white cushions. She didn't appear the least bit embarrassed to be naked while he stared at her.

He couldn't keep his eyes off her. She'd cast a spell over him and he wanted to do nothing more than touch, taste and look at her for hours. Her breasts were rosy from his kisses and her hips and thighs were lush and ripe. The subtle, sexy perfume that was such a part of her mingled with the scent of their lovemaking and did nothing to help slow down his pulse.

It was well after midnight and he had to be to work early in the morning but he couldn't care less. He'd gladly spend every waking moment worshiping the very pores of her skin.

Bending over, he scooped her off the couch and cradled her in his arms. "I hear walking is overrated anyway. Where's your bedroom?"

Sareena let out a purr of contentment and nuzzled his neck. "I like how you think, Officer Donahue. Now I'm even more upset it took me so long to get you in my clutches." She curled her fingers into claws and raked his chest lightly.

"I'm making up for lost time. The bedroom?"

"Down the hall, last door on the left."

With every step he took over the plush carpet her body rubbed against his, reminding him of what it felt like to have her under him. The hallway seemed to stretch for miles as he hurried to get to the bedroom.

"How big is this freaking place anyway? If your bedroom's much farther I'm not going to make it."

"Umm." She licked the hollow over his collarbone. "I think it's nine thousand square feet, give or take. But most of that is the gym and pool. My bedroom isn't much farther."

Nine thousand square feet? His entire neighborhood wasn't nine thousand freaking square feet. "You have a gym and a pool in your apartment?"

"Pretentious, isn't it?"

"I wouldn't think a cat would have much need for an indoor pool."

"Actually, jaguars love water. If you think you can handle it, I'll take you for a swim sometime."

"Later. Much later." Brogan captured her lips with a kiss to tide him over until he could find her damn bedroom.

The differences in their lifestyles were as wide as the Grand Canyon. At least when he was touching her, the disparities didn't seem so bad.

At last, he made it to the bedroom. Light from the full moon shone down through the skylights onto an acre-wide bed. A black satin comforter covered the mammoth piece of furniture and red, black and white pillows lay piled against the headboard.

He was too preoccupied with picturing Sareena spread out on there to pay attention to the rest of the room but he vaguely noticed a bathroom off to the left and a door that must lead to a closet on the right.

Brogan laid her down amongst the pillows and admired the picture she made in all her naked glory. "I'm going to dream about this for years to come."

Sareena knelt on the bed and pulled him down to her. "I'll give you something much better to dream about."

With a strength that surprised him she flipped him on his back so he now lay across the silky pillows.

"Stay here, I'll be right back."

"Honey, I'm not going anywhere."

A jolt of heat slammed him in the gut when she tossed a sultry smile over her shoulder. She scampered across the bed to what looked like a built-in closet on the other side of the room. It was actually a refrigerator, and the light from it caressed the curves of her breasts and ass.

When she bent over to fumble around for something, Brogan felt his cock twitch with desire. Unreal. He'd come twice and already he was gearing up to pounce on her again. What the hell had gotten into him? Had someone slipped an aphrodisiac into his dinner?

Sareena closed the refrigerator door with her hip and walked toward the bed. Even with her arms full of containers she moved with power and grace. His heart flipped over in his chest as he watched her approach him, her slanted eyes gleaming with satisfaction.

"Lana must know something I don't, because she stocked my private stash before she left tonight."

"Oh really? And what did the ever-resourceful Lana pack for you?"

"If I tell you, it'll ruin the surprise. Just lie back and enjoy."

"It'll be tough but I think I'm up to the challenge."

She placed the items on the nightstand and pulled a few more things out of a drawer before crawling on the bed.

"So, Officer Donahue, how do you feel about handcuffs?"

Her smile sent a thrill straight to his groin. A pair of red, fuzzy handcuffs dangled from her elegant fingers. Anticipation and excitement snaked down his spine.

"Only if I get to return the favor."

"But you get to handcuff people all the time," she pouted but her eyes gleamed. "I've never had a chance to use these before."

Wasn't that interesting? She had a kinky side but hadn't done anything about it. Considering how tightly controlled she was that wasn't a big surprise. What shocked him was that she trusted him enough to explore her sexual fantasies with him. Could he convince her to trust him further?

"I'll make it worth your while."

She appeared to think for a minute before smiling at him. "Okay, but I get to cuff you first."

"Go right ahead." He held out his wrists.

As she leaned over to secure his hands above his head, Brogan couldn't help but swipe his tongue along her pointed nipple. A shudder shook her body and he hid a smile. She might think that by cuffing him she was in control but he could do a hell of a lot without using his hands.

"You're a naughty boy," she said but didn't move away.

He drew her luscious tip into his mouth and bit it gently before laving it to take away the sting. Sareena trembled and finally pulled back. Her breathing had increased and her eyelids lowered partway.

"You look like the innocent boy next door but you sure hide an evil streak behind that guileless face." She grabbed a few more things and put them in easy reach before moving between his legs.

"I have multiple layers." He watched as she clicked a remote and soft bluesy music drifted through unseen speakers.

"And I plan on uncovering several of them tonight."

Brogan's pulse raced as she knelt between his thighs and shook her hair back over her shoulders. The moonlight kissed her full breasts and made her look like a goddess come down to Earth.

"I hope you like strawberries," she said in a throaty whisper.

She took one of the juicy berries from a bowl next to her and bit it in half. Staring him right in the eye, as if daring him to look away, she trailed the sweet fruit down her sternum and under the curve of her breast.

Searing heat filled him as he watched the circular path she made over her luscious mound and then around her nipple. When she finished one creamy globe, she took another bite of the strawberry and traced her other breast.

"I think they've become my favorite fruit."

Sareena said nothing but a sly smile crossed her beautiful face. Her skin glistened with sticky juice and he couldn't wait to lick it off her. His mouth watered for a taste of her sweet skin.

The smoky music surrounded them and Sareena swayed to its beat. She picked up another strawberry and took a bite of it. Her white teeth and full lips sucked at the berry, making him envious of the tiny fruit.

With no regard for what the sticky juice would do to her comforter, Sareena slid down between his legs and ran the berry up his thigh. Brogan jumped from the coolness of it against his overheated skin. Her warm breath against his thigh sent licks of flame straight to his cock.

When she traced his balls and his length with the crushed fruit he thought he'd shoot off the bed.

"You know, they say you should get at least five servings of fruit a day," she said as she wrapped her berry-stained lips around the head of his cock.

Brogan could do nothing but groan in pleasure as she licked and sucked him into a pleasure coma. He strained at the cuffs preventing him from clutching her hair but didn't break free. Sweat trickled along his forehead as he fought to hold back his release for the third time that night.

"I just love fresh produce, don't you?"

"I'll never look at a fruit salad the same way again."

Heat rolled off him in waves as he watched her take yet another berry and crush it between her fingers before popping it in her mouth. She ran her sticky hands over her breasts and squeezed them like he was dying to do. He licked his lips, anticipating what she'd do next.

Sareena threw her head back as her fingers parted her sable curls and teased her clit. Little cries of pleasure blended with the music and she traced her pussy lips and circled her nubbin.

Every single muscle in his body tensed as he fought for control. His eyes flew from her enraptured face, over her glistening breasts to where she played with herself and back up again. He couldn't decide which was hotter—her fingers toying with her pussy or her reaction to it.

She gave a low moan as her hips bucked with her pleasure. Brogan had to bite down on his cheek to keep from following her over.

"Holy Mother of God." He closed his eyes for a minute to recover his senses.

Unfortunately, his lack of vision only made his other senses sharper. He could smell the sweetness of the berries mingled with the musk of Sareena's womanly cream. The feel of the cool satin next to his heated body competed with the hot silk of Sareena's fingers across his chest. And when she leaned down and brushed her lips against his mouth, his taste buds exploded with the varied flavors that were uniquely hers.

"Would you like a strawberry of your own?" she asked, holding a plump berry to his lips.

He ate it, relishing the burst of wetness over his desert-dry mouth.

"Good, huh?"

"Not bad. But it isn't the berry I really want."

"Oh? And what berry might that be?"

"The one between your legs."

Sareena gasped and her rapid breath fluttered over his lips. He couldn't use his hands to move her into position but he didn't need to worry. With a lithe twist she scooted on top of him, her dewy pussy just inches from his waiting mouth.

Her clit was red and plump like the berry he'd named it and when he sucked it into his mouth, it far surpassed the fruit's sweetness. He wanted to drink her juices for hours, to gorge on her flavor and drown in her essence. Her taste and texture had him so enraptured he didn't realize what she was doing until her hot mouth captured his cock and sucked him deep.

No longer could he keep his hands still. With a flick of his wrist he unsnapped the toy cuffs and freed himself of his restraints. He pressed a finger into her slick channel and searched for the slightly different texture of her G-spot. A sudden flood of cream told him he'd found it and he pressed harder.

He used his free hand to caress her delicious ass. He couldn't stop from giving her behind a tiny nip—it was too rosy and inviting to pass up. Her derrière was nicely rounded and slightly muscled. Gathering moisture from her dripping pussy, Brogan pressed his finger against her tight, pink rosebud. He stroked the sensitive nerves at her rear entrance and smiled against her pussy lips as she shouted in pleasure around his cock.

When she stroked the soft spot beneath his balls and pressed his nerve-rich perineum it was his turn to gasp in pleasure.

"I want to be in you." He blew a hot stream of air over her swollen clit. "I want to fuck your brains out. I want to drive into you until all you can think about is the next thrust."

Sareena whimpered and rolled off him only to turn around and straddle his hips. She didn't try to tease him or prolong the agony but sank her warm sheath over his throbbing cock until he was in deep.

"Sonofabitch that feels incredible," he swore softly, reaching around to gently pinch her ass.

"Uh huh." Sareena's eyes were closed and her head thrown back as she rocked her hips over him.

With every lift and fall of her hips she tightened her inner muscles and squeezed his cock in a fist of hot velvet. Brogan leaned forward and captured a berry-covered nipple in his mouth. He rolled the bud over his tongue and sucked it hard. When she didn't protest the slight pain, he bit down then laved away the sting.

"I can't hold back," she panted, her head whipping side to side.

"Don't."

Brogan sucked her other nipple and flicked her clit at the same time. The combination pushed Sareena over and she spasmed around him before collapsing across his chest.

Thank God.

He didn't think he could last another second. Clenching her hips, Brogan thrust up into her still quivering warmth. It barely took three strokes before 'he too found a welcome oblivion.

It was only when Sareena finally rolled to his side that he realized they hadn't used any protection.

FOUR

UCK!"

"Again? I need a few minutes," Sareena murmured sleepily.

"That's not what I meant. Not that I'd mind, but that isn't what I was saying."

Sareena forced her eyes open and peered at Brogan. He appeared flustered and upset. "What's the problem?"

"I didn't exactly come dressed for the party. We didn't use protection."

"Oh that. It's not an issue. One of the benefits of being a shapeshifter is immunity to diseases. It counterbalances our low birthrate. I'm clean as a whistle. The only reason I didn't mention it the first time was because I didn't want to freak you out and have you stop."

"Like that was gonna happen. But what about pregnancy? You can still get pregnant. That could be a problem."

A tiny pang of sadness rang in her heart. It was too easy to imagine carrying Brogan's baby. The fact that it was not only a long shot but also not something he'd want hurt a little bit.

"Don't worry. It's the wrong time of the month. And even if it was the perfect time, the chances of me getting pregnant are slim to none."

She pushed away from him and grabbed one of the bottles of water she'd taken from the fridge earlier.

"I didn't mean to insult you. It's just . . ."

"It's just you hadn't planned on sleeping with Sareena the heiress, never mind Sareena the shapeshifter, and the thought of an unwanted pregnancy scares the freckles off your face. I understand. I'm not insulted." *Much*. She slid off the bed and headed toward the bathroom to wash.

"Now just wait a damn minute!" He followed her to the bathroom and cornered her against the vanity. "Don't put words in my mouth. Just because I hadn't *planned* on having sex with you didn't mean I didn't *want* to."

Sareena sighed and forced her irrational irritation away. Brogan had handled the strangeness of the night admirably. It was ridiculous for her to feel hurt because he wasn't doing handsprings of joy at the thought of getting her pregnant. *Grow up, Reena.*

"I'm sorry. You've explained about your discomfort with my bank account. That's not going to go away just because we had good sex. And you've handled the whole shapeshifter thing a lot better than I could have ever hoped for. I didn't mean to act like a spoiled brat."

"Come here." Brogan pulled her into his arms and she nuzzled the valley between his muscular pecs.

His musky, manly fragrance rolled over her and she cuddled closer, trying to absorb his scent. Unconsciously, she rubbed her cheek against his slightly sweaty chest. Her inner cat purred at the marking of so strong a mate.

Hold on there a minute!

Brogan wasn't her mate. Sure, she'd worked with him for months but this was the first night they'd ever spent together. It was way too soon to start thinking about anything permanent.

"So tell me, which bothers you more? My money or the fact I turn into a jaguar?"

He chuckled and she felt it vibrate through his torso. "Apparently it's your money because seeing you turn fuzzy didn't stop me from making love to you the first chance I got."

"Oh good. I could give my money away but there's not much I can do about being a shifter."

As soon as the words were out of her mouth she wanted to yank them back. When Brogan stiffened against her she could have kicked herself. She racked her brain for something to break the tension oozing from him.

"Not that *that* will ever happen." She slid to the side and smiled up at him. "But, since you're here now, would you like to go for a swim in my hot tub?" She pointed to the black marble bathtub that took up half the room.

"Swim is right. Do you realize I've been in pools smaller than your damn tub?"

"Ah, but I bet they didn't have jets. If you're really nice to me I'll even put in some of my sandalwood bath salts so you won't smell like a girl when you leave."

She bent over and turned on the faucets, not waiting for him to answer. His low groan made her smile to herself. He might not be sure about everything that had happened tonight but he still wanted her. It wasn't perfect but it was a start.

"That would go over big at the precinct. I'd never hear the end of it. The guys busted my balls already for wearing a tux."

"But you looked so good in it."

"It was a rental. I don't go around wearing monkey suits on a regular basis."

"That's a shame." She flicked the water from her fingers in his direction.

"We can't all attend black-tie events every night, princess."

She narrowed her eyes at him. "Don't call me princess. It makes me sound like either a spoiled poodle or a pampered rich girl. I don't know which is worse."

"Are you trying to tell me you're not rich?"

"Yes, I have money, but I don't spend all my time jet-setting from one hedonistic playground to another. I know having great wealth also means having great responsibility."

He grabbed her hand and pulled her close again. "I was kidding. I know how hard you work. I've seen you covered in paint from when we did the renovations on the shelter. A lot of folks would have just been happy giving the money to make the construction possible. Not many of them would have pitched in to help do the grunt work."

"I didn't think I'd ever get that awful ceiling paint out of my hair."

"You made a pretty good painter, for an heiress."

"I did a great job with the paint. It was the drywall that beat me. Every time I go in the recreation room I see that damn seam in the wall. It mocks me."

"I'll buy a picture to put up in front of it so you'll never have to see it again."

Sareena's shoulders relaxed as the tension evaporated. She might only have this one night with Brogan, she didn't want to waste it arguing. Leaning over again, she checked the temperature of the water. It was nice and hot so she added the bath salts and turned on the jets.

"Can I ask you a personal question?" Brogan asked as he settled into one of the carved-out seats in the tub.

"Sure. It's not like I have much more to hide."

"Why the battered women's shelter? There are a lot of charities out there, how come you picked domestic violence?"

"You couldn't ask me something easy, could you?"

"You don't have to answer it if you don't want to. I was just curious."

"How much do you know about animal behavior?"

"I know dogs poop a lot, especially on the damn sidewalk outside the precinct."

Sareena laughed and let her legs float over to mingle with Brogan's. "Jaguars aren't pack animals, but there's still a pecking order. In my clan, my father and mother are the Alphas, which is why I can't live too near them."

"I think I get it. It's like the old saying, you can't have two women in one kitchen, or something like that."

"Exactly. I love my parents but if you think two women in the same house is rough, two Alpha women in the same house is a nightmare. Cats need to have their own territories. Which is why I'm here in New York City and my folks are in London. Having an ocean between us helps keep family harmony."

"I bet."

"Someday I'll be the Alpha of my own clan. Someday far, far away if I have any say about it." Just the thought of juggling all the responsibilities she already had with those of a clan leader was enough to give her hives.

"So if there are Alphas that means there has to be . . . Betas?"

"Bingo. It's not as bad as with some of the wolf packs but there's still a pecking order. Anyway, one of my good friends was a sub—a Beta. The thought of being in charge of anything was enough to send her into a panic attack. She liked being told what to do and liked to be dominated."

A shudder of revulsion snaked down Sareena's spine. She had to force herself to relax and not let the anger control her. She'd already changed twice tonight—if she let herself turn furry again she'd be too exhausted to move.

"Theresa, my friend, seemed to attract the worst men for her. She could be in a room of a thousand nice guys and manage to find the one wife beater there."

"I know the type. It's like they have a bastard magnet on their foreheads."

"Exactly. I can't tell you the number of times I picked her up at the hospital with broken bones, concussions and internal injuries. No sooner would she heal then she'd find a new guy to beat her up. It got to the point where I set aside a special fund for her to access in case she needed to run away and I wasn't around."

"Did she use it?"

Pain slammed her in the gut and tears burned her throat. "Not soon enough. I was in India, acting as an ambassador in my mother's place. The cell phone coverage in the mountains is spotty to say the least. Theresa called for help but I didn't get the call until days later. By then it was too late. Her boyfriend had beaten her to death in front of a bus station full of people."

"Why didn't she turn into a jaguar to save herself? I mean, that's what you did tonight, right?"

"She wasn't a full-blooded *jaguatium* so she could only shift when the moon was full and with a great deal of effort."

Brogan swore a blue streak as Sareena tried to fight back the lump in her throat.

"What happened to the guy who killed her?"

"He got seven years in prison for manslaughter and was out with good behavior after five."

"Fucking figures. Is that why you set up the legal fund for the shelter?"

"Yes. It's important that women trying to get away from their abusers have a safe place to go. But it's also imperative that they legally protect themselves and their children."

"You got that right."

Silence stretched between them as they were both lost in their thoughts. The rushing of the water through the jets was the only sound.

"So," Sareena cleared her throat to get rid of the huskiness. "Why do you volunteer at the shelter? I know you work close to sixty hours a week for the department. Why use your precious free time to fix holes in the walls and leaky plumbing?"

Brogan's gut clenched at Sareena's question. He owed her an answer, a real answer, not the usual bullshit he told everyone else. But how could he explain it to her? She'd either be repulsed or, worse, pity him.

He looked around at the opulent bathroom, gleaming with chrome and black marble. How could she ever look at him again with anything but loathing if she knew the truth?

"You don't have to tell me if it's something personal," she said, obviously sensing his apprehension.

Oh Christ. Now he felt like an ass. Here she'd laid out all her deep dark secrets, trusting him with her very life, and he couldn't even utter a peep about his shitty father. What a fucking hypocrite.

He sunk lower in the bubbles, feeling vulnerable and massively uncomfortable with what he was about to say.

"I volunteer at the shelter because I used to live there. My father beat the shit out of my mother on a regular basis. When I was seven he hit me so hard he broke my arm. That was the last straw for Mom. She could handle him hitting her but when he went after me she ran."

Tears swam in Sareena's eyes and he could see her struggling with what to say.

"Look, it could have been a lot worse. At least my mom got out in time. She was one of the lucky ones—she never went back. It wasn't easy for her either. She had to raise me on her own working minimum-wage jobs and accepting food stamps. Her pride took a beating over that but she never went back to him."

"I'm so sorry."

"Don't be. I got over it and so did my mom. Neither one of us want your pity." He pushed himself up and prepared to get out of the tub but Sareena flew at him and he splashed back down.

"I don't pity you. I admire you and your mother for escaping that vicious cycle. I know how often it doesn't happen."

"You and me both." He released a pent-up breath. "I worry

that someday I'll turn into him. That I'll become an abuser too. I don't just work at the shelter because I owe them, I'm there so I don't ever forget what it's like to be a little kid watching your mom get smacked around."

"You could never do that. Just because your father was a batterer doesn't mean you'll turn into one."

"How can you say that? You barely know me."

"Bullshit. I've been working with you for almost a year now. I've seen how you play with the kids to give their mothers a break. And I've seen how you interact with the women there. You treat them with respect, you never look down on them. You're the only man they'll let in there, did you know that?"

"Yeah, I know that. But part of the reason is Janice was the director when I was there too. She's known me most of my life."

"Do you think she'd let a potential batterer into her domain? She's more protective of her clients than a mother bear."

Brogan relaxed slightly and considered Sareena's words. A tiny knot of fear he carried around inside of him loosened slightly. It was still there but not as strong as before.

"You know, you're pretty damn smart."

"I know. It's just one of my many qualities," she laughed.

"You're already rich and beautiful, how many more qualities do you need?"

"A lot, apparently, since it's taken me this long to get you into my bed."

"I wanted to be in your bed the first time I looked at you, it was only when I found out who you were that I eighty-sixed that idea."

"You know, I've always had to worry about men coming on to

me because of my money. You're the first guy I've met who *wouldn't* come on to me because of it."

"Nope, I just want you for your mind." He wiggled his eyebrows suggestively.

"Right, and I bet you read girlie magazines for the articles too." Her wet breast slipped over his chest and her legs tangled with his. Any remaining anger or sorrow was pushed aside by the feel of her skin against him and her hands on his body.

"You can never do too much research. In fact, I think I'll do some right now." He ended the conversation by capturing her mouth with a kiss.

Sareena sighed into the kiss and relaxed against him. Her nipples pressed into his chest and he felt his cock stir yet again. She might not be the only one unable to walk by the end of the night.

Brogan's cock thickened against her thigh and Sareena's pussy tingled in anticipation. His large hands, strong but so gentle, stroked her back and she arched into the delicious pressure.

"Does my little cat want to be petted?" he teased.

"Depends on where you're talking about touching." She slipped her hand between their bodies and grasped his rock-hard cock. "And with what."

"You're insatiable. I like that in a woman."

Sareena laughed and faked a punch at him. The movement sent her sliding and she splashed him with bubble-laden water. "I'm not the only insatiable one here. You're the one with a tent pole sticking up between your legs. For the fourth time tonight, I might add."

"It's your fault. I've never recovered so fast or so often in my life."

"That really could be my fault. During a full moon *jaguatium* emit pheromones for mating. That could be influencing you and getting you more worked up than normal."

"Honey, being in the same room with you works me up. If the pheromones are helping me recover faster, I say bring 'em on, this is a new record for me."

"Well, you know what they say about records. They were made to be broken." She crawled across the tub to him and jumped when one of the jets sprayed water over her clit. "Oh my." She closed her eyes and enjoyed the feel of the hot water teasing her nub.

"Do you want a moment alone?" Brogan asked, watching her with hungry eyes.

"I'd rather have you but this feels damn good. I may have to start using this thing more often."

"Cripes. After only one night I'm being replaced by plumbing." He reached out and fondled her breasts.

Her position made them hang down, ripe for his touch. She closed her eyes and enjoyed the double assault on her senses.

"Guess I'll have to find some way to make myself more memorable."

Brogan wrapped a steely arm around her stomach and moved her to the other side of the tub. "Put your hands up here and don't move them. I don't have the handcuffs to make sure you hold still so I'm going to have to trust you."

"Like the cuffs held you for long."

"Are you complaining?" He gave her a swat on her wet bottom.

The stinging slap took her by surprise but didn't really hurt. In fact the burn quickly turned quite pleasurable.

"I wouldn't dream of arguing with an officer of the law."

Another slap, this one on the other cheek, increased the fire heading straight for her pussy.

"Don't you forget it."

The echo of Brogan's spanks reverberated through the marble-filled bathroom—and through every atom of her being. Juice ran freely down her legs and her pussy lips were swollen and achy. Another jet of hot water pulsed against her nipples like many tiny tongues licking her. Sareena whimpered in frustration but didn't want the sweet torture to end.

When her butt was as hot as her pussy, Brogan stopped spanking her and began kissing every inch he'd abused so pleasurably. The feel of his soft lips over her super-sensitive ass made her groan out loud. She was the closest to begging that she'd ever been in her entire life.

"Please," she gasped.

"Please what?" he murmured against the soft flesh where her thighs met her ass.

"Lick me, fill me, fuck me!"

Tears leaked down her face but she didn't move her hands to wipe them away. Her grip on the edge of the tub was the only thing keeping her anchored. She was afraid if she let go she'd fly into a million pieces.

"All in good time."

His finger probed at her entrance and she thrust her hips back to give him better access. He stroked her slowly, never building her high enough to come. Her breath came in heaving gasps as she strained for the orgasm he held just out of reach.

She was sure she'd explode as soon as his hot mouth lapped at her clit but he backed off before she could go over.

"Brogan!" Her chest heaved with her labored breathing.

"Do you want me, Sareena?" Another fleeting lap of his tongue on her nub.

"Yes!"

He drove into her forcefully but Sareena didn't care. Her pussy welcomed his cock like a hand in a glove and she lifted her hips to let him in as deeply as possible. Water sloshed over the sides of the tub as he thrust into her from behind. His balls slapped her super-sensitive skin and added another caress to her overloaded body.

Brogan held her hips still, preventing her from rushing the pace. She cried out with frustration. She wanted him hard and fast and *now!* He was killing her. There was no way she'd survive another minute without an orgasm.

"Hurry!"

"Not yet, sweetheart." He leaned over, pressing his entire body over hers.

Almost every inch of their skin touched. She could feel his legs brushing along her inner thighs and his pelvis against her stinging behind. His hand crept down from her hip to part the curls of her pussy. One finger swirled around her clit as he slowly pulled his cock out of her and then pressed back in.

Sareena could feel the pressure ready to explode inside her. If he'd only move a little faster she'd fly over the edge in a second. She tried to move back against him when he withdrew but he bit down on the cord of her neck and stopped her.

The feel of his teeth against such a vulnerable spot sent an eruption of lust through her. Whether knowingly or not, Brogan had laid claim to her in an age-old feline manner and the cat inside her responded with a ferocity that shook her to the core.

The orgasm that tore through her ripped the very fabric of her being. It felt like her soul burst through the thin shell that was her body and scattered to the stars. Brogan's hips pistoned against her, making the orgasm go on and on. If it weren't for his arm around her middle, she was sure she'd have slipped under the water and drowned.

God knows she didn't have the energy to move.

"Shit. I think I might have bit a little too hard when I came." He kissed her gently.

"'S okay," she murmured in a daze. The slight sting on her neck barely registered. Her body was still humming from the most incredible orgasm of her life. He could have bit straight down to the bone and she probably wouldn't have noticed.

"No really, you're bleeding."

Brogan pulled out of her and Sareena shuddered from another wave of pleasure. Her legs shook as he pulled her to her feet. She felt loose and boneless and sublimely happy.

"Can you stand on your own?"

"Maybe."

A satisfied chuckle rumbled from him as he grabbed a hand towel off the rack. Her body fairly sang when he held her close to dab at the tiny bite mark he'd left on the back of her neck.

"I guess it's not too bad. I don't know what got into me. I just *had* to bite that sweet spot and then you convulsed around me and I couldn't hold back any longer."

"Your bite was what made me come so hard. It's a cat thing."

"I'll have to remember that for future reference."

He took another towel off the heated rack and rubbed it over his hair. All too quickly he wrapped the bath sheet around his waist, hiding his delicious ass from her view.

"Will there be a future between the two of us?" The warm towel she patted herself with did nothing to warm the chill of nervousness in her blood.

Brogan ran a hand through his hair. "I want there to be."

"But?"

"But it isn't going to be easy."

"Most relationships aren't. At least not the ones that mean anything." She pushed out of the misty bathroom and plunked down on the couch in her bedroom.

"Yeah but most relationships don't occur between the son of a batterer and a fucking heiress."

Sareena looked up in shock. "I turned into a jaguar in front of you tonight. Twice! And the biggest issue you have is with my money? What is wrong with you? There are a million reasons why things might not work. My family, my race, your schedule and any number of other things but the fact I'm rich should be the least of the problems."

"I know. Damn it, I know I shouldn't care but all I think of is every time we're out together people are going to think I'm with you for your money. Or that you're using me as some sort of boy toy. The flack I caught for going to the benefit dinner will be nothing compared to what I'll have to deal with if you pick me up at work in that goddamn limo."

"Do you want to pretend we're just business acquaintances?" Anger and frustration boiled in her chest. She was trying her hardest to understand his point of view but he made it seem like he'd be embarrassed to be seen with her.

"No. I'm not going to sneak around and see you on the sly. That isn't fair to you."

A lump formed in her throat and she pushed it down before it strangled her. "It's not too late to back out. Even if you don't want to . . . be with me, I know you'd never betray me."

"Damn it, I do want to be with you!" he shouted and kicked a throw pillow across the room. "I just don't know how. I can barely remember what fork to use at those fancy-schmancy dinners. I'll end up doing something to embarrass you."

"Oh, Brogan, you could never embarrass me. I really don't give a damn what others think. You're a kind, caring, intelligent man. Let people believe what they want. I know that you're not with me for my money. Shouldn't that be what matters?"

"No offense but that's easy for you to say. It's not you who'll be branded as a gold digger in the supermarket tabloids. I may not have much but I do have my pride. No man wants to be seen as a sponge."

"Oh please. I can't see you quitting your job to be my boy toy."

"Hell, if the paparazzi hound me as badly as they do you I won't have a job. I can't see my captain being too pleased with me if I screw up a bust because a mob of reporters is on my back."

"I-I never thought of that." Damn. How would they ever work this out?

"Trust me, I have. Otherwise I would have knocked on your door the minute you gave me a second glance. I've wanted you for a long time. I just couldn't figure out how we could make it work. I still don't."

She took a deep breath and prayed for patience. "Listen, we don't have to figure this all out tonight . . . err, this morning.

Why don't we have some breakfast and we can talk about it later?"

"Breakfast? What time is it?" Brogan looked at the clock glowing by the bed. "Sonofabitch! I have to be to work in an hour." He dropped the towel and searched for his clothes. "I have to go. I need to change into my uniform and get downtown. Christ, I have to return the damn tux too."

Sareena followed him and couldn't help but admire the view of his tight ass hustling down the hall. While he jerked on his pants she picked her robe off the living room floor and slipped it on.

"I'll call a cab for you while you're getting dressed. I'd offer the use of my limo but I don't think you'd appreciate it."

"No! I definitely don't want to pull into my neighborhood in your limo. Maybe someday but not yet."

"I understand." She made the call from the kitchen phone to give Brogan a few minutes to pull himself together.

Once he was dressed, she slipped on a pair of sandals. "We'll take my personal elevator, it leads to a private entrance. There's no guard posted there so you won't be seen with me, although there are security cameras. Maybe you can turn your face away so no one will recognize you if they see the tapes. I'm sure if you move fast enough none of your police buddies will see you getting into the cab so no one will know you spent the night with me."

"Sareena, I'm not embarrassed to be seen with you, okay? It's just going to take me a little time to get used to it. A shitload has happened in the last twelve hours."

She took a deep breath and let go of her lingering irritation. Patience wasn't her strong suit. Just because she didn't have a problem seeing them as a couple didn't mean it would come as quickly to him. She had to back off and let nature take its course.

"Okay. C'mon, I don't want you to be late for work." She led him through the laundry room and into her private car that would drop him off near the servants' entrance.

When the doors opened at their stop, Brogan stepped out first and scanned the area. Her heart did a slow tumble in her chest. Even though he'd seen her turn into a jungle cat that could tear him apart with one swipe, he still felt protective of her. *How sweet.* Sareena waited for him to drop the arm blocking her from exiting the elevator but he left it there.

"Why don't you go on back up? I'm sure the cab will be here shortly, and you're not exactly dressed to be out in public."

"This is a private entrance and I'm covered from neck to ankle."

"But I keep remembering you in that same robe last night and I don't want anyone else to see you like that."

"Well, in that case—look out!" Sareena shoved him aside just as a knife slashed at his back.

The doors to the elevator slid closed without Brogan's arm to hold them open. In seconds, she dropped the robe and flowed into her cat form. Nudging the button with her nose, the doors opened in time for her to see Brogan scramble away from another attack. Her snarl of rage echoed through the tiny hallway as she leapt from the elevator.

Brogan and the man from last night wrestled across the tiled floor, grunting with the force of their blows. Sareena's tail lashed as she waited for an opportunity to pounce on the wretch who dared to harm her mate.

Finally her chance came when Brogan used his feet to throw the wife beater over his head. Sareena was on him like a terrier on a rat. She used her entire body weight to slam into him, sending his head crashing against the wall. Blood flew everywhere, its coppery scent inflaming her senses. Just as she raised her claw for the killing blow, Brogan jumped in and pulled the attacker away before she could slash him with her claws.

"Stop it! He's not worth it. Go!" he ordered.

Bloodlust raged through her and she growled with frustration. She wanted to kill the sorry piece of meat on the ground.

The wail of sirens whined in the distance and sent a thread of panic into her fiery thoughts.

"Get back to your apartment before the cops get here. I'll get you when it's safe."

Sareena shifted into her human shape and almost dropped to her knees. It was all she could do to press the elevator door button and stumble inside the car. A fog of exhaustion blurred her vision and tried to drag her down into its depths.

Her head pounded and she slumped down against the cool, metal wall. The ride to her floor seemed to take forever and every second that passed made her muscles ache that much more. She fought to remain conscious until she reached the safety of her home. Nausea rolled in her stomach as her vision faded in and out of focus.

Thank God she'd left her door unlocked because she didn't have the strength to fumble with it. Her white robe had streaks of blood smeared across it and she made a mental note to have Lana clean up the elevator and check for traces of blood that could lead to her condo.

It took every iota of willpower to wash off in the laundry room and not just lay on the tile floor and go to sleep. She didn't want the wife beater's scent on her or she would have done just that.

The bedroom was way too far away for her to make it. With the last ounce of energy left in her body she staggered into the living room and collapsed on the couch. Her brain registered Brogan's scent wafting up from the cushions seconds before she fell into oblivion.

FIVE

UNLIGHT WARMED HER FACE and the smell of fresh coffee woke her from the sleep of the dead.

No, not dead just damn close to it.

Her eyelids felt like they weighed a hundred pounds each but she forced them open. Lana stood at the side of the couch with a tray of coffee and a pitcher of orange juice.

"Lana, you're a goddess."

"I know," she said with a smile as she set the tray down on the table. "Overextended ourselves a little, did we?"

"I don't know if you did, but I sure as hell pushed the envelope last night."

"More like two nights ago. Last night you were unconscious on the couch. You didn't even stir when that policeman came banging on the door."

"Policeman?" Sareena perked up.

"Yes, Brody or Brogan or something. He's come by at least ten times since last night and he's called nearly twice that."

"What did you tell him?"

"I told him you were indisposed and you'd call him back when you were able."

"Did he leave his home number?"

"And his cell phone number and his work number and his pager. Now drink some of that orange juice as well as the coffee while I make up your eggs."

The icy juice felt heavenly against her parched throat as Sareena chugged down a tall glass.

What did Brogan want? Had seeing her in full feline rage destroyed any hope of a relationship with him?

Her heart jumped into her throat as someone pounded on the door.

"Come on, Nurse Ratchet, she can't still be sleeping. It's been over twenty-four hours!" Brogan's voice came through the door loud and clear.

Lana stepped from the kitchen and made to answer the door. Sareena waved her off and crossed to the foyer herself. Every muscle in her body screamed in protest but she was better off than she'd been when she came home yesterday.

"Don't shout, I just woke up." Sareena opened the door then stepped back as Brogan barged in.

"Finally! I've been a nervous freaking wreck. I thought you'd slipped into a coma or something." He yanked her to his chest and kissed her hard.

Shock held her in place for a few seconds before she melted into the kiss. God she hoped the orange juice she drank would disguise her morning breath.

"Are you okay? The last time I saw you, you were pale as a ghost and stumbling."

"I'm fine now. What about you?" She ran her finger lightly over the multiple bruises on his face. One eye was swollen and his nose looked puffy too.

"Just some bumps and bruises, I'll live. Thanks to you."

"I didn't do anything."

"You saw him coming at me with the knife when I'd missed him completely. If you hadn't shoved me out of the way I'd have been a goner."

"I'm just glad you're safe. Is that bastard behind bars?"

"Yeah, now that he's out of the hospital. They're sending him for a psych eval after his bond hearing. He tried to tell the doctors that the slashes on his stomach were from a huge cat."

"Really? And did anyone believe him?"

"Not after they read the part of my report where I stated he got caught climbing the fence and hurt himself as he flipped over it. The consensus is that he's faking insanity to get out of his charges." Brogan smirked then winced.

"Talk about crazy. A huge cat in the middle of the city. Who'd believe that?" She nuzzled his neck, inhaling the scent of soap and man. Delicious.

"I don't know, I think you could convince me of just about anything."

SIX

Six months later

"YOU'RE SURE ABOUT THIS? I don't want you doing anything that makes you uncomfortable." Sareena's gut twisted with nerves.

"Oh really? That's pretty funny coming from the woman who pulled out a vibrator and told me 'just relax.' I'm fine, honest."

"I just don't want you doing this for me. I want it to be your idea."

"Reena, it was my idea. If you remember, *I'm* the one who suggested it."

"I know, but—"

"But nothing." He shut her up by placing a finger over her lips. "I want to meet the rest of your family. And I want to try my hand at running my own business. I only took a leave of absence from the force. If things don't work out I can always go back. My captain thought it would be a good idea to take a break until the heat died down anyway so it works out for everyone." He kissed her softly and stroked her hair.

"You wouldn't have any heat if it wasn't for me." Sareena leaned into his caress. Damn but Brogan had great hands.

The pilot of her private plane approached them. "Miss Wilton, we've been cleared for takeoff. We'll be leaving shortly."

"Thank you." She settled into the leather seat and fastened her seat belt while Brogan did the same.

"I'll never get used to this, you know. I've never even been on a plane before and here I am, getting ready to fly to freaking Europe on a private jet."

"And that's a bad thing?"

"Not bad, just different. Don't worry, I think I've mostly gotten over my hang-up about your money. As long as you don't try to make me a kept man I'll try to check my ego."

"I could always give it all away. You know I'd do that for you."

"Not that argument again." Brogan took her hand and kissed her knuckles. "You can do a lot more good by using your money to help people in need. I'm not so selfish that I'd sacrifice all the work you do for my pride. I know I love you for you and not your money. Even if that is what every freaking tabloid across the country prints."

"Screw them."

Her heart flipped over with a slow thump at his words. She'd never get tired of hearing him tell her he loved her.

The last six months had been both the most amazing and the most difficult of her life. Amazing because loving Brogan was mind-numbingly incredible. He turned out to be just as considerate out of bed as he was in it.

Unfortunately, balancing his job as a cop and her public image was a nightmare. His picture had been splattered over every tabloid in the city. He'd had to get an unlisted phone number because the darn thing rang all day and night. Every talk show and radio program in America wanted to hear about the cop who managed to snag the Wilton heiress.

His captain hadn't been happy when the paparazzi stormed the precinct house trying to get pictures of him at work. Brogan had been confined to desk duty, which nearly broke Sareena's heart. He was too good a cop to be taken off the streets because of her.

She shuddered a little, remembering when she tried to break things off with him.

"What's wrong?" he massaged her shoulders, sensing her tension.

"I was just thinking about the time I tried to dump you."

Brogan snorted and lifted the armrest so he could pull her closer. "Don't ever try that shit again. You almost gave me a heart attack. I can't stand the thought of losing you."

"It nearly killed me but I had to try. It was for your own good."

"Why don't you let me worry about what's good for me?"

"But you love your job. I hate seeing you punished because of me."

"Oh? I thought you enjoyed punishing me?" His smile bordered on a leer and shot sparkles of heat straight to her pussy.

"Only in bed."

The plane rolled down the runway, jostling them a little as it prepared for takeoff. Brogan used the movement as an excuse to press even closer to her. His hand stroked her breast covertly.

Instantly the barely banked fires of lust he stirred in her just by breathing flared to life. Her nipples hardened into little points and poked through her silk turtleneck.

"Damn, I wish I wore a low-cut shirt."

"I don't know, the way this one clings to your every curve works for me. And that long skirt you're wearing just makes me wonder what you have on under it."

Sareena shivered as his provocative words rumbled against her throat. His touch burned through her shirt and bra and made it almost impossible to hold still.

"The co-pilot will be coming back here as soon as we take off and you've got me all hot and bothered."

"It works both ways. At least you don't have an erection threatening to break your zipper."

She glanced down and saw he spoke the truth. His hard-on stood up like a tent pole in his dress slacks. Her hand drifted down to caress his length. He was hard enough to pound nails.

Another shiver trailed down her spine.

Sareena scrambled for a magazine to hide her erect nipples as the sound of the cabin door opening reached her super-sensitive ears. By the time the co-pilot made it back to the lounge area they appeared to be engrossed in their respective reading material. She hoped.

If the co-pilot noticed Brogan held his sports magazine over his lap and Sareena had her fashion magazine practically pressed to her chest, he didn't mention it.

"We've reached our cruising altitude and there's no turbulence as far as we can tell. It should be a pleasant flight to London."

"Wonderful, thank you."

Under the cover of his magazine, Brogan stroked her upper thigh. Tiny jolts exploded between her legs and her pussy dripped cream.

"You're welcome. Can I get you a drink or a snack?"

"We're all set for now. We may want a light dinner later but I think we're going to take a nap first." She fought to keep her breathing normal as Brogan continued to tease her. His fingers found the strap of her garter belt and traced it.

"Yes, ma'am. Shall I dim the cabin lights on my way back to the cockpit?"

"Yes, please." Sareena ignored Brogan's snort at the word cock.

"Enjoy the flight." The co-pilot left without the slightest flicker of emotion.

She waited until she heard the snick of the cabin door closing before she turned on Brogan.

"You beast! I could barely string two words together coherently. He's going to think I'm some sort of flake."

"Why do you care what he thinks?"

"Because I don't want to be thought of as an oversexed trust fund baby."

"I think you're far from oversexed. In fact, I think you're decidedly undersexed." He tugged on her long skirt, pulling it up inch by inch. "So tell me, Miss Wilton, what do you have on under this skirt?"

"A very damp thong."

He'd exposed the tops of her stockings and she heard his breath hitch at the sight of the black lace. She'd worn them just for him but hadn't expected to show them off before they'd landed in England.

"So, have you ever had an orgasm on a plane before?"

"Ah, no," she gasped as he followed the lacy strap of the garter with his finger.

"There's a first time for everything."

He drew a small circle over her clit, rubbing it through the wet silk of her thong. Sareena squirmed in her seat as he teased her. Flames of lust shot through her bloodstream and she arched her hips to get closer to his touch.

"I love how you respond to me."

"If you move my underwear, I'll show you one hell of a response."

"All in good time."

"Easy for you to say."

"Would you prefer I do something else with my mouth?" Brogan slipped out of his chair and knelt between her splayed knees.

Sareena had barely a second to thank God for having a private jet with plenty of room before Brogan tore her panties and her world exploded. His hot mouth descended on her pussy and lapped at her juices. Hot bursts of pleasure bubbled through her like the finest champagne, intoxicating her more than wine ever could. She had to bite her lip to keep from roaring out her pleasure.

His finger slipped inside her dripping channel as he licked her clit. The pressure in her core built to the breaking point with every stroke of his knuckle along her slit. She gripped the seat with all her might to keep from flying apart.

It didn't work.

One final stroke of his hot tongue against her clit and she exploded into a million pieces. Her pussy spasmed and her legs shook with the force of her orgasm. The plane might be flying over the Atlantic, but Sareena was among the stars.

"Dear God in heaven, that's a beautiful sight. I could watch you come apart for hours."

"Don't let me stop you." Her eyelids weighed too much for her to open her eyes. She was so relaxed she could melt into the leather seat and not move again until they landed.

Except Brogan practically vibrated with sexual energy next to her. She could smell his arousal mixed with her orgasm and it stirred her blood.

"You know the best thing about wearing a skirt like this?" she asked as she unzipped his fly.

"Easy access?"

"That too. But I was thinking more along the lines of coverage."

His cock sprung out into her hand as she pulled his pants and boxers over his raised hips. She couldn't resist running her tongue along his length just once before standing.

Gathering the yards of material of her skirt, she climbed onto Brogan's lap. Leaning forward she angled her body until she worked her way onto his stiff cock. Her heart almost burst in her chest as he filled her. Every inch of his length pressed against the slick walls of her pussy, setting her nerves aflame. His groan of pleasure washed over her and she squeezed him tightly, loving the feel of his hardness surrounded by her softness.

The folds of her skirt fell down over their legs, hiding their actions should the pilot or co-pilot emerge from the cockpit.

She fervently hoped they stayed put.

Brogan ran his hands under her shirt and up her rib cage. He circled her breasts, drawing closer to her begging nipples so slowly she almost cried. When he finally reached her tightened points she was ready to whimper with need.

"Do you know how sexy you are? How great you feel in my hands?"

"Do you know how fucking hot you are inside my body? How much I love feeling you in me?"

His rock-hard chest pressed against her back and his steely thighs bunched under her as he thrust slowly into her. She reveled in the feeling of all that power surrounding her. His large hands toyed with her breasts and she rested her head against his shoulder, pushing her chest out for more of his touch.

"I love you so much, Reena," he whispered against her, pushing down the fold of her shirt to reach her neck.

"I love you too, my Brogan."

"God, I never get tired of hearing that." He bit down on the tendon of her neck he'd exposed. Arrows of lust speared her at the touch of his teeth on her and she bucked as the wave of her orgasm overcame her.

Vaguely she felt him join her but she was too busy exploding to be sure.

Her body still quivered even after she'd cleaned up and returned to her seat. Just being near Brogan had that effect on her.

"So is there anything I should know before I meet your pops? I mean, are there any faux pas I should avoid? I'd kind of like to make a good impression."

"Are you nervous about meeting my family?"

"I just don't want them believing any of the crap they might have read."

"My parents know better than to believe any of that." And she was sure her father had already had Brogan investigated thoroughly. But Brogan didn't need to know that. "As long as you're kind to me they'll love you as much as I do."

"Like I could be anything but good to you. If I tried to smack you around you'd disembowel me," he teased.

"Then I guess you'd better take care of me."

"That might take the rest of my life."

"I can make it worth your while." She snuggled into his arms.

"Oh yeah? Convince me."

And as the plane sped through the night sky, she did.

SATURN UNBOUND

ANN VREMONT

ONE

*T*HE HOUSE STOOD AT the edge of The Forest, fronting the westernmost tip of Pebble Beach's 17 Mile Drive and overlooking Monterey Bay. From where she waited at the front gate, engine idling, Izzy Kirsch could see little more than the main dome centered off the back. Trees and the eight-foot-tall stone wall hid the rest of the structure. She had been inside once before—six years ago. New to the area and living in a cheap studio apartment in Pacific Grove, she had shelled out fifteen dollars to tour the home while it was in probate and uninhabited. A few months later, the will was settled and the house was auctioned off. The winning bidder Maceo di Silvio still owned it.

In the six years that had passed, she hadn't forgotten the house or its owner. Mediterranean in style, most of the structure was low-roofed, the interior an aged eggshell in color. Four turrets with cone-shaped roofs rose up, only to be dwarfed by the rotunda with its pale blue dome. Twelve windows were cut into the rotunda walls and paned with Austrian crystal. Floor-to-ceiling glass doors opened onto a marble patio with more blocks of the timeworn stone leading down to the water. The patio doors faced west, letting in the evening sun, while through the day she imagined the room bright with the light filtered from three-hundred-and-sixty degrees through the crystal panes. It was an artist's dream room, although she personally knew no artist capable of affording the house that held it.

Still, she had bluffed her way into an auction that was supposed to be by invitation only. Finding a seat in the middle of the bidding audience, she had hoped her neatly pressed but inexpensive black pantsuit and her mother's string of pearls didn't mark her as an outsider among the rows of Armani and Versace. Keeping the bidding paddle pressed tight against the top of her thighs, she avoided any eye contact with the auctioneer. Instead, she watched the other bidders and imagined how one would fill the house with post-modern sculptures and another with a string of mistresses.

Only one bidder looked as if he would be at home in the house—Maceo di Silvio. But then she may have been typecasting him as the perfect owner for the perfect home. The black hair that fell to his shoulders managed to look silky and untamed at the same time with its mass of soft curls. The broad, muscular body was draped in a linen suit that matched her memory of the house's eggshell walls. At the cuff of his pants, she caught a glimpse of tanned masculine feet clad in walnut-colored sandals. The sandals had shocked her. The bare skin had seemed almost scandalous among the Gucci penny loafers. Her eyes kept returning to the floor in front of him, imagining the arch of his foot as he dug his toes into the sand at the end of the property's marble staircase. He'd turned once, treating her to more than just his chiseled profile, and she had found herself staring into eyes as pale blue as the dome. Finding that Mediterranean blue gaze on her, she'd jerked back, catching her breath at the strength of her reaction. A smile had curved at the edge of his firm lips before the auctioneer recognized another bid and di Silvio turned back to the front, raising his paddle once more. Whether he had looked back again, she didn't know. The instant connection had both frightened and aroused her. If she hadn't been terrified that any significant movement on her part would be interpreted as a bid, she would have left in the middle of the auction.

Now, here she was at the same gate, called there at his request and with a commission almost in hand, to fill the blank space of the rotunda with a mural. Rolling down the window to her Jetta, she reached out. A visible tremor bounced along her outstretched finger as she zeroed in on the call button. She pressed the button, waited, and then glanced down at her dashboard clock. She was right on time—to the minute. Had he forgotten? Had she mixed up the date? She reached out again, ready to push the button a second time when the box squeaked once before di Silvio spoke.

"Miss Kirsch?"

The voice was sun-coated, warming her face and thighs. Izzy closed her eyes, hoping the security camera on the callbox was off—hoping that he hadn't, in fact, been watching her sitting at the front gate for the last five minutes.

She cleared her throat, fighting the urge to look at the little lens and nod. She didn't need to ask if it was him. They'd talked at length last week over the phone, discussing his ideas for the room long enough that she could work up some preliminary sketches. But she had an almost perverse need to hear the seductively low voice again before the thirty seconds it would take to navigate the circular drive. "Yes. Mr. di Silvio?"

"Maceo, please," he answered, and then the gate buzzed open.

The trees that filled the center of the circular drive provided a striptease of the house, slowly revealing what was hidden from the street. The landscaping had been redone. The assortment of flowers brought a smile to her face as she wondered whether the entirety of the grounds and house would reflect di Silvio's status as a world-class astrologer.

The smile faded as she pulled the car to a stop and glanced at the entryway. The door was open, framing di Silvio as he waited. Izzy had an instant's sense that he was posing for her. His arms were stretched over his head, fingers gripping the top edge of the door frame. His arms were bare, his torso covered by a clinging black silk tee that hugged the sculpted muscles of his chest and abdomen. The tee was tucked into pleated black slacks that hinted at equally sculpted thighs and calves. When her visual journey reached the bottom of his pants, she blinked once. He was barefoot. She looked up, meeting his gaze through the window of her car, and frowned.

He shouldn't be sexier than last time, she told herself. If anything, he should be less so—six years had passed and he must be closing in on forty.

Realizing she still was staring at him, Izzy looked down at her dashboard and turned off the Jetta's engine. Hand halfway to her hair, she caught herself before she could give a quick primp in the rearview mirror and reached instead for the small portfolio on the passenger seat. Climbing from the car, she popped the trunk release, conscious of his return inspection as she bent down to retrieve a larger portfolio that had slid to the back of the trunk. She imagined what he was seeing in return and her frown deepened. Not that she didn't like what looked back at her from the mirror—she just didn't drop ten thousand a year on face cream or make weekend shopping trips to Rodeo Drive. She wasn't the sort of artificial beauty that epitomized the world in which he lived.

By the time she pulled her head from the trunk, Maceo was standing next to her. He took the heavy portfolio from her before she could protest. Charging up to the house, he paused in the entryway with the barest backward glance to make sure she was following.

"I thought we'd go straight to the rotunda," he said.

Attention focused on keeping her eyes off his tight behind, Izzy gave a grunt of assent.

Double doors matching the floor-to-ceiling patio doors at the opposite end of the rotunda were open. The floor was partially sunken, with its walls cut to form a bench that ringed its perimeter. Twelve marble columns circled the depression. He had described it on the phone, not knowing that she'd been inside before. She could have stopped him, but she needed an idea of his vision of the room. And, of course, his voice had its own hypnotic effect on her. She could have been listening to him read the back of a cereal box and she would have made the same appreciative noises to indicate her understanding.

Face it, girl, she thought, and watched Maceo plop down in the middle of the lower level's floor and open her sample portfolio, *you were practically mewling.*

Glancing behind him, he caught Izzy studying his back and shoulders. She raised one brow to communicate that her lingering gaze was no more than professional appreciation of a well-formed body. Too bad the blush ruined her intended effect.

He gestured at the floor next to him. "You don't mind, do you, Miss Kirsch? The open space will let me take it all in at once."

Resisting the impulse to look at the breezy summer skirt that fell just past her knees, she shrugged the question off and sat down next to him. Her first smell of Maceo had Izzy biting down on a moan. Honeysuckle with a touch of caramel. Christ, she hoped he wouldn't smell like that all the time, or that she wouldn't have to be so close again. Honeysuckle in the middle of the day, no less, when the flowers usually scented only at night. The man belonged in bed, the taut muscles of his back and stomach oiled, all of him slick and—

Izzy snapped open the smaller portfolio and began spreading the concept drawings on the floor next to him.

"You can call me *Izzy*," she said. She was having trouble breathing and the words came out with a faint pant.

"But it's not *Izzy*, is it?" He was leaning close to her, examining the preliminary sketch she had done of Mars fighting a ram. "*Isa*, maybe? *Kirsch* is German, no?"

"German, yes, but it's *Isold*," she answered, and took another lungful of his scent. There was no avoiding it, as close as he was. She could count the hairs that had stubbled up since his morning shave, see the fine strands of silver hidden beneath the mass of jet-black hair.

"You're oddly colored for a Capricorn," he said.

Izzy pulled back, her gaze dropping to the thin chain of silver around his neck and its crescent-shaped pendant. She hadn't noticed it earlier, though the contrast only served to deepen the sweet caramel of his skin. *Honeysuckle, caramel, oil* . . . She coughed and turned her attention back to the spread of concept sketches.

"And you're not moon-faced," she answered after another small hesitation. From the corner of her eye, she saw him reach up and finger the pendant.

"The moon and silver are common to many signs," he said. A light tease ran through his tone. "How do you know that I'm a Canc?"

Izzy chewed her bottom lip for a second before reluctantly confessing, "I Googled you."

Maceo laughed. The bassoon-like quality of his voice vibrated through Izzy's body and she turned, presenting her shoulder to him. If she kept letting him affect her like this, she was going to lose the commission.

He lifted a lock of copper-colored hair from her bare shoulder and examined it in the room's perfect light. "I don't cheat," he said, and gently replaced the strand, the back of his fingers delivering a brief caress.

Flesh bumps rose along her arm and she brushed them down, disguising the motion with a backward glance of disbelief. "So how did you know?"

Cocking his head, Maceo studied her for another second, the open gaze so intense and inquisitive that she could have been sitting for one of her own murals. "It's all over you, really," he said. "The way you walk, talk, paint . . ." He paused, the gap between his words as sultry as the smell of honeysuckle rising up from his skin. "I bet it's even in the way you make love."

Izzy gave a little huff, indignation coloring her cheeks pink. "What do you mean, it's in the way that I paint?"

"How you're holding back—"

"That's called *structure*," she said, carefully enunciating her words to keep her breathing under control.

Leaning in, Maceo shook his head. "No, Isold, it's called *ice*."

She felt her mouth quirking into a pout and tried to smooth it out, her brows arching high from the attempt. "If you think there's something lacking in my work, why did you ask me here to pitch the mural?" She'd be damned if she would acknowledge how accurately he had pegged the meaning of her name.

Maceo's hand returned to the silver moon pendant and he smiled, his gaze sliding over her bare arms and the modest show of leg she unsuccessfully had tried to hide beneath her skirt. "I've seen enough of your work to know that there's more than Capricorn in your horoscope," he answered. "Though I think the Goat is heavy in your chart."

Shaking her head, Izzy reached to gather up the smaller concept sketches and shove them back in their portfolio, but Maceo caught her hand. He turned it palm up and traced small, calming circles. She wanted to ask him if he'd taken up palmistry as well but couldn't muster the sarcasm, not when the sensation of his fingertips over her palm mentally translated to her clit.

"I'll have to do your chart before I make my final decision, but I really do like what I see, Izzy," he said. He raised her hand, his lips not quite close enough to deliver a kiss, and then he let go without warning.

Her hand fell hard, bouncing off her knee and hitting him in the solid muscle of his abs. She had been melting beneath his touch and the realization made her wince. Did he really think she was as gullible as his clients?

"I don't work that way. It's . . . it's . . ." She fumbled over the irony of the pending word. "Dammit, it's capricious! You don't choose an artist based on their chart!"

The smile that curved along his firm mouth was indulgent. "Izzy, people pay as much for my charts as I'm paying you for the mural." He gestured around the room at the scope of the project she would be undertaking. "IPOs and campaign announcements are timed to my charts."

It was true, she knew. He had gotten her name from Maya and Craig Norrin. She'd done a mural for their nursery—Maceo had done a series of charts pinpointing when they should conceive. They had, indeed, paid him more for his chart than Izzy's art and Maya was a month away from delivering what the couple intensely believed would be a perfect baby boy.

"Now, why wouldn't I want to satisfy myself by my own standards and means?" he asked. "You're going to be living here while you work, after all. I must know your character."

Already starting to rise, Izzy stumbled and he caught her. "Live here?" she stammered.

"Of course. I have to travel a lot, the hours are odd and we'll need to consult. How else do you propose we do it?" he answered. "Your boyfriend won't mind, will he, Isold?"

"I most certainly won't be working or living here if you keep calling me that," she answered. Her voice strained over the final words. That she didn't have a boyfriend was none of his business.

"But you will," he said. His smile twisted the statement into a challenge.

She dropped her head, squaring her shoulders as she prepared to launch into a rant on the size of his ego.

"Oh, come on, Izzy!" He laughed and grabbed her shoulders, the effect of flesh on flesh immediately stilling her. "Just let me do the chart and then you can decide if my offer's worth it, eh? Don't be stubborn just to be stubborn."

She pushed away from him and managed to stand without falling all over him once again. "Will it get me out of here quicker?" she shot back, silently adding, *Before my legs go all jelly again and I have to be carried out.*

"If that's what you want," he said, and turned to gather up the samples he had taken from the larger portfolio.

She blocked him. There was a notepad and pen in the outside zip pocket of the case and she quickly scribbled her date of birth. Shoving the piece of paper at him, she busied herself with rearranging the samples back into their original order.

"I need the city and time too," he said.

"Phoenix, six-thirty-two p.m.," she answered, the growl in her voice dropping the final word an octave. Bad enough she had to confess to being thirty-five without being interrogated on the minutia!

Studying the slip of paper for a second, Maceo nodded and then let his head roll back onto his shoulders. His eyelids were closed, but Izzy could see the rapid movement beneath them, as if he were outlining the exact lay of the heavens at the moment of her birth.

When he dropped his head and looked at her, a smile lit his features. Crooked at one end, it was sly—the kind she'd expect to find in a fox's den.

"Your ascendant is Cancer," he said, still smiling.

"What, you've got things memorized down to the hour and

minute?" she asked, and snorted at the possibility. And so what if her ascendant was Cancer? It wasn't like they'd both owned neighboring ski lodges in Aspen.

"It's incremental, only the bases and patterns need to be memorized," he answered. "And I have enough clients your age—"

"Why are you still smiling?" Impatient, she stamped her foot on the marble flooring, digging in for the impending fight.

"Venus is in Capricorn."

His tone was almost joyous. It was definitely smug. Izzy leaned the portfolio against the wall and tucked her hands behind her back—the urge to thwack him was one degree shy of overwhelming.

"You'll excuse me, but I haven't been practicing astrology for the last three decades." The arrow hit home and she smiled as she saw some of the arrogant puff leave his chest. Maybe there was a little of the Sagittarius Archer in her chart too!

"Well," he started to explain. "It's an extremely curious position . . . particularly when combined with a Canc ascendant."

"Huh . . . Really?" She tried to pretend disinterest but Maceo was moving closer. She hadn't even dented his ego, he'd merely exhaled before moving in for the kill.

"Really." He pressed his chest against hers and raised his hand to tug at the corner of her mouth. "Of course, I'll have to do a more thorough chart to know the polarity of the two influences."

"Polarity?" She stumbled over the question, the word gaining urgency as he stroked her bottom lip. Christ, every time he touched her she felt it at the surface and deep down—the urgency threatening to send her to her knees in supplication.

"All these past lovers, including the current one . . ." He

paused, flashed a ravenous grin and then continued. "No, no current one, is there?"

She didn't answer, but the tremble in her body seemed to confirm his suspicions.

"They've never satisfied you. Too dominant, not dominant enough?" His other hand fastened on her hip and Izzy leaned against him, turning her head the instant before he could taste her lips. "Not dominant enough, I think."

He squeezed her bottom, drew her tighter to him. He was hard, his erection jumping against the press of her stomach as he dropped his lips to her neck. He ran his teeth over the sensitive skin, lightly biting down when she arched against him.

"So much control, four layers of Saturn's reserve, including in the bedroom . . . they'd never dare order you down on your knees, would they, Isold?"

Izzy didn't answer. She was beyond speaking. But he wasn't going to let her get away without an answer as her other lovers had. He broke contact, held her swaying body at arm's length and forced her to meet his gaze.

"A month's time is enough for me to get my answer from you, one way or another." His gaze traveled over her at a leisurely pace, his mind seemingly lost in anticipation of just how he would pry the truth from her body.

"You. Can't. Think. I'll. Take. The. Job?" Every word broke through in stilted gasps, her mind screaming for control while her body couldn't even hold itself up without Maceo's supporting brace.

He tilted his head, studying her expression as if it were an accurate gauge of her resistance. "Sorry, Izzy, but you can't afford not to, can you? A recent investment? A little over your head with it, yes?"

The gallery. She felt a measure of control seep into her body, anger promising to fortify her rebelling flesh. How could he know that? She certainly hadn't told Maya or Craig that she had purchased a gallery, let alone that the costs of opening it were running too high. And it hadn't become an issue with the bank yet—not that she could hold out much longer. Still, she had a choice. The building would sell quickly, leaving her debt-free but back at ground zero with a depleted savings account.

"H-how?"

He gave a shrug, the motion both casual and indignant. "You don't believe in what I do, so what's the point in answering?" Another shrug, but the hand that curled around her shoulder gripped her a little tighter.

"Come on, Izzy, thirty-five thousand to do the mural and a month in *Casa di Silvio.*" He looked around the room before pinning her with his pale blue gaze. "You like the house, don't you? This room . . . you can feel the sunlight pouring into you here, warm . . . filling you with his heat."

She nodded, oddly struck by his masculinization of the sun, but unable to deny the room's pull or the heat that was steaming her blood and threatening to mist the air around her. Not just her blood, she thought, and ran a shaking hand through her hair. She was humid everywhere, the warm pocket of her cunt slick with her melting reserve.

Releasing her completely, he took two steps back. "Go home, pack if you want to, take a cold shower if you don't. I'll be here until noon tomorrow and then I have to fly to New York."

He took a half step toward her and then stopped, shoving his hands deep into the pockets of his black slacks. His fists twisted beneath the fabric for a few seconds and then he pulled out a silver-toned key.

"If you show up before then, I'll give you the key and be back in a few days." The key flashed as he dropped it back into the pocket. "If you don't show, then I'll find someone else for the job."

"That simple?" The question came out as a dry bark, worthy of the seals that could be found sunning themselves a few miles northeast of the house and its rocky beach.

"Pretty much," he said, turning and leaving her to find her own way out.

TWO

*M*ACEO KICKED THE BEDCOVER and sheets down to the end of his king-size bed. The air-conditioning was on, the chilled air trying its best to caress away the heat rising from his nude body. Not that it could. He needed a woman's cool fingertips to stroke away the fire that had built inside him while he slept. Not just any woman's touch either.

Izzy.

She had found her way into his dreams nightly since his undetected visit to her gallery three weeks ago. Even before that, her murals and paintings had been haunting him. The conflict of hot and cold, of water and earth, puzzled him and he no longer had to ask whether a painting at one of his clients' Monterey homes was an *Izzy Kirsch*. He knew immediately, his body and mind reacting with the same growing sense of intrigue and desire. The last mural he had seen, the one for the baby Maya and Craig were expecting, had caused him to seek her out.

The baby would be a Leo, and the Norrins had requested the sign's symbology to be heavily present in the mural. The beast she had delivered was magnificent. Powerful and raw, with a human intelligence sparkling in its tawny gaze, it was a creature that would either inspire the baby to the full potential of his sign or have him sleeping the first decade of his life in between Maya and Craig.

But underlying all that was a golden sensuality, and he was instantly struck by the image of the still unseen artist with her throat cradled between the lion's bone-crushing jaws and razored teeth. Here was a woman who hadn't yet surrendered to love but needed desperately to do so.

And so he'd made his inquiry with the Norrins, and then a few more until he had learned she was opening a gallery and that most of her time was spent there when she wasn't on-site at a client's, painting a new mural. He could have called—he had the number to her answering service and to the gallery. He could have, but he didn't want to. He wanted to see her in person. Until he actually saw her in person, and then, like a schoolboy catching his first glimpse of a woman's bare breast, he'd hidden and watched—afraid she would disappear into thin air if he announced his presence.

Though the gallery wasn't open to business, the doors were. Workmen were on the inside—one putting up a temporary sunscreen on the windows, another installing a security system. He could hear a woman's voice talking with a third worker at the back of the gallery—the moveable display walls blocked his view. Maceo moved toward the voice, noticing the precision and underlying chill of her words and tone as she discussed the dollar figures the workman was throwing at her. He had seen that ice in her work too—her women often aloof and frigid. Cold, pale creatures who would accept none of the heat offered them.

Stalking her through the maze of walls, he paused every few seconds as one of the already hung pictures demanded his attention. Her first showing, it seemed, would be a trip to Dante's vision of hell. From the canvas women looked at him, their heads on backward, ripe asses pushed high in the air as a lake of flames lapped at their stomachs and breasts. One canvas, simply titled *Suicides*, showed a forest, but when he looked closer, he saw that bodies formed the trees, their branch-like arms thinning and vining back in to coil around their own necks and strangle them to death. Everywhere, fire threatened destruction.

By the time Maceo had turned the final corner and caught his first glimpse of Izzy, he was trembling from the combined effect of despair and beauty. Seeing her stopped him dead in his tracks. She was stunning but, more than that, she was familiar. He had a second to wonder whether she had painted herself into any of the murals when it hit him—the auction he had purchased his home at. She'd been there, in the crowd, watching him even. Until he caught her shocked gaze, and then she seemed to look anywhere but at him. He had searched for her after the bidding was through, unable to force his way past the congratulatory handshakes in time to prevent her leaving.

Little had changed in those six years. If anything, time had enhanced her beauty. The hair that had hung in copper coils that day was tied back, but a few tendrils had managed to escape and curve along the line of her jaw. The pale skin was still unspoiled by the touch of too much sun and her lips were flushed a pale mauve as she argued over the price to fix the gallery's air-conditioning system.

It must have been the failed air-conditioning unit that had caused her to shed the jacket to her pantsuit. Whatever the reason, she wasn't wearing a bra beneath the thin silk shell of the pantsuit's blouse. It was, he thought, another example of the conflict within her. Outside she presented a cold exterior, but beneath that wisp of fabric were two small, pert breasts slick with sweat from the unusually high July temperatures—wet and salty, begging to be licked and suckled if only the icy shell could be stripped away without damage to the hot interior.

Sure that her little fashion tic was a prime example of everything about her, Maceo had retreated. He would meet her, but not in the safe cocoon of her private domain. He would pull her into his, into his home and the rotunda with the walls that he now felt fate had left blank for this very purpose.

Groaning from the heat that still infected his body and thoughts, Maceo pushed up onto his elbows and squinted through the dark at the clock on his bedroom dresser. The clock was fashioned from moonstone and silver, both materials representing his Cancerian birth. The moonstone, lit from within by a thin filament, had been fashioned into a bull's horns—another play on his sun sign with the crescent shape, but also signifying his ascendant sign of Taurus. The shadow of the silver clock hands over the curve of the horns told him it was a quarter past five, or maybe it was three twenty-five. He could never tell at night. In his profession, time was everything and nothing to him, and the ambiguity of the many clocks in his house was a testament to that odd fact.

He swung his feet up and over the side edge of the bed until he was in a sitting position, the tip of his erection nuzzling the dip of his navel. For a second, he considered finding relief of one sort or another in the bathroom, if a cold shower could drive away thoughts of Izzy's breasts or any other part of her body. He decided, instead, to put on a robe and go into his study.

Flicking on the light, his gaze wandered over the floor-to-ceiling bookshelf opposite his desk in search of a distraction. The subjects on his shelves were an eclectic mix—or would be to any other mind. There were the expected tomes on astrology and tarot, half a dozen of which he had written or co-authored. More shelves were filled with psychology, philosophy, art, ancient history, semantics, calligraphy, astronomy, computer programming, advanced mathematics and physics. As with the astrology and tarot, the math and physics sections housed titles with his name on them.

A smile played at the edge of his mouth as he wondered what Izzy would think of his master's degree in physics. The smile deepened and he turned away from the bookshelf and skirted the desk. A sheet of metal hung on the wall. Globes, dancing with deep swirls of electric colors, had been cut onto the surface with a plasma arc welder and were strung together to represent the solar system. Maceo let his hand play over the surface of the metal for an instant before he felt along the top and released a spring lock.

From the small safe hiding behind the artwork, he pulled a silver box and placed it on his desk. The inside of the box was lined with black velvet and held slim metal cards. Like the sheet metal behind his desk, a plasma arc had been used to bring out shapes and colors, but the metal was a Bali silver—the pewter content giving it strength and a darker tone. There were seventy-eight cards, each precisely designed according to his specifications and one of a kind now that their creator had passed away.

He removed the cards and placed them on his desk next to the box. Next, he picked up a dark-charcoal pencil and a piece of bond paper. From the top center drawer of his desk, he pulled a printout detailing the astrological alignment at Izzy's birth. As he had suspected, the Goat was heavy in her chart. She was a quadruple Capricorn—the sign being present in the Sun, Moon, Mercury and Venus at her birth. But the restrictive influence of Saturn—Capricorn's planetary ruler—was opposed by her rising sign of Cancer and the creative freedom the Moon bestowed on her children. Depending on other aspects of her chart, a Cancer ascendant could be good or bad. The two signs were polar opposites, with the positive influences of one potentially offsetting the negative influences of the other. For some, however, they could be fatal opposites, the dueling natures rending the mind in half and leading to a lifetime of misery.

Starting to sketch a visual depiction of Izzy's chart, Maceo sighed. As a Canc, he was Izzy's astrological opposite too. No wonder he had felt an instant attraction—an attraction that seemed to frighten her and that her Saturn nature would do everything to quash. As he continued sketching her chart, he became more concerned. Saturn's position in Mercury indicated an early interruption in her education and Jupiter in Scorpio hinted at profound troubles with one or both of her parents.

Putting down the pencil, Maceo picked up the tarot deck and gently shuffled the silver cards. Focusing on Izzy, her pale oval face framed by copper curls and her gaze a cloak of emerald ice, he started with an astrological spread. He laid twelve cards down on the table, one for each house. The pattern resembled a clock's face, but started at nine and ran counterclockwise. In the first house was the Queen of Swords upside down. It was not the card he would have picked for Izzy with her warm coloring, but it was meant to signify her personal issues. Even knowing the card's purpose, he still wondered if the cold, inflexible queen was all there was at Izzy's core.

Remembering her heated reaction when their bodies had touched the day before, Maceo brushed the thought away. When he reached the seventh house, opposite the first and signifying relationships, he glanced back at the Queen before returning his attention to the upside down King of Cups. A betrayal, then? Or did the Queen and King represent her parents—an emotionally blank mother and a devious father? Whichever it was, he knew he had to proceed cautiously but with persistence. Her walls wouldn't yield with a few smiles and caresses—but they would yield.

He would make sure of that.

THREE

*I*Z! IT'S TEN-THIRTY ALREADY, are you going to do it or not?"

Sitting in her car at the gas station near her condo, Izzy jerked the cell phone away from her head. The shrill excitement of her sister Millicent's voice threatened to drill a hole in her eardrum.

"I'm in the car now," Izzy answered, hesitating before she put the phone back up to her ear. She could almost hear the whir of Millicent's industrious mind.

"He's loaded, right?"

"He has a house on 17 Mile Drive and he's paying me thirty-five thousand plus materials for a mural." Izzy sighed, her mind jumping ahead to the next question. *Click, whir.*

"And he's interested in you? I mean *interested?*"

Izzy glanced at the dashboard clock and then closed her eyes. An image of her sister rose up. More glamorous, though no prettier in the abstract, Millicent was the type of Rodeo Drive Queen she would expect to see on the arm of a man like Maceo. *Or at least the public Maceo,* she thought, and opened her eyes before she could summon a full memory of the expression he had worn as he left her in the rotunda. *Hopeful—not needy—but wanting, desiring . . . and something so deep and soulful in his expectations that it could only be her imagination or her own needs projected.*

"Is it really that hard to believe, Milly?" she asked. The *click, whir,* turned to the sound of her sister backpedaling.

"I didn't mean it like that, Iz! Just . . . I mean, how cool is that?" There was a pause as vanity and self-pity snuck into Millicent's voice. "And ironic."

"You'll catch your own millionaire one of these days, sweetie." She managed to keep her tone light. Any note of disapproval in Millicent's apparent career choice of snagging a filthy rich husband would result in an argument Izzy didn't have time for.

"Maybe I'll find one at your wedding," Millicent teased.

"Yeah, right." The answer came out in a snort and Izzy strummed her fingers against the steering wheel until she caught sight of the uneven nails and their creases filled with an ever-present line of paint and clay.

"Look, hon, don't shoot yourself in the foot before you even walk in the door!"

"*Nothing* is going to happen, okay?" Glancing at the clock again, Izzy started the car and put it in gear. She really couldn't be late, not with a commission hanging in the balance that would cover the remaining costs of opening the gallery and tide her over for its first six months. "He's just another smooth, rich guy trying to play with the hired help—I run across them all the time."

Except she'd never run across another man like Maceo. Sighing, she rested her head against the top of the steering wheel and tried not to look at the clock while Milly continued arguing.

"He's not Ron," Milly said. "None of them are, hon. You have to learn that sooner or later."

Izzy's mouth quirked and she leaned back in the seat, trying to turn Milly away from the subject of their biological father without opening up old wounds. "I wouldn't know," she answered, her voice soft and contemplative. "I never really met Ron. For that matter, neither did you."

"You're so stubborn—" Milly started, not yet ready to relent.

"Look, I've got to get going," Izzy interrupted. "You do want me to go, right?"

"You're insufferable when you're like this, you know?" Milly asked. Her tone was indulgent, as if she were the older of the two. "And you're *always* like this."

"Milly, please—"

"How are you timing it?" Millicent asked, gears running smoothly once again as she moved the topic back to Izzy and Maceo. "He's leaving at noon, right?"

"I'm not—"

"Puh-leeze, don't lie to your own sister, or yourself." Millicent said, the admonishment softened by her light laughter. "Of course you're timing it. Too early and he'll think you're desperate, too late and you're some cold-ass bitch playing hard-to-get."

"Okay, okay." Izzy relented. She checked the time—*ten-fifty-nine*. It would take at least twenty minutes this time of day to get through the community gate and to the front gate of Maceo's house if the traffic on Forest Avenue stayed as light as it was. "But wouldn't you say I'm timing it awfully damn close right now?"

"Just don't you dare turn your cell off," Millicent said. "I've got a hair appointment at one—but then I want to know *everything!*"

"Okay, okay."

"You said that already!" Another laugh, her words splitting like wind through silver chimes.

"But, I . . ." Izzy stopped, looked at her nails again. One had less than a millimeter of white showing above the quick. She could picture Millicent's nails, each one a perfect matching length, the color one shade darker than the day's lipstick. "Look, I—"

"It's eleven-oh-five, hon. Just say goodbye!"

"Good—" The sound of Millicent hanging up cut Izzy short and she switched her phone off, tossing it onto the front passenger seat. Checking her rearview mirror before backing from the parking space, she gave a low growl. "Does she ever *not* get the last word in?"

Leaving the gas station, she turned left onto Forest Avenue. She was aware of the rapid tic of her pulse and the odd little backbeat that developed whenever she was nervous. The car in front of her was doing five miles under the speed limit and she switched her turn signal on.

"Of course, I'm nervous," she said, and started pulling into the left lane. Her foot pressed down on the gas pedal before she cleared the bumper of the slower car. She jerked farther to the left as the other driver pulled far right. "Thirty-five thousand dollars, the gallery, it's not like . . ."

Great, now I'm talking to myself. Raising her hand, she returned a slightly less impatient gesture than the other driver had offered and then pulled to a stop at the traffic light. Another light and then she would be able to see the curved wall of the Presidio before she hit the tunnel. The route was circuitous but still twice as quick as trying to find a more direct path across the little enclave of the rich and richer.

Passing the southeastern links of Pebble Beach some fifteen minutes later, Izzy glanced down at the dashboard clock and allowed herself to relax a little. She still had thirty minutes despite underestimating how much time the curving drive and slower speeds would eat up. *Not to mention the foot traffic!*

"Just stop it!" Window down, she spoke too loudly and a young woman with a golf bag on her slim shoulders jerked her head to look at Izzy.

Izzy waved and mouthed the words *not you*. So what if Maceo did think she was playing hard-to-get? That wouldn't stop him from writing the deposit check. It wouldn't cause her to lose the job. And she wasn't really interested in him. Not *that* interested, at least.

Rounding the last turn, she saw that the gate to *Casa di Silvio* was open. At least he hadn't left early. Or maybe he had and someone was waiting there to let her in. Slowing down, she pulled into the drive, her gaze jumping ahead to catch sight of the house and the front door.

The doors were open again, the trunk of a black Crossfire up. She parked behind the sports car and took a few seconds to compose herself. Her attention flitted half a dozen times to the doorway but it remained empty. Drawing a deep breath, she unlocked her car door and stepped out. No sound came from the house as she walked up the short path. Stepping over the threshold, she instantly felt an ocean breeze and noticed that the doors to the rotunda were open. Was he waiting where he'd left her?

Izzy started to call out, but something checked her words and she moved quietly across the expansive entry room. She felt ungrounded, as if she were floating toward the rotunda and then down its steps into the center depression. She didn't see him and turned slowly, trying to mask a rising sense of disappointment. When her gaze landed on the section of wall that would house Sagittarius, a smile broke past her tight-lipped façade.

"I thought," Maceo said, and stepped away from the wall, "you'd start here. If you don't mind, that is?"

Izzy shrugged and turned to examine the remainder of the room. "I don't, but why?"

"It was the most finished sample you showed me." He had used the built-in bench as steps and stood directly behind Izzy, his breath whispering against her shoulders as he answered. "Or Scorpio," he added after a second's pause, just long enough for the hairs at the nape of her neck to relax before being thrilled all over again.

She gave another shrug, the motion serving only to transfer the trail of flesh bumps from across her neck to her breasts where the nipples hardened against the thin linen of her blouse.

"Your vision for those signs is excellent, even with your horoscope's placement of Jupiter in Scorpio." He wanted to push the issue of her childhood and the relationship he had seen reflected in her chart and the two tarot readings he had done that morning. But, more than that, he wanted to touch her and he ran a fingertip along the curve of Izzy's neck.

Maceo's touch made the flesh on her thighs crawl with a pleasant anticipation and she moved away from him with an abrupt sidestep. She rolled her shoulders, trying to throw off the sensation of his touch and keep the meeting as businesslike as possible. "I'll need the deposit for supplies," she said, turning back to him once she was at the opposite end of the lower level, "and the key."

He was dressed in a light-gray suit, the silk shirt beneath a perfect match for his eyes. If there was any flaw in his form, the cut of the fabric hid it. Shaking her head, she turned away. The fabric hid nothing. It molded itself around him, caressing the narrow waist, lingering over the powerful thighs and chest, reaching up to wrap around the broad shoulders. She felt her exterior temperature spike despite the first cool breeze in weeks filtering into the room from the open patio doors.

"Everything's in order," Maceo said.

Hearing the crisp snap of paper, Izzy risked another glance at him. He was holding a thick envelope up, his expression playful as he motioned for her to come and take it.

Like a cat dangling a cube of cheese, she thought. Moving toward him, she felt an uncharacteristic sway working its way into her walk and tried to straighten it out before he noticed. She took the envelope and dropped her gaze as a warm blush fanned across her cheeks. A twin flush circled her chest and thighs, making her wet as she stood in front of him, waiting to find out what he would do next and how she would respond.

He gestured at the envelope. "Deposit, keys, contact information for me and security . . . there are more numbers by the phone in the kitchen." He paused, not quite reaching out for her, and then shoved his hands into his pockets. "You're welcome to enter any room that's not locked."

"And where am I going to sleep?" Izzy asked. She felt childish but she couldn't bring her gaze up to meet his.

"I-I thought you could sleep in here," he said. His right hand snuck its way out of the pocket only to play at the edge of his jacket. "A bed's being brought in and a wardrobe to hold your things . . . I thought you'd like it."

Touched by his perception and a little confused, she nodded.

"But sleep anywhere you like . . . in the house, that is." Clearing his throat, Maceo glanced at his watch. "Well, I've two more bags to stuff in the trunk before I can leave. Do you need help unloading your car?"

"No, I'm fine," she answered. She looked up, caught his blue gaze and offered an awkward smile. "The platform equipment won't arrive until tomorrow."

"Well, when they're bringing in the bed—if you need anything brought in"—he stopped, leaned toward her and then abruptly pulled back—"just tell them."

Feeling like a kindergartener on her first day in school, she nodded again, her head bobbing to convey her understanding. The unexpected hesitation in his voice and manner made her heart flutter. Had he thought to kiss her just then, she wondered? Why hadn't he?

Maceo nodded back and then, for the second day in a row, left her standing alone in the middle of the rotunda.

FOUR

ARS WAS BATTLING A white-fleeced ram when Maceo returned from New York four days later. Using her projector and half a dozen computer graphics programs, Izzy had the first layers of Sagittarius and Scorpio done, their completion waiting the arrival of a few special paints and more drying time before she could apply them.

"It's more like you're fighting with Ares than he is fighting the ram, you know?" Maceo said after he inspected the other two sections of the mural.

Izzy took a step back, reaching behind her to place a brush in the tin of cleaner. It was already dark, the natural daylight gone, and she resisted the urge to brush past him and shut off the freestanding lights she had been working with. She cupped her elbows instead. "What do you mean?"

His gaze traveled the contours of her forearms. She was hugging herself, the fabric of her blouse drawn across the delicate morsels of her breasts. They were bare underneath, just as he had seen her at the gallery, and the knowledge distracted him. Could she appreciate the dichotomy, he wondered? The way she simultaneously pushed and pulled, seeking to be free and restrained at the same time.

He scratched absently at the rough shadow of a beard that had formed since she last saw him and forced his attention back to the image. "You're viewing Ares as a brute," he answered after a few more seconds of thought. "And the ram's relationship to Ares—Ares is his sovereign, the ram may not wish to submit at first . . . but how can he not?"

She moved in front of the painting, letting her silence serve as an answer to his criticism.

"You don't feel it?" he asked.

When she shook her head to indicate she didn't, he continued on, his words tumbling out in an apparent attempt to keep her from interrupting or running away.

"Mars is in Pisces in your horoscope, you see? Mars is determined, hot, not at all like the gentle water sign of Pisces. And Mars is in its aversion, here—a full zodiac away from the sign it rules. That's a hard mix, particularly with another water sign as your ascendant . . ." His hands tried to shape the air in front of him into meaning. "With this layout, forcing submission only meets with absolute obstinacy." He gestured at the ram. "And yet, with the right pressure—gentle pressure—submission becomes the most natural thing in the world."

Maceo pointed at Ares's hands on the ram's horn and shoulder. "There's no gentle pressure here." He turned, his gaze sweeping over her face and shoulders. "Think about the touch that would make you yield and paint that."

"This isn't about my horoscope or me submitting or—"

He interrupted Izzy, moving closer to her with the wary grace of a predator. "It's about an unyielding inability to—"

"Nu-uh," she said, sidestepping him to turn off the nearest lamp.

Maceo grabbed her by the shoulders before she could reach the light. Unbalancing Izzy, he gently spun her until her back was flat against one of the cool marble columns. His hand raced up to cushion her head before it could touch the stone. As part of the same fluid motion, he moved closer to her until his chest brushed against her nipples.

The threat of further contact, of his chest pressing harder against her breasts or his hips meeting hers, kept Izzy pinned in place. She told herself to stay cool, but caught the telling direction of his glance as it measured the distance from the column to the queen-size bed centered on the floor of the rotunda's lower level.

"I'm here to paint the mural, that's all!" she said.

He smiled, his gaze and mouth sleepy with the need to move her to the bed. He leaned closer, holding her in place with his torso while he eased his hand from behind her head to release the rich coils of copper-colored hair she had roughly tied back. His other hand moved down to cup her breast.

"You don't really think you can separate yourself from your art, do you, Izzy?" Adjusting the press of his weight against her, he thumbed slow circles around her erect nipple. He caressed her temple, the pace of his touch against her breast and the side of her face hypnotically asynchronous.

She looked over his shoulder to see their position reflected in the mural, the black and gold eyes of the ram seeming to mock her. "You're wrong," she whispered. "You're seeing what you want to . . . or trying to convince me—"

"This isn't a pick-up gimmick, Isold," Maceo said, his lips played against the curve of her jaw and the faint growth of beard brushed her check.

She pressed closer to the column, but the marble had lost its chill and offered no relief from the heat spreading out from the press of his mouth on her throat, or his warm breath as the veil of her hair trapped and magnified its effect against her skin. "I-I don't want this," she said, the last word catching as she gasped from the sudden press of his erection against her stomach.

He slid against her, rising up to kiss the crown of her forehead before trailing his lips over her closed eyelids and against her trembling lips. Her skin ached, every muscle drawn tight in resistance to the pleasure his touch offered. Knees locked, she felt a swoon threaten, and then he was sliding downward, his mouth moving over the cloth that covered her breasts. His knees met the floor, his descent over her stomach slowing until he stopped, his mouth nuzzling against her mons as he breathed new heat through the thin fabric of the shorts she was wearing.

Head lolling, she opened her eyes and looked at him kneeling in front of her. *Mars abeyante.* Her hands, held stiff at her sides the entire time, brushed once against the dark, black curls and then she knotted her fingers through his hair. He lipped the front of her shorts—the sharp tease of his teeth played at the surface of her labia and she moaned. Eyes closed once more, the mural filled her mind even as the sensation of Maceo's touch claimed her body. The arrogance of Mars disappeared and she saw only the gentle subduing of one fierce creature by another.

She was moving against him now, against the questing mouth as she telegraphed more than mere consent. Maceo tugged her shorts down. Her panties clung to her skin, the fabric wet with her desire and from the moist sucking he had teased her into submission with.

Transitory submission, she told herself, watching his tongue lift the edge of lace that lay against her thigh before disappearing beneath the fabric. *Mutual submission*, she amended and spread her legs as far as Maceo's firm grip on her hips would allow. She wouldn't lose herself, wouldn't give more of herself than he offered in return.

His tongue parted her labia, thrusting into the well of her cream before attacking her clit. Near collapsing from the strain, her body trembled against him, deepening the vibration of his mouth on her pussy. Her hands grew clumsy and rough in his hair, her breathing down to sharp pants as the first clench of orgasm approached.

Supporting Izzy's weight, Maceo jacked her tight against the marble column. She folded around him, crying out with each tremor of her climax.

More. She wanted more. She wanted the thick cock she had felt pressed against her sliding through her slick folds. She wanted the weight of his heavy balls slapping against her ass as he held her legs wide and rammed into her.

Untangling her hands from his hair, Izzy ran her nails up her stomach and underneath her shirt to squeeze her breasts. Maceo released her hips and covered her hands as he rose up. His mouth crushed hers and he forced her hands away from the sensitive tips of her breasts, pushing the fabric up and out of the way. Pinching her nipples, he teased them to a darker shade of crimson before flicking his tongue against the tips and blowing cold air around the circles of her areolas.

She was still in her underwear and he grabbed one edge, cinching her to him as he moved down the impromptu steps of the bench to the bed. He pushed her onto the mattress, pulling her panties roughly down to her ankles. He twisted his fist in the delicate material, the motion forcing her knees to bend so that she was on her back, ass thrust an inch off the mattress and the front of her thighs pressed hard against her breasts.

With his free hand, he reached into his jacket pocket and pulled a condom out. Holding the foil packet with his teeth, he quickly unzipped his pants and pushed his briefs down. His erection, full and curving in its length, jutted forward. He ripped the condom's wrapper open with his teeth and sheathed his cock in one extended pass.

She wanted him in her—in her pussy, in her mouth—fucking something, anything, and she gave an urgent little moan for him to enter her before she exploded again.

"Oh . . . oh, gawd," she said, groaning as he thrust into her. She could feel his cock stretching her, his erection plump and solid. She wriggled against him, trying to accommodate the girth of his cock. Its weight pressed deeper into her, massaging her clit from the inside out as he rocked back and forth, still holding the impromptu binding of her feet so that she was forced to rock with him.

Maceo's other hand reached between her legs to rub her clit with hard, matching strokes. Izzy moved to cover her face, to find some shelter from the intense pleasure building inside her, but he ordered her to look at him. She obeyed, startled that no trace of arrogance creased his mouth as he roughly conquered her pussy.

"I'm coming," she breathed out, embarrassment flushing her cheeks only to be instantly washed away by the first rush of the announced orgasm.

Maceo tossed his head back, his expression squeezed tight as he thrust into her and froze. His body pulsed in climax and then he rotated his hips, grinding deeper into Izzy's cunt as his fingers started their dance over her clit once more.

"Please, no . . ." Another desperate moan robbed Izzy of the rest of her protest. His orgasm hadn't robbed Maceo of his erection and was still thrusting inside her slick pussy. Her cream coated the condom and he smeared his fingers in it before continuing his assault on her sensitive button.

"Ah, Isold, don't go cold on me now," he pleaded, intent on wringing another orgasm from her. She was bucking against him now, her hands flung over her head and knotted in the bedspread. "I've seen the fire inside you," he coaxed. "You're so hot right now, I can feel you holding me, feel each flutter."

She *was* fluttering around him, the walls of her cunt mimicking an epileptic butterfly as she gave up all control to his touch. She came again, the third wave of pleasure drowning her in its force. And then he was withdrawing from her, unbinding her ankles and pulling her up into the center of the mattress. He stepped away for an instant to the trash can waiting for the filled condom. He returned to the bed, covering her with his body. His kisses, meant to calm her electrified flesh, only made her hotter, and she arched against him.

"Shhhh . . ." He pulled the bedspread around her shoulders, wrapping her tightly to him so that she couldn't move. He kissed her neck and shoulders, pulling her shirt off before peppering more kisses across her cheeks and closed eyelids. When her body calmed, he bundled her back up in the covers and caressed her until she fell asleep.

Izzy felt Maceo trying to wake her early the next morning. He ran his fingertips lightly over her cheek, at the corner of her eye, across the full width of her lower lip. He nuzzled her ear, his voice alert as he softly called her name. When she kept her responses to half mumbles, he rolled onto his back, one hand still toying with her hair.

"Morning-after remorse, Isold?"

She ignored the question. "You're flying to Sacramento this morning?"

He gave a little growl at Izzy's non-answer and turned back, tossing his leg over her and drawing her to him. Chin resting against her shoulder, he sighed. She curled against the brush of air along her neck and Maceo rolled her onto her back. Bringing her hands up, she tried to create a barrier between their bodies even as her hips rose up to press against his erection.

"Why do you regret last night, Izzy?" he asked. He grabbed her wrists and pulled her hands above her head. "I remember you as not wanting to stop last night." He was kissing her as he spoke, moving from lips to neck to breast and back up again, his erection sliding across her mons, in the shallow valley the press of her thighs created, and back over her swelling labia.

Her nipples were hard and the telling smell of fresh cream coating her pussy wafted up as the sheets moved with him. Answering him, she tried to keep her voice a cold contrast to her body's signs that he was making her hot. "I wasn't thinking last night."

"You should do that more often," he said, nuzzling against her throat a second before his lips fastened over the crook of her shoulder and he started sucking.

"Not. Think?" she asked.

Maceo stopped and chuckled, heating the skin on her throat and reminding Izzy of the firm press of his lips as he had knelt before her, his tongue sliding across the smooth silk of her pubic hair to part her labia. He'd have her back to an unthinking state before the bruise of his sharp little kiss could surface if she didn't get him off her. He still held her wrists above her head and she twisted against him. Feeling his hard body against her as she moved only ensnared her further, but he pulled back, releasing her.

"And what is it you think about that makes you pull away?"

Spreading his legs and planting a hand on each side of her, Maceo hovered over Izzy without touching her. The bedspread slid halfway down his back, revealing the strong expanse of his shoulders and thick biceps.

Izzy's gaze flicked lower and then she had to close her eyes to keep from staring at the erect cock. Swollen, suffused with blood from his desire, the skin was a polished caramel, darker where the network of veins pushed at the surface. "You." The word erupted with a petulant tone, pushed out with a thick need to curl around his erection.

"What are you afraid of?" he asked. His voice was low, contemplative, and she imagined he was tilting his head at her, studying her with those eyes as blue as a Mediterranean bay. "Pleasure? Losing control? Losing it in or out of bed, Isold?"

"Stop calling me that!"

"Why? It's your name," he said. Waiting for her response, he dipped his head. Not touching her, he blew lightly across her collarbone, over her shoulder. "Who gave you that name? Your mother? Father?"

Seeing sadness and then anger flit over Izzy's features, Maceo dropped the question.

"*Ice*, that's what your name means. You would think Saturn icy, so far from the sun . . . You know it has its own heat, Izzy?" He had slid farther down her body, the little wisps of air he was blowing kissed her nipples before leaving a trail of flesh bumps down her stomach to her navel. "It radiates more heat than it receives. Isn't that how it's been with your lovers, Izzy? With everyone in your life? You giving so much more than you receive—but because you hold back from satisfying your own desires." He shook his head, his expression perplexed. "Whatever caused it, it doesn't need to be that way anymore." When she still said nothing, he pressed on. "Why deny yourself that pleasure?"

Maceo was almost all the way down the bed now, his head even with her pussy. He stopped, no longer teasing her with the touch of his breath against her skin, and waited. After a few seconds, he gave another small puff. "Look at me, Izzy."

She opened her eyes and pushed up on shaking arms to look at him. His lips were flushed a dark carmine and his irises had darkened, something primal flickering in the black of his pupils. Resting his weight on one arm, he ran a hand over the exterior of her pussy, sliding his thumb between the swollen lips. Finding her wet, he centered his thumb in the tight exterior circle of her cunt, rotating it around the muscled rim until she squirmed against him.

"I'm just not looking for a fling," she said, at last trying to back away from his touch but finding her body incapable of anything but a sharp thrust to draw his teasing thumb deeper into her. *Was this what her mother had felt with Ron?* Izzy wondered. *Something so intense, she was nothing but a drained shell after he abandoned them both?*

"And I am?"

The low growl that held his question interrupted Izzy's thoughts and warned her against making any assumptions. Watching her move with him, a sensual grin flashed across his face. He pulled out, moving away from her completely and holding his hand out to her.

Izzy looked up, slightly dazed from the sudden loss. She thrust her head back into the pillow so she could see Maceo's face. His jaw was set, his gaze inflexible, but there was a look of gentle kindness around the edges of his mouth. Maybe she already was an empty shell and he meant to fill her.

"Come on, get up," he said, hand still extended. "You need a little water play before you get back to work."

She shook her head at him but took his hand and let him lead her naked to the suite-like master bath. She had been in the room already, curiosity and his open invitation for her to enter any unlocked room leading her to explore the house on the first night. She hadn't used the master bath, though, just stood in awe at the threshold while she described it over the cell phone to Milly. Every surface—floor, walls, ceiling, even the tub and separate double shower—was covered with small Mexican tiles of varying shades of blue. The faucets and handles were polished chrome, light winking along their surface at every angle.

"What do you mean, water play?" she asked, hesitating as he tried to guide her into the room.

"Just a shower, Izzy," he answered. The curve of his smile and the hungry way his gaze dropped to travel over her breasts suggested it would be anything but *just* a shower.

Half relenting, she let him coax her into the center of the unenclosed shower. Unable to stop herself, she glanced down as he followed her in. Still erect, his cock pushed forward only to have its length force it to curve back to where the thick head rested just below his navel. She drew her lips in, wetting them as he pulled the showerhead from its cradle and turned it on in slow degrees.

"You've a plane to catch," she reminded him.

"Plenty of time, love," he said. Satisfied that the water was neither too hot nor too cold, he put it back into its cradle and then pulled her into his embrace.

Izzy closed her eyes, telling herself it was because of the warm spray and not because of the word he had used. He was just being Italian—calling anything he fucked *love* but not loving everything he fucked. That's all it was, all it could be. *Fucking.* Fucking was safe—at least emotionally.

"Don't be so stiff, Isold," he said, leaning his back against the shower wall and taking a bar of soap from the small corner ledge.

"I told you—"

"Then don't be so stiff," he laughed, rubbing the soap over her breasts and flexing his glutes so that his cock twitched where it was nestled between the cheeks of her bottom. "Leave that to me, 'kay?"

"Shouldn't we . . . umm." She turned, avoiding his mouth as he kissed the curve of her jaw. She scanned the counter of the double sink, half expecting a bowl of silver-wrapped condoms to be there.

"Just a shower, Izzy," he said. His soapy fingers slipped lower, ran light circles over the taut muscles of her stomach, dipped into her belly button before racing back up to her nipples. "I want your Pisces at ease and open when you're finishing up Ares and his ram."

He was soaping her clit, the feather strokes doing anything but putting her at ease. "And how many little lessons are you proposing before the mural is finished?" she asked, ending her question with a sharp bite on the fleshy lobe of his ear.

"As many as it takes."

Holding her to him, he was tugging at her clit while he pinched her nipple. The pressure was gentle at her clit, sharp on her breast, the erect tip darkening with abuse and need. Izzy moaned, her hips moving in small circles as she followed the play of his hand over the spine of her pussy.

"And what lesson is this?" She panted the question, arching and gasping as he pinched the nipple harder.

His touch slowed and she responded with a mewling protest.

"It's intuitive, love," he answered, slowing further.

He sighed and even the sharp rise of his chest against her back aroused her. She brought her arms up and around him, interlocking her fingers behind his neck and turning her head to kiss him.

"The water or your methods?" she asked after breaking the kiss.

Eyes sparkling, he smiled and kissed her back. "Both. I want you floating back to the rotunda on a wave of endorphins . . . I want you thinking about me all day." He slid his fingers across her labia, over her thighs. "Each brushstroke, I want you to remember this. I want you to be in touch with your creative center."

Izzy arched against him, rose up on the tips of her toes as she tried to guide Maceo's cock to her. He shifted, denying Izzy the thick treat, sliding his other hand down her back and coaxing her away from him. Unknotting her hands from behind his neck, she leaned forward and braced herself against the opposite wall of the shower.

Maceo teased her cunt with both hands, rubbing her rigid clit, rolling its engorged hood between thumb and forefinger as his other hand massaged the exterior ring of her pussy. Hands soaped, he invaded her one finger at a time. Impatient, she ground against him until he rewarded her by joining first two fingers and then three. His hand left her clit and she heard him lift the showerhead from its cradle. The muscles of her pussy contracted in anticipation as she felt the powerful pulse of the water against the small of her back, the nozzle a few inches from her skin.

The slow, tight throb of the water's spray moved down her back. She contracted again, her muscles viselike around his fingers as the pressure danced over the nervous pucker of her ass. The steady pulse, lingering at the swollen entrance to her pussy, followed the motion of his fingers inside her, slapping her sensitive flesh only to dart away. And then Maceo trailed the nozzle across and around her leg until the steady rhythm was against her stomach, promising sharp licks and kisses against her clit.

Izzy's legs began to tremble from the strain, from the need to

come as she felt him pounding inside her with the same irresistible thrust the water delivered. Clenching and rotating her
hips, she worked his probing fingers. She forgot her morning remorse, ignored its potential return as she ground harder against
him, letting the sensation of his hands and the water violently
whipsaw her senses until she bowed her head against her arms
and came in one long cry of pleasure.

When she was finished riding the last wave of her climax,
Maceo pulled her back to him, his hands once again rich with
lather as he caressed her flesh. She sought his mouth, kissing him
between entreaties that he fuck her.

Had she ever asked a man that before, she wondered? Had
she said those words before? *Fuck me, please. I want to feel you inside me,
filling me, fucking me.* Izzy shook her head, sure she hadn't—that it
was a first.

"Hmmm?" Maceo asked, seeing the sharp toss of her head.
"What is *no*, love?"

"Nothing . . ." He was still stroking and pinching her aroused
flesh, sending her back to the edge of another orgasm and she
turned a circle in his embrace. "Cancer is a water sign," she said,
her kisses turning to light bites as he evaded her hands. "Show me
that, please."

He caught her hands and brought them up to his lips, slowly
sucking at her fingertips. "When it's time," he said, and gently
forced her back so he could rinse the soap from her body.

Flesh impassioned, she pushed at his hands and ran her fingers
wildly through her hair. "I want . . . mmm . . ."

He wrapped an oversized towel around her, drawing her tight
within it when she wiggled against it.

"Maceo . . . I need . . ." Frustration cut her words short and she snaked her arms from the impromptu binding. He let her kiss him, let her deepen the contact until the towel was on the floor and she was covering him.

"You need patience," he teased, turning her until she was resting against the countertop.

"I thought that was a problem."

Stepping back, he smiled at her. "Nothing about you is a problem, love—merely a challenge." Reaching out, he trapped her head between his two strong hands. "Stop shaking your head at me."

"You're teasing," she said, her tone chilling from the steamy heat it had held a few seconds before. The light humor he used in rejecting Izzy irritated her. Hadn't her mother always gone on about Ron's laugh and his smile—how he could end any argument they had with a mere wink and a crook of his finger? When Maceo shook his head again to deny her, she pushed against him. "Then why say *no*?"

Maceo raised an eyebrow at her. "That plane you were so worried about me catching?"

"So you're punishing me." He was still holding her head and she trailed her hands up over the veined forearms to the hard curve of his biceps.

Dropping one hand, he rolled her nipple between his thumb and forefinger as he stepped between her parted thighs. His cock, rigid and swollen, butted between her labia, probing but stopping just shy of entering her. "Punishing you with pleasure?" he asked, amusement and incredulity mixing in his voice.

"Incomplete—" she started to accuse, and then stopped short with a moan as he rolled the nipple a little harder, the tumescent head of his cock sliding up to stroke the hood of her clit.

Almost indignant, he gave a rough twist to the tip of her breast while the pressure of his cock bore down on the spine of her sex. "Incomplete? How many times did you come this morning, Izzy?"

Leaning into his hand, she wrapped her legs around his hips and locked him to her. "But *you* haven't." She had promised herself earlier that she would offer no more than what he would give in return—but he was giving too much, the inequality of it making her feel needy. She slid against him, sweat from the room's heat and her own frustration kept her skin slick as she tried to coax him into taking her. "I want *your* pleasure."

"Something to think about before you entomb yourself again in all that Saturn reserve," Maceo said, and dropped his hands to his sides.

Seeing the hard set of Maceo's jaw, Izzy glanced down to find that he seemingly had turned his arousal off with the flip of some inner switch. She unwrapped her legs from him and bounded off the countertop, stopping only long enough to scoop up the towel and cover herself with it.

She turned in the doorway, glancing back over her shoulder. "How is that not punishment?"

He shrugged. "You'll see it as you want until you see it as it is, love."

She felt her mouth screw tight at the use of *that* word. "Don't call me that!"

"What, *love*?" Seeing her curt nod, he threw his hands up in resignation. "Fine, Isold."

Her mouth began to tremble, strain vibrating through her

while her mind bounced between the need to cry and the desire to hit him. She thought back to her last lover and their six-month engagement. No tears had marked the dissolution of their relationship—there had been only a quiet and equitable division of the things they had jointly acquired over the three years of living together. She'd be damned if Maceo was going to make her cry after only a few days and as many climaxes.

"Why are you being so difficult?" she asked, reining in the tight warble of her throat before he could guess at how upset she was.

"That question from a woman who defines *difficult?*" He was smiling, but the expression was restrained and never reached his pale blue gaze. "Ah, I forgot, that's *structure*, right?"

"Fine." Turning away from him, she moved to the bedroom door. "Any instructions on the mural before you go?"

"Umm, no," he answered.

Thoughtful and low, the quality of his voice called Izzy back but she forced herself to move through the open door, wrapping the towel tighter around her as she went. Safely back in the rotunda, she closed the doors and stomped over to the freestanding wardrobe. She pulled out a sleeveless T-shirt, shorts and undergarments. Her breasts were sore, still heavy with the sensation of his touch, and she shoved the bra back inside before roughly pulling the rest of the clothes on and taking up her station in front of Mars and his ram.

Arrogant creature! Had she really thought otherwise last night, if even for the briefest of seconds?

• • •

Hand hanging uselessly at her side, holding an equally useless brush, Izzy still stood in front of the unfinished section that held Aries when Maceo entered the closed rotunda half an hour later. He was dressed in a midnight-blue silk suit, his shirt an antique maize broken by the straight line of a silk tie that matched the suit's dark hue. Through the open doors, she could see three bags. Some Republican convention at the state capital, she remembered—he'd be gone until the following Monday.

"Stuck?"

He didn't approach her, choosing instead to sit on the unmade bed. Hands resting casually between his powerful thighs, he waited for her to answer. Izzy turned, tossing the brush into a can of cleaner. Her gaze dropped to the V of his crotch and she noted how relaxed he seemed. She looked up at the rotunda's dome and counted the crystal-paned windows that were within her field of vision.

She chewed at her bottom lip, counting backward from the last pane. *Just a game. He really must think I'm a dupe, like one of those pressed and starched politicians whose money he'll be pocketing this weekend.*

But then a trickster Maceo was hard to reconcile with that other Maceo, the one she'd found in his library and online, though she had refused to believe they could be the same man until she'd seen the author pictures—an astrologer and an astrophysicist? Dropping her gaze to meet his, she pointed a finger at him, trying to pin him down. "How can you do astrology when you were a scientist *first*?" she asked him.

A single tic flashed once at the corner of his mouth. "You're deflecting my question. Are you stuck?"

Izzy walked back to her worktable and picked up a brush as if to prove she wasn't stuck or deflecting his question. "I think," she started, her voice as neutral as the pale taupe she was loading her brush with, "you're accustomed to asking the questions no one wants to answer and now I've asked you one and *you're* deflecting."

"I'm asking as a concerned patron—you're spoiling for an excuse not to answer."

Izzy lightly pointed the paintbrush in his direction, careful not to let the tension running through her arm send a spray of droplets across the rotunda floor. "That's not . . ." she paused, her thoughts jumping from *maybe* to *yes* to *no*. "That's not the whole truth of it."

"Fine," he said, and smiled.

Damn, there was no reason for that indulgent smile, she thought. He wasn't indulging her and it was too damn sexy.

"To begin to answer your question, I wasn't anything *first*." He closed his eyes, his expression growing soft and sentimental. "I grew up in San Mamete, in Italy but just a few minutes from the Swiss border."

Shifting on the bed, he opened his eyes, his gaze sliding from sentimental to seductive as he studied Izzy's face.

"Why don't you come here, Izzy?" Maceo asked softly.

Too softly. Why did he have to possess a voice that would melt a glacier?

"Because you're not done answering my question." *Because, if I stall long enough, you'll have to leave for Sacramento and I can pretend the last twenty-four hours never happened.*

He continued, but gave a soft growl first, as if he could read her plan just by the way she canted her hip at him or pursed her lips. "My grandfather was Swiss—my mother's father. He'd fallen in love with Nonna Vecchio when her family fled into Switzerland while the fascists were in power. He helped my mother raise me when my father died."

The tic came again, pulling the corner of his mouth down for an instant's frown. "He was Swiss through and through—fell in love with a dark-haired girl who had a gypsy's soul and an aristocrat's upbringing. Each of his three daughters were mirrors of their mother, adept at astrology, tarot and herbal medicine. I guess I was his first chance at injecting some Swiss culture back into his bloodline."

Izzy nodded. Abandoning the charade of the loaded brush, she cleaned it and dumped it back into its container. "So you studied astrophysics to keep both sides happy?"

"Yes."

Maceo shifted, seemingly impatient again, and she wondered if he was getting ready to leave. Did she really want him to?

"But along the way," he continued, relaxing again, "I realized physics and metaphysics are far from incompatible—the best answers come when the two systems are used together. No one else was combining them, at least not as reputably as I could with my academic and research credentials. And when my grandfather passed away, well—" He gestured at the house in general and the finished sections of the mural.

"Now, Izzy, I've answered your question." He flicked his hand, glancing down at his wristwatch, and then smoothed his cuff back over the timepiece. "Why don't you come here?"

"I don't want to," she answered, looking at the floor in front of him. He was wearing black Italian leather shoes, Maglis maybe. She remembered how shocked she'd been at the auction to see him in sandals. She wanted him barefoot again, not ready to walk out the door in comfort. Biting down on the inside flesh of her cheek, she shut off the rising fear that she had already grown too attached to him. She had the weekend, she reminded herself, to regain her former detachment.

"Why?" Maceo asked. "Because you're angry? Insulted?"

Did he really want to know? How could he not know? Her mouth twitched. Maybe she should tell him to consult his magic ball or an event chart? Instead, she gave an angry little shrug of her shoulders.

"Thank you, Izzy."

She looked up, intending to merely glance into those soulful eyes to determine if the words had been masked sarcasm. "What do you mean, *thank you?*" she asked, finding that she couldn't look away.

"For not insulting my profession," he answered. His hands slid over his thighs and he spread his arms behind him as he leaned back. "It was there, dancing on the tip of your tongue, wasn't it?"

Izzy nodded, her attention drifting in and out of focus as her gaze wandered over his body. The semi-reclining position pushed the muscles of his chest out and narrowed his waist even further so that she found herself pulled back to the split of his thighs. He was hard again, the thick press of his cock against the pants so evident that the fabric might as well have been transparent. That he could switch in an instant from talking about his dear old grandfather to having a raging hard-on from her perusal of his body made her wet.

"So, again, Izzy—why don't you come here." His voice was still soft but there was no question in its tone.

Izzy moved toward the bed, feeling each inch covered with a sort of slow-motion glide until she was kneeling before him. Eyes moist, she looked up to where he was leaning over her. "I-I don't want any games," she said. But she did want him, knew now that a month or a year full of weekends wouldn't help her regain her former detachment. She frowned, trying to decide if she'd actually ever been detached—one brief sighting at an auction had fueled six years of him floating in and out of her thoughts and into more than the occasional fantasy.

"I know." He caressed her cheek, his thumb lingering over the flesh of her bottom lip. "No games, no fling. I promise. But you have to give yourself to me, Izzy . . . and let me give myself to you."

"I don't know how," she said. The words echoed like a secret in a church confessional, fitting since she was on her knees in front of him, her mouth watering with the need to do penance for the way she kept pulling back from him.

"I do."

She hesitated and he caught her gently by the hair, his mouth closing in on hers with a demanding kiss. She turned her head, breaking contact with his lips and resting her head against his silk-clad thigh.

"I . . . I just want . . . . to taste you," she said, and shrugged away from his attempt to pull her up onto the bed. Couldn't he let her control one thing? "Please, just let me do this."

Maceo eased back, a thoughtful frown creasing the sides of his mouth and eyes as Izzy's hands moved with an artist's precision to undo his belt. When she had the fly unzipped, she relented to his touch and let him brush back the hair that had fallen across her profile. He kept his hand on her cheek, stroking the line of her jaw as she delivered the first tentative swipe of her tongue up the base of his cock. Maceo's cock tasted of all the scents she had come to associate with him. Honeysuckle entwined with caramel and joined with a new layer of vanilla. She could smell the same scent on her skin, the sweet, tantalizing aromas still lingering from the body wash he had massaged onto her breasts and thighs.

"When I get back," he started, his voice clogged with some emotion Izzy didn't want to guess at, "you'll be just as distant as you were this morning."

She shook her head, gently lipping the tip of his erection as she mined the thin slit for the few precious beads of pre-cum that had glistened at its edges. She wanted to taste his cum, to discover if it was sweet or sharp, knowing that it would fill her either way.

"Swear you won't, then," he said.

More of that unnamed feeling vibrated through his words. She shook her head, harder, and sucked the length of his cock into her mouth in one quick descent. She bobbed up, releasing him with a wet pop. "Let me"—she covered him again, her nipples thrilling at his uncontrolled groan—"taste you . . . please you."

She didn't voice her other need, the one that went deeper than her need to see him shiver in pleasure at the slide of her mouth over his erection. She didn't tell him she needed to know that he had no more control than she did over what was building between them. But, somehow, she felt he understood without her saying it.

She devoured his cock in slick, fast mouthfuls, releasing the tip only to cover down to the base an instant later. Maceo was panting, trying to touch her without squeezing her to him. His hands traveled through her hair and across her shoulders until he gripped the thin straps of her T-shirt and froze in place, the ripple of cum through his cock and her mouth working the shaft the only movement in the room.

"*Il mio dio!*" Maceo tumbled back onto the bed, his strong hands demanding that Izzy follow him. He rolled onto his side, half pinning her on her back, his tongue invading her mouth.

He held her head immobilized, pausing only for a heartbeat. "Promise me."

She didn't want to speak, only wanted to savor the taste of him before it faded. But it felt as if he wasn't going to let her breathe until she promised him. "Your plane—"

"*Don't* say that." He was on her, chest to chest, his mouth roaming her face and throat while he kept her trapped. "Swear."

Izzy started to shake in his embrace. *I will.* That's all she had to say. *I promise.* She wanted to, the dull suction in the center of her chest told her as much. It shouldn't be so hard, shouldn't feel that giving into the need to let him possess her would cause something else inside her to shatter and break. But she was on the verge of breaking, a brilliant explosion of white shards that would shred anything close to her.

"Shhh." He pulled back, sensing the conflict in her and calmly smoothing her clothes into place. "I'm sorry . . . I just . . . I . . ." He tucked his hands to his sides. "It's okay. You don't have to say anything—anything you can't."

She nodded, her gaze layered with tears that spilled onto her cheeks. Did he know that she wanted to?

Please, know . . . I can't.

He shushed her again and brushed away a loose tear. He kissed her forehead, the tremble of his lips raising flesh bumps on her skin as he spoke.

"There's always the fun of starting back at square one, yes?" He offered the question as a joke, but the words seemed ragged and pained.

Izzy gave a wild shake of her head and wrapped her arms around him. There would be no going back, she promised herself, even if she couldn't promise him. *Just yet.*

FIVE

ON HIS FIFTH MORNING back from Sacramento, Maceo was sitting on Izzy's bed. In front of him was a tray he had taken from the dining room server and the deck of silver tarot cards. At his back was a rather irritated female. Glancing over his shoulder, he caught Izzy staring at him. He clamped his lips together. Smiling only seemed to make her madder when she was like this.

He couldn't help it. The smile erupted as he stared back. Almost four in the morning, she was dressed only in cream-colored satin panties and a matching camisole. There was a smudge of blue on the underwear from where she had stopped to watch him earlier, hand on her hip while she absentmindedly held her palette. Another streak of blue ran along the inside of her thigh.

That she wanted him out of the rotunda was obvious. *Tough,* he thought, and wrinkled his nose at her before turning back to shuffle the cards. *Tough, tough, tough. Not gonna budge, no way, no how.*

At least she didn't make me start back at square one, he thought as he laid six cards facedown in the shape of a crescent. *Close, but not quite.*

She had been working in the rotunda when he returned from Sacramento. Seeing her standing next to the finished Ares, the warrior's hard domination softened to a persistent coaxing for the animal to yield, he had felt an immense and immediate pleasure. That pleasure multiplied exponentially when Izzy took her instruction from the mural and yielded to his gentle pressure that night in the bedroom. But when he woke the next morning, the bed was empty—just as it was the next night and the night after that. It didn't matter where they made love. If they fell asleep in his bed, he would wake to find Izzy in hers. If passion took hold in the rotunda, he would wake in her bed to the sounds of her mixing paints in the kitchen.

When she had tried to slip out this morning, he followed. He ignored the squinty-eyed *go away* looks she gave him, kissed the edges of her mouth until she couldn't hold her frown any longer and had to push him away, mumbling that she'd never met someone so obstinate. When she seemed resigned to letting him stay, he had fetched his cards and the tray to keep from falling asleep.

Hand hovering over the first card, Maceo glanced over his shoulder again. She was cleaning the brush and wiping the unused paint from the palette. She hadn't, he realized, made a single new stroke on the wall this morning. Pouting, she shook the cleaner from her brush by banging it between two dowels wedged inside a cardboard box.

Tossing the brush into an empty coffee can, she stalked back to the bed. Her eyes lit on the cards and he saw a spark of interest shine in Izzy's eyes before she seemed to remember that she was mad at him.

"I can't sleep," she told him.

"Neither can I."

"You should try, you have a trip today."

"I'll sleep on the plane."

She shook her head. "But I have to work!"

"Go ahead," he answered. "It doesn't bother me."

"It bothers me," she protested.

"Don't let it." He knew the solution was as impossible as it was simple. Dropping his chin, he pretended to study the back of the cards. Unlike the front that had been individually painted with a plasma arc, the backs were stamped with the same design.

Izzy sat down at the end of the bed, cross-legged and facing him. After a second, she reached out to pick up one of the cards. "Obstinate," she accused.

"Ditto." Gently, he took her hand before she could touch the card. Bringing her hand to his mouth, he kissed the back of her fingers and then placed her hand on her thigh. "I have to work with these today, love."

"Are you saying I'll taint them?"

She sounded like she was spoiling for a fight, looking for any reason to take offense and demand he leave the room. Sighing, he turned the first card over. Again, he was staring at the upside-down King of Cups. In this spread, the card's position was bad. Very bad.

Looking up at Izzy, he tried to smile. "I only meant that your energy would linger . . . and how could I think of anything else?" Izzy's mouth pinched tighter. She thought he was being smooth, nothing else. Tapping the card he had just turned over, Maceo drew her attention to it.

"Who or what am I reminding you of, love?"

The look she gave him was puzzled. "You aren't."

"Izzy, we both make a living studying people, their expressions—*who* do I remind you of?"

Turning her head, she looked away. "So, the *card* is telling you that, huh? I thought you were an astrologer."

She hadn't ridiculed his profession since their first meeting. Now she wanted to escalate the push factor? Fine. He knew how to push back harder, particularly when the prize already meant more to him than any other person he'd ever known.

Maceo gave a sharp smile that went unseen before he answered her. "So, instead of answering my question, you want a lecture on the symbiotic relationship between astrology and tarot?"

Is that shame coloring her cheek or anger? He shook his head. It didn't matter if she regretted the derisive remark or was just plain pissed off. Picking up the card, he thrust it forward until it was an inch from her face. "This card, first to be read—it's the present pulling up the past. This king, upside down, he's treacherous. And a father figure to you. An older lover?" He waited, his blue gaze studying her face for confirmation that it was something else. "No? Your father then? Grandfather? Uncle? Who betrayed you, Izzy?"

She was chewing on her lip, near tears and still refusing to look at him. Fear crawled up from the bottom of his stomach and wrapped its black tendrils around his windpipe. What if she did tell him and he couldn't handle it—couldn't fix the pain he saw stamped across her pale features? He swallowed hard, forcing the tendrils to loosen their grip.

"Izzy, please, trust me. However bad you think it is—"

She shook her head, watching him from the corner of her eye. "It's . . . it's not what you think it is."

"I'm not thinking anything," he assured her.

She shook her head again, harder—hard enough that Maceo could hear the sound of her hair slapping against Izzy's skin. She looked at him, stared into him.

"Like . . . like I haven't been asked this before, you know?"

She pulled back, ready to bolt, and Maceo gently placed his fingertips on her knee. "Trust me," he pleaded.

Her gaze hardened. "You're afraid."

"So are you." He whispered his reply, softening the words until she couldn't read them as another challenge.

Her hand shot out. Too fast for him to stop, she flipped the remaining five cards over. "Why can't you get your answer from them?"

She was angry now, enraged, and Maceo felt on the verge of losing her. He took his time choosing the words he would answer her with, hoping the delay would mute her temper. The second two cards horrified him. The Hanged Man should have signified no more than limbo until Izzy could let go of the past and embrace the future. But it was followed by the inverted Queen of Swords. He shook his head, trying to remember when he had experienced cards so persistent from reading to reading.

"I feel so close to you, it's like I'm trying to read for myself— there's no clarity, Izzy."

She jabbed the third card with her index finger. "Who is this?" she asked, and pushed the Queen toward him.

"Your mother, I think"—he hesitated before adding—"and, more and more each day, it's you."

At his reply, the tears she had been holding back started to spill down her cheeks. She pulled her hand back to her lap, twined it together with its mate and stared at them as more tears fell onto them.

"Six months before my eighteenth birthday—" She stopped, and Maceo strained forward, mentally urging her to continue.

"Six months before . . . it was the last day of my senior year. We were signing yearbooks, I remember."

She looked up, her gaze landing and locking on the section of the mural that housed Scorpio. Izzy had filled the section with a woman. Her hair was as black as Maceo's, but streaked with a more prominent network of silver. She was dressed in a fantasy gown and robes—both dyed a menstrual black. Vines, thorned and dripping poison grew at her feet, their source hidden beneath the wide sweep of her skirt. The thickest of the vines curled behind the woman to climb in spirals around a standing mirror until its leafless end hung like a scorpion's tail over the woman's head.

"I was late getting home from school."

Izzy's voice hitched and Maceo reached out to comfort her, but she flinched and he drew back.

"But not so late that they had time to cut my mother down from the roof."

Suicides. The painting that had so disturbed him when he saw it in her gallery. It wasn't something she had imagined—it was something she had seen.

"Why?" It sounded so useless, but he couldn't stop it. He pushed the hair from his face while he tried to think how to un-ask the question.

Izzy shrugged, her left hand jumping up to her mouth. She nodded at the King of Cups. "Because he left her . . . almost seven-teen fucking years before?" Biting down on a nail, she gave another, more exaggerated, shrug. "Because she spent all her money on private investigators and was losing the house she hung herself from?"

She jerked her hand away, hitting her leg. "Because I cried when I was nine months old and he couldn't stand the sound of it."

Maceo placed the tray on the floor and moved down to the end of the bed. Wanting to hold her, to shield her from the memories he had forced her to dig up, he reached for her. This time she didn't flinch and he folded her into his embrace. "Your father didn't leave because you cried, love."

"I know that," Izzy answered. He was stroking the side of her face and shoulder while he rocked her. "But she didn't."

Maceo delayed his business trip another day—his mind playing over the remaining three cards while he tried to make Izzy feel adored without smothering her. He wasn't sure he succeeded and when early morning rolled back around, he woke to an empty bed and the soft sounds of her retreat.

"One step forward, two steps back." Sighing, he pushed the bedspread from him and slipped into silk pajama bottoms before following her down the hall.

Izzy saw him coming and waited, her hand hovering on the door handle. Stopping beside her, Maceo reached out and caressed her collarbone. The midnight hunt made him half think she should come with a warning. *Noli me tangere—for ice I am and wild to hold though I seem tame.*

"Am *I* just being needy?" he asked as she pushed open the doors. "Or are you compelled to get up and leave before you wake up unexpectedly alone?"

Ignoring his question, Izzy flipped on the rotunda's main lights. The current section of the mural framed the interior doorway and she turned on a set of freestanding lights positioned around it.

"Just four signs left," he said, dropping the question as he stopped in front of the ill-started section that would house the Gemini twins. He traced a faint outline she had plastered over. "You've·undone part of it? Why?"

"I wanted to use a different material." She left the rest of her answer unvoiced. The twins were giving her trouble, more than the others she had finished to date.

"Which one?" he asked, and pawed through the cans and tubes on the prep table.

She took the tubes of paint he was holding away and pushed his hands behind his back. "I need to order it."

"In the meantime?" He turned and looked at the remaining empty sections.

Izzy had personalized the layout of the signs, borrowing from Maceo's chart where she could and filling in the remaining sections according to their ruler or the progression of the signs. That meant Gemini would flank the doors on one end of the rotunda and Taurus and Cancer—Maceo's ascendant and sun sign—would flank the doors that led to the patio. The fourth unfinished section, shouldering Taurus, was her own sun sign, Capricorn.

"I'm ahead of schedule," she said. "I thought I'd wait for it to be delivered."

"Can you get it locally?" he asked. He was standing in front of the twins' section again, his sharp gaze picking out the other areas of the mural she had started and erased and restarted.

Again, the remaining three cards from yesterday's reading surfaced in his thoughts. The Lovers, the Empress and the Queen of Cups—could she possibly go for what he was thinking and, more importantly, would it help her?

"Closest supplier with it in stock is in Santa Monica." Izzy was standing behind Maceo, her head cocked to the right as she tried to read what was going through his mind. He was definitely thinking about something. His thumbs were lightly moving over the first three fingers of their respective hands. She had noted the habit before but now realized he was mentally shuffling a deck of tarot cards—just as he would tap the thumbs against the first two fingers when he was calculating a chart element.

He stopped and turned to her, flashing a smile that made his eyes twinkle a deep cerulean. "Your sister lives on that side of Beverly Hills, right?"

She nodded. Because of her earlier reluctance to disclose childhood scandals, Izzy had only briefly mentioned Milly. "That's right."

"How old was she when . . . well, you know . . ."

"She's a little younger than me," Izzy half answered. She didn't fear his rejection if he found out that she and Milly didn't share the same mother, that they both were, in fact, bastards, their mothers having been duped into offering their wedding vows to a man already married on the east coast. But the men Milly sought—they'd be a different story and it was a secret Izzy wanted to protect, if not for herself, then for her half sister.

"I mean . . . it's something that I just don't get, even with you having Mercury in Capricorn," he said, and returned his attention to the twins. "You're drawing this like you're an only child."

"Well, kind of, yes." She caught the glance he threw her way, saw the twinkle fade when he realized she didn't want to share any more information with him. "We didn't grow up together."

Maceo nodded, accepting the explanation she offered. "Look, you should pick up the material today in Hollywood. Visit your sister—it will help with Gemini. I'll charter the plane."

She tried to push the offer aside with gratitude and a firm demurral, but he covered the distance between them and grabbed her by the shoulders before she could finish saying *no*.

"I'll pick you up tomorrow in time for dinner with friends—twins!"

"Twins?" The line of his mouth, the sensuous twist to it, made Izzy uncomfortable. It felt like another lesson. But all the other lessons had been sexual in nature.

"Well, astrologically speaking—they have the exact same natal chart."

Izzy shrugged. "Is that uncommon? Seems like everyone would have a couple thousand astrological twins."

"Not at all . . . location and timing down to the minute. Not even birth twins automatically have the same chart—Gil and Hugh were born at the exact same time two hospital rooms apart."

"Maceo . . ." Some wicked desire to find out just what he was proposing made her hesitate. "Just dinner?"

"Whatever you want on the menu, love."

Her head moved in a diagonal path somewhere between a *yes* and a *no*. "I'm not sure I can deal with being any more attuned to my natal nature," she said, her will caught in the dancing blue of his gaze.

They were about a foot from one of the columns and he

deftly steered her toward it until her back was against the cool marble and her breasts were pressed against his warm chest. Only the thin fabric of the T-shirt she had slipped on before leaving his room divided their flesh.

"It's annoying, you know?" she asked while she tried to ignore the fact that he was erect again. His instant readiness and ability to take her at any hour of the day seemed almost unnatural for a man his age and she half·expected pharmaceutical reps to show up with briefcases full of little blue pills.

"Not this?" he asked, and rotated his hips against her.

Hands resting on his shoulders, she dug little crescent moons in his bare skin, the fight to keep her body from sliding against him in kind, a battle she was barely winning. "The way you're sure you know what's best," she answered through clenched teeth.

"You're right, I don't know best," he said, dipping his head to nuzzle against her cheek.

"You. Said. That. I'm. Right?" She couldn't see his expression but felt he was teasing her. Hell, she knew he was teasing her. He had firmly pressured her legs into an open stance and was flexing one of his powerful thighs against the crotch of her thin shorts.

"So right," he breathed against her neck, twisting the meaning of her words while his hands moved over her bare arms to cup her breasts. He trailed his lips over her collarbone to the flesh of her shoulder and bit down. The gentle cupping of her breasts turned into a hard, erotic squeeze and Izzy broke down and squirmed against him.

"If you don't know what's—"

Maceo interrupted her with a kiss, his finger replacing his mouth to keep her quiet. "Don't get carried away with that admission, love." He dropped his hand to the bottom hem of her shorts and pushed the fabric to one side. "I may not know what's best for you . . . but I know how to facilitate your discovery of it."

"I don't . . . ah, stop that." She groaned from the slide of his hand parting her labia and his thumb's unerring ability to find and tease her clit. "Your negotiations are . . . mmm"—she sucked a sharp breath in and finished as she crested against the hard ridge of his palm—"unfair."

"Just dinner . . . no expectations on their part . . . however you want to play it, love."

Like a cat scenting its master's leg, she caressed him with her head and shoulders, rubbing herself all over his upper torso and face as her squirming grew more insistent. "I want to play you. Be played by you. Now," she panted.

"You'll spend the day and night visiting your sister?"

Knotting her fingers in her hair and tugging upward, Izzy nodded.

"And I'll pick you up from the airport tomorrow for dinner back here?"

She was biting her lip too hard to answer and nodded again.

Maceo bent down, folding Izzy at the waist and hoisting her up over his shoulder, his hand still cupping her mound to keep her balanced. Placing her in the center of the mattress, he stripped her before stepping out of his silk pajama bottoms and descending on the wet folds of her sex. He allowed himself a few leisurely swipes of his tongue along the length of her pussy and then he launched a full assault on her cunt, his lips trembling against her clit in their hunger while he drove four fingers deep into her creaming interior. She closed her eyes, a starburst patterning the black of her inner eyelids. The pattern melded and divided until only two stars remained.

Sensing the end of her climax, Maceo moved up the mattress and cradled her body to him, gently restraining her hands as she sought to return some fraction of the pleasure he had just given her.

"Shhh . . . you need to sleep still, love." The room was warm and he pulled just a sheet up over their sweat-covered bodies. Resting alongside her, he kissed her eyelids and closed his own.

When he woke a few hours later, Izzy had already left the bed.

SIX

ILLY WORKED IN THE marketing and public relations department at an investment advisor firm. It was a job that paid well and allowed her to meet potential husbands in a way that wasn't blatant. Not that she wasn't great at what she did. She organized investor-specific events and made sure that the advisors in her office were invited to high-profile events within the community. She had the best florists, best caterers, best chamber musicians, best everything on speed dial. Her ability to successfully orchestrate a social gathering of five to five thousand people on short notice was a talent Izzy couldn't hope to possess. Trying to orchestrate a gathering of just two was beyond Izzy's abilities most days and Izzy knew she would be on bended knee begging Milly to help her with the gallery's first show.

It was surprising, calling Milly on the drive to Monterey's airport, to have her insist on taking the day off from her uberschedule and chauffeuring Izzy to the art supply shops she needed to visit. Not that they weren't close, but more on the level of friends than sisters.

What wasn't surprising was the rapid series of questions Milly shot at Izzy the instant she spotted her in the baggage claim area of the Santa Monica Airport.

"You checked that? Why'd you check luggage? Never mind. Is that all of it? I thought we'd get some lunch first, okay?"

When Milly paused long enough to pull in another lungful of air, Izzy gave a nod and a quick, "Okay."

Grabbing Izzy by the elbow, Milly weaved in and out of the light afternoon crowd of travelers, popping out one question and then another before Izzy could answer the first. "He really chartered a flight for you? You were the only passenger? Why didn't he come?"

Milly paused as they stepped out of the airport, feeling a tug on her arm as the heat pushed against Izzy. "Sorry," Milly said, and let go of Izzy's arm. "Forgot how sheltered Monterey is from the heat."

"Not a huge difference," Izzy said, and wrapped her hand around her sister's. "Just enough of one."

Reaching the car was a relief. Milly had managed to park out of the sun, with the car's interior still cool from the fading effects of the air conditioner. And Milly was an obsessively quiet driver. Music was allowed, phones were forbidden and conversation was kept to a minimum. But she was practically jumping with the need to ask Izzy more about Maceo.

"What do you mean, *you can't say?*" Milly asked after the hostess had finished seating them. "You're either in love or you aren't!"

"Why does it have to be one side or the other? I mean, maybe I am and maybe I'm not . . . maybe I just don't know?"

"You could just say *no*," Milly pointed out. "I mean, if you're not sure, then I guess it's a *no*, right?"

"I . . . I really can't say."

The smile Milly flashed as she snapped open her menu was sharp and knowing. "So you are. What do you want to order? The lobster bisque is good."

"Eh, ocean cockroach. I think I'll have the chicken breast."

"Is the sex as vanilla as your lunch?" Milly asked, her face was partially hidden behind her menu, just the arched brows and bright twinkle of her gray-green eyes showing.

Izzy started to say something but a shadow literally settled across her sister's face. Izzy glanced over her shoulder to find a rather imposing and oddly familiar man behind her. His hair was a rich brown, warmed to red around the edges by the sunlight filtering through the restaurant's windows. When he dropped his gold-flecked gaze for an instant to acknowledge her presence at the table, Izzy recognized him.

Without saying anything, he turned and left, stopping just long enough to pay his bill.

"What the hell was that about?" Izzy asked. "You've never dropped *that* name."

"Barely know the guy," Milly answered as she unwrapped her silverware and unfolded the linen napkin. She examined the white square of cloth, picking a few knots of lint off it before placing it over the black skirt she was wearing.

"Seemed like he could cut diamonds looking at you, but you barely know him?"

Milly tilted her glass at Izzy in accusation. "You're just avoiding giving me the dish on di Silvio."

"There's nothing to dish. Why'd he look at you like that?"

Milly sighed and turned away. "He thinks I'm a call girl or something."

Izzy sat back in her chair and studied her sister. "You make, what, one-ten at Goulden's—and he thinks you hook on the side?"

"Call girl, gold digger . . . all whores to him, I imagine."

Milly continued looking away and Izzy reached across the table. She took Milly's hand, examining the French manicure as she lightly prodded. "You're not a gold digger or anything like that, and who the hell is Jason Covington to talk trash with his playboy reputation?"

Pulling her hand away, Milly nodded at the approaching waitress. "Well, you know how men are—they only like the whores they own, right?"

"I—"

Milly cut her short. "End of conversation—all I want to know is that you aren't going to torpedo what you have going with Maceo." She looked up at the waitress, handing both menus to the woman. "Lobster bisque and chicken breast with mineral waters, please."

When the waitress was gone, she turned back to Izzy. "Now, is he looking for a relationship? Something long-term?"

Izzy nodded. "I think so. It all seems so insane."

Milly's light silvery laugh was back and she shook her head, the sandy blond curls fluttering around her face like a bird's wings. "It's so not you and about damned time."

"He's pushy."

"You need that."

"Did he call you and tell you what to say in advance?"

Izzy's gaze had widened, her expression just shocked enough that Milly could tell the question had been asked in earnest. Another light laugh and Milly reached across the table to squeeze Izzy's hand.

"I'm really beginning to like this guy—when do I get to meet him?"

It was Izzy's turn to look away. "When he debuts the mural?" She shrugged. "I have to go, even if, well . . . you know. Either we'll still be seeing each other or I'll need a social crutch."

"*Lean on me*—"

"Oh, hell, not that! You promised we'd never have to sing it again!"

"You don't . . . and *whatshisname* is gone, so who cares what kind of idiot I look like?"

Izzy tilted her head but Milly was quick to raise her hand to stop her. "No. Closed conversation. I forgot, but it's still closed."

"Not if you're going to sing that song—that's my price, little sister."

"Eight and a half months," Milly snorted.

"Don't care if it was eight and a half seconds, *little sister*, that's my price. Don't sing, or spill the beans."

"I'm so leaving it on your voice mail."

"3–7–7," Izzy answered, snapping her napkin open as the waitress arrived with the mineral water. "It's the 9–1–1 of voice mail."

The waitress brought their food a few minutes later and Izzy and Milly found other things to talk about through lunch. Each one reluctantly called a truce to avoid talking about her own love

life. Stopping at a video store once Izzy had found all the material she needed, they rented sappy romance movies to fill the
void the truce was causing. And in the morning, Milly dropped
her off in front of the airport where a second charter was waiting
to take Izzy back to Monterey, *Casa di Silvio* and, perhaps, a night
with three men.

SEVEN

GIL AND HUGH COULD have been biological twins, Izzy thought as she watched them across the dinner table. They certainly seemed as close as brothers, occasionally grabbing something off the other's plate or pushing something on to it that it was imperative the other try. And though they had only known each other for a few years, they had picked complementary career paths. Hugh was a musician. He played jazz piano and had a few records out. Gil was a record producer. They had met working on one of Hugh's records and grew closer after they found out about their hometown and then their astrological connection.

They looked like brothers too. Both were gray-eyed and blond-haired, Hugh's was a darker shade of blond—as if all the smoky clubs he played piano in had left a permanent tint. Gil was the bulkier of the two, still fit, but with the shoulders and broad chest of a linebacker. Almost a bear of a man, but all of it seemed to be muscle.

A blush crept across Izzy's cheeks as she contemplated finding out whether it was just the flattering cut of his clothes or if the promised thrust power of Gil's thighs and ass were real. Trying to pull her gaze away from comparing the two, she picked through the food Maceo had catered. Izzy's chest tightened as she realized that she really was considering going to bed with three men at once. To go from plain vanilla, monogamous Izzy, who had more fingers on her right hand than she'd had lovers, to almost doubling that count in one night—it seemed scandalous, naughty . . . almost dirty, but for the fact that she didn't see a hint of that opinion reflected in the men's faces or bodies.

Hugh's hand, slim and artistic like her own, brushed against Izzy's as he reached for the fruit platter. With a tentative smile, he selected a fat cube of cantaloupe and handed it to her before choosing his own. The creamy light orange color of the fruit glistened with its own juices and she tried not to stare as he popped it into his mouth, his tongue surreptitiously sneaking out to lick the light coating of juice from the pads of his thumb and index finger. She tried. Really, she did.

Feeling Maceo's gaze on her, Izzy turned her head and offered her own tentative smile. Or was she offering consent? She still wasn't sure. She was wet enough—she knew that—as wet and slick as the second cube of cantaloupe Hugh was pulling into his mouth, his tongue curling around the fruit to trap it. She had the sudden desire to suck on his lips, run her tongue over his, taste the fruit and feel his tongue curl around her.

Running a shaky hand through her hair, she offered Maceo a second glance and then pushed away from the table.

"Excuse me."

The words came out shaky too, and she left the room quickly, almost running to Maceo's bedroom once she was out of view. In the master bath, she let the water run cold in the sink and dampened a washcloth while she thought about Gil and Hugh. Watching the way they interacted with one another, she wasn't sure Maceo was working solely on her issues tonight. Hugh in particular had a certain way of holding back in his interactions with Gil, reminding Izzy of a pitcher waiting for the opposing team to clear the field.

She was still holding the washcloth to her face, trying to cool her hot flesh, when Maceo came into the room.

"Are you done with *dinner?*" he asked, his voice dropping to stress the last word.

"I-I don't think I can go back in there," Izzy confessed. She was wearing a backless dress, a thin layer of perspiration making the skin glow.

Maceo ran his fingertips over her exposed skin. She leaned into him, her hip pressing against the base of his erection. Izzy sighed and he put his hand on her other hip, tightening the embrace.

"What do you want next, love?" he asked.

She turned into him, so that they were chest to chest, his erection thick and hard against her stomach. "You."

Izzy was trembling, her whole body vibrating so hard she might have been standing naked in a walk-in freezer but for how hot her skin felt. She knew that if Maceo really touched her, if he so much as lifted the hem of her dress and brushed the inside of her thigh, she would come.

"You think I'm decadent, don't you?" He was nuzzling the right side of her neck, his voice a rough purr against her skin.

Shaking her head, she buried her face against his shoulder.

"It's not what I think . . ." she started, and then shook her head again.

"It's what I'll think of you?"

Izzy wouldn't answer, that would be an admission of how badly she wanted tonight, of how excited she was at the thought of being securely wrapped in Maceo's strong embrace while other hands toyed at her clit and mouths sucked at her nipples. She wanted to be wet and sore and possessed by the movement of three beautiful bodies.

His hands moved to her shoulders and he looped a finger under each strap of her dress. Slowly, he began peeling the fabric down her body. His palms caressed the skin on her upper arm while he extended his thumbs wide enough to coax the front of the dress down the rise of her breasts.

"You're trembling," he said.

Only his hands touched her, but he held his mouth and the promise of the rest of his body less than an inch away. Izzy could feel the energy vibrating in the small cushion of air between them.

He stopped the striptease long enough to pull her tight to him and bite down on her neck. She pushed up against him and felt his erection. The tremors in her body magnified ten times over and she felt a new wave of cream coat her lower lips.

"You could come right now, love," he said the second before his mouth covered hers. Izzy moaned and he pivoted until her ass was against the counter, and then pressed harder against her. The position and the tight skirt of the dress kept her from wrapping her legs around him, and so she ground against him in sharp circles.

Maceo pushed away and spun her around until she was bent over the counter and staring at herself in the mirror.

Is that really me?

Her cheeks were flushed, the skin a rose red prominent against flesh that had grown pale everywhere else. Except for her lips. The colored gloss she had put on earlier was gone but her lips were still a dark crimson. They seemed swollen, pouting, almost a perfect mirror to the way her pussy lips felt trapped inside the black lace panties she was wearing. Almost a perfect mirror— not quite. She licked her lips until they were shining, wet, trembling.

Is it?

The humidity, inside and out, had untamed her hair until it formed a coppery halo around her face. Her eyes had a feverish shimmer to them. She looked wild and dangerous . . . a completely sensual animal ready to dig her claws into the back of the next prey she scented.

Is this what Maceo sees?

She met his gaze in the mirror. The fact that he'd obviously been watching her self-contemplation only made her hotter. She wanted to show him she was ready, but he had her trapped in her state of partial dress, the lowered straps and bodice of her dress forcing her arms tight against her body as he pinched the dress's waist.

Keeping the fabric around her waist tight, Maceo knotted his other hand in her hair and drew her straight. He guided Izzy like this, a prisoner of her own heat, toward the bed and again forced her into a bent position. Her stomach flat on the mattress, she felt his hand leave her hair and immediately push down between her shoulder blades. He bent over her, stripping the rest of the dress away along with her heels, but leaving her panties on. Putting pressure on her legs, Maceo forced them apart until she was presented ass high in the air with her feet almost separated by the bed's full width. He ran his hand under the band of her panties, finding her wet and swollen.

"Shhhhh . . . not yet," he cooed at her as she began to shake from the tension of an approaching climax. He slid two fingers into her pussy, trying not to add any more fuel to the sensual fire consuming her flesh. When his fingers were coated with her juice, he pulled out and held them in front of her face. Her lips parted with a sharp moan and he offered her a taste of just how hot she had become.

"Don't lose that," he said, gathering her up to the center of the bed. He propped her against the massive bed pillows and pulled a decorative shawl of pale rose silk from one of the bedroom's reading chairs to cover her with.

"Don't lose that," he repeated, dimming the lights before he backed from the room.

Heart beating rapidly in her chest, her breasts rising and falling in waves from the deep breaths she was taking, Izzy waited on the bed. An obsidian clock curved along the surface of the dresser, and she watched the slim, silver hand tick away the seconds. A minute passed, and then a few more as her body slowly came down from the fevered pitch Maceo had left her in.

Maceo returned, chest and feet bared. Leaving the door open, he stood at the side of the bed and pulled his pants and briefs down over the slim but powerful hips. His cock was swollen, its length and width making her mouth and pussy wet all over again.

She reached out and curled her fingers around it, sighing at the fat girth that wouldn't let her fully enclose his cock in her grasp.

He drew the silk away from her and then took her hand and pressed it against her stomach. Sliding onto the mattress, Maceo coaxed her forward until he was spooned against her. He rolled onto his back, partially pulling her with him so that she was half on him, her backside against the hard planes of his chest and stomach. He slipped one arm under Izzy, cradling her while his other hand caressed her thighs open and dipped beneath the band of her lace panties.

She could feel his cock nestled between the half globes of her bottom and she contracted around him, her smile warm and sleepy from the groan it produced. The hand that cradled her found her opposite breast and began kneading it, tugging at the ripe nipple while he rubbed her clit. She was squirming against him, sliding and contracting her ass muscles, a naked, dry fuck but for the fact she was so very wet from his touch.

Izzy didn't realize Hugh had entered the room until she heard the slide of his zipper, the sound almost lost in the small mewling pleas she made as Maceo teased her to a more frenzied state. Like Maceo, he came dressed only in his pants and briefs and he stripped slowly, his airy gaze watching her expression. She glanced at his face only once, her attention mesmerized by the play of Maceo's hands over her and the slow unveiling of Hugh's lithe frame. Of the three, he had the lightest skin and, in the room's low lights, his body was infused with a diaphanous glow. Blue veins stood out against the pale white of his chest. Her gaze followed the network of blue against white across his flat stomach and narrow hips to the proud jut of his erection and dark blond mass of pubic hair that curled around it. He grabbed his cock and Izzy became lost in contemplation of the slim fingers working his shaft. He was teasing her as much with the promise of a musician's touch as he was the solid strength of his rod.

Hugh eased his way onto the bed and Maceo withdrew his hand from beneath the band of her panties and started easing them over her hips. Hugh reached out, his mouth pressed against her navel as he took over the operation of removing the last barrier to her sex. As the panties slid lower, so too did his lips. When the lace was at her knees, he slid his tongue between the top split of her labia. Wet, wriggling until he could press it flat, the organ quickly covered her clit. His tongue curled at the edges until he was spooned around her sex button. She felt the panties pass over her heels and tickle the soles of her feet before Hugh dropped them to the floor and began to move his tongue in small waves.

The need to wrap her legs around Hugh's head pressed hard at Izzy's flesh, but Maceo kept one hand on her exposed thigh, tempering the sharp, wild movements that sizzled through her body. Maceo arched his hips and pulled her legs wider until her cunt was greedily presenting itself to Hugh. Hugh pressed his lips against the hollow where thigh met mound. His fingers trailed slowly up her leg, parting her labia and playing in the wet pocket of her cunt before beginning a languid dance along the spine of her clit.

Hugh had explained at dinner how he would open the piano up and play the strings by hand sometimes, but Izzy hadn't expected the fingertips to be calloused. The sensation of Hugh's strong, rough hand against the silk of her pussy was slowly driving her mad and she twisted against Maceo to find the anchor of his mouth. One hand on her thigh, the other teasing her breast, he kissed her, the thrust of his tongue as dizzying as the slick glide of Hugh's thumb over her clit. She was moaning into Maceo's mouth, trying not to bite down as warring sensations from both their touches kept her sharply on the edge of climax. Afraid she would bite down—she broke the kiss.

And then Gil was there, his clothes seemingly abandoned in one of the other rooms. He had one knee on the bed, the other foot planted firmly on the floor. Both hands were fisted, one enclosing wrapped condoms, the other wrapped around his magnificent cock, his thumb pressing hard at the base as if he were trying to control a building climax. Izzy swallowed hard, her gaze widening to take in the full measure of his cock so close to her face. Unlike Maceo's length, which reached deep into her to awaken nerves that had never been touched before, Gil's cock was no more than five or six inches.

But the width!

Izzy blinked and drew in a lungful of air as her gaze refocused. Maceo's breath was hot against her neck, urging her forward. She reached out, her open palm flat against the bottom curve of Gil's testicles. Heavy, cum laden, their weight produced an overwhelming sense of fullness in her. She curled her fingers and rolled his balls in her hand, her touch firm but sensitive to their fragile nature. Gil gave a deep grunt and released his cock and the handful of condoms. He laid a gentle hand on the crown of her head, his fingers playing in the coppery silk as he leaned closer.

As her tongue darted out to circle Gil's swollen cock head, she felt the loss of Hugh's touch and impatiently wiggled her ass, her entire body greedy for the sensations that each lover delivered. She heard the crinkle of a condom wrapper and then Hugh's hand slid past the slick opening of her cunt to wrap around Maceo's cock. Maceo groaned, his grip on her breast tightening as Hugh put the condom on him. Izzy jerked in anticipation, her mouth suctioning around the tip of Gil's erection. Releasing her hair, he steadied himself by planting one meaty hand on the mattress.

Maceo moved his hands until he was gripping her hips. He slid her body higher, Hugh's hands guiding his cock to the waiting slit of Izzy's pussy. Maceo slammed into her and then eased back out. Another slam and his mouth found the soft flesh of her shoulder. His strokes gentled as he delivered sharp, sensuous love bites. When Hugh's mouth descended on her once again, she moaned, the expression stretching her lips far enough that she could swallow Gil's full length into her mouth. He murmured her name, his hand caressing the side of her face before he took her nipple between thumb and forefinger and began rolling the sharp-tipped bud.

Already blind from the pleasure racing like warm acid across her chest and legs, Izzy closed her eyes. Hugh's mouth kept her clit locked in an ecstatic state, his talented tongue dipping down not only to tease the upper rim of her pussy, but to stroke Maceo's cock as it thrust in and out of her. Hugh's little journeys up and down the length of her clit and along the base of Maceo's cock whipped both lovers into a frenzied state. Maceo's fingertips dug into her hip each time Hugh dared to go a little lower.

Head bent so that his lips were close to her ear, Gil gave a little warning cry. "I'm going to come. Now . . . coming now."

Izzy grabbed Gil's ass, her nails forbidding him to pull out. She sucked harder, her mouth moving with the ripples of cum through his cock, her whole body shaking as her own climax rumbled through her. When she had wrung the last drop of cum from Gil, she tossed her head back. Her body, like jelly, moved separately from her mind as Maceo continued to thrust into her.

Moving onto the bed, Gil laid down to where his head was even with Izzy's chest. His mouth covered one areola while he squeezed and massaged both of her breasts. Hugh stopped laving her pussy, and then there was the sound of another condom leaving its wrapper. When he had finished sheathing his cock, he formed his middle three fingers into a triangle and rolled another heavily lubricated condom onto them.

Maceo pulled out until just the head of his cock remained inside Izzy. His knuckles flat against Maceo's erection, Hugh began to stroke the ring of Izzy's cunt with gentle side-to-side caresses. Gil's hand moved over the flat of her stomach to find and tease her clit while his hungry mouth feasted on her sore nipples and swollen breasts. Lids fluttering as her eyes rolled back, Izzy tightened around Maceo and thrust her hips forward.

"Relax, beautiful." Hugh kissed the inside of her thigh as he bent over her pussy.

While Maceo held his own hips and cock rigid, Hugh's fingertips breached the circle of muscle protecting her center. The lube from the condom mixed with her cream, letting his fingers join with Maceo's cock in a slow push forward. Her taut muscles relaxed with each deep incursion into her body.

Maceo stopped, half his length inside Izzy as Hugh worked her cunt wider. And then Hugh was torso to torso with Izzy. His arm embraced Gil's broad shoulders and his erection rested flush against Maceo's. Slowly Hugh pushed into Izzy until the head of his cock was nestled just below the tip of Maceo's.

Their bodies were a knot of pleasure. She could feel a masculine hand between her hip and Gil's stomach, the fingertips rubbing against her side as the hand worked Gil's thick cock. She wasn't sure whose hand it was—only that it wasn't Gil's because he had one hand cupping her breast and the other curled around the bottom curve of Hugh's ass.

Izzy gave a gnarled cry and then Maceo and Hugh began to move in unison. Maceo's mouth pressed hard against the hollow of her throat, Izzy had lost the safe purchase of his kiss and she wrapped an arm around Gil's head as he suckled one breast and then the other.

"Don't stop," she whispered to no one, to all three, to her own body.

Gray danced against the lids of her closed eyes as Maceo and Hugh moved inside her. Four bodies held tight to one another. Kissing, sucking, fucking. She cried out again, the last of her air leaving her, every inch of her body frozen and incapable of drawing in more as she felt the twin swells of cum traveling in a wave through Maceo's and Hugh's cocks. Everything seemed to explode around her, the shattered fragments of her three lovers absorbed through her skin.

Izzy collapsed into Maceo. His hands left her hips, protectively curling around her shoulder and waist. Sensing the exhaustion that infected the other three, Gil drew up, stroking and kissing Izzy's face as he said goodbye. Hugh followed, kissing her on the mouth for the first time that night. She brought her hand up, tangling it in the mess of long blond curls and deepened the kiss for an instant. The taste of her cream was still sharp on his tongue and she broke the kiss slowly, her tongue circling his lips before she released him completely. He scooped his pants from the floor, closing the door behind him as he followed Gil out of the room.

With the other two men gone, Maceo wrapped her more tightly in his embrace. He was still embedded deep within her, little contractions racing in circles around his cock as she fluttered around him. As he had throughout the day, Maceo thought of the cards again. He thought of the Lovers who had just left, and the Empress Izzy had become for the evening, adored and in command of her own harem of lovers. But mostly he wondered whether she would be able to embrace the last card—her true nature—the Queen of Cups.

He snuggled into the fabric of Izzy's hair, his mouth at the edge of her ear. "Don't leave me tonight, love," he said.

Izzy brushed her cheek across his lips. His voice was sleepy, heavy with the same bone-deep tiredness that held her in its grip. She brought his hand to her mouth, kissed the knuckles then drew it to her chest. *I won't*, she thought, her mouth too relaxed to shape the words. *I won't*.

Izzy woke to Maceo's light startle sometime later. His hand brushed her bottom and then closed around the base of his cock. She remembered that he was still wearing the condom and shifted, trying to ease his withdrawal. Drifting back to sleep, she had the impression of him completely turning down the lights and going into the bathroom.

. At some point, he must have pulled a light quilt from one of the linen closets because they were covered when she woke again. No light peeked around the edges of the bedroom curtains, so she guessed it couldn't be past four in the morning. She rolled onto her stomach, Maceo's relaxed hand sliding from Izzy's hip to rest against the back of her thigh. The casual contact warmed her skin and she slid farther toward the edge of the bed until his hand was on the mattress and she was partially uncovered.

He really should have a real clock in here, she thought. The house wasn't completely devoid of electronics, but most of the gadgets were hidden behind stone or wood, with all of the natural façades rich with astrological symbology. Each room formed a section of a larger piece of collective art. His bedroom was a perfect example. The dresser was black mahogany, the top inlaid with mother-of-pearl. More of the stone framed the front face of a matching chest of drawers. Reflecting both his ascendant Taurus and sun sign Cancer, the adjustable lighting was hidden behind thin shells carved from rose quartz, their edges banded with silver. And she had noticed him bringing other things into the room to make it more astrally accommodating for her. The obsidian clock with its silver hands was a union of both their signs. To each side of the clock were carved silver boxes large enough to hold a few personal items. The box on the right had the wild, looping seven inset with garnets that represented her birth sign, while the other one had the familiar sixty-nine curving in on itself done in black pearl.

But, really, a clock that could be read at night wasn't too much to ask for, was it? She turned her head to the side, but her eyes hadn't adjusted enough to the darkened room to read his face. He breathed with a deep, even pace. Obviously, he never suffered insomnia. She turned onto her side, completely out from beneath the quilt.

She went through phases, her insomnia most present, she realized, when there was a lover in bed with her. She could feel her brows knitting together at the thought. But it was true. She had been exhausted after the first few weeks of living with Cory, the lover she had almost married. It began to affect her moods too— peace coming only when she would slip out to sleep on the couch for a few hours before coming back into their bedroom.

Izzy pushed up on one elbow, her other hand reaching beneath the quilt to find Maceo's. It was palm up and she momentarily rested her fingertips in the cup his curled fingers created. She thought she heard him sigh in his sleep as she pulled her hand away.

Just a few hours, she told herself. She crawled out of bed and eased the bedroom door open. Knowing Gil and Hugh would not have stayed, she didn't bother to grab her clothes but crept down the hall and into the rotunda.

Izzy rolled onto her side, pushing her arms up over her head, a huge yawn kept her eyes shut. The stretch ended and she opened her eyes. Next to her, the little black dress she had worn the night before was folded neatly on the pillow beside her with the slip of lace panties placed on top. Gaze widening, she bolted up

in the bed. Instead of the curved walls that enclosed Maceo's bedroom with their slate-gray coloring, she saw the painted sections
of the rotunda.

Shit! She grabbed the dress, struggled her way into it and jumped
out of bed. Not stopping to put the panties on, she smoothed the
skirt down and dashed out of the rotunda. The sound of women
talking in the kitchen slowed her down. The caterers were back,
cleaning up and retrieving their containers.

Izzy tried to inch past the kitchen. When one of the women
spotted her, she gave a weak smile and picked up her pace. Just as
she had fled the dining room the night before, she was almost
running by the time she reached Maceo's bedroom door.

His shut bedroom door.

Reaching out, she tried to turn the handle but it wouldn't
budge. She lifted her hand, her first double knock tentative.
Nothing. She knocked again, a little more loudly, and then
pressed her ear against the wood.

Izzy wandered back to the kitchen and stood quietly in the
doorway. An old white woman was rinsing the containers and
then stacking them with a slowness that would have made a
turtle impatient. The other, a pretty little Latina, was bagging
garbage. When she caught sight of Izzy, she smacked her
forehead, a tumble of words Izzy didn't understand spilling
from her.

"Senora Isold?" the girl inquired.

Izzy shook her head. *Isold.* Not a good sign. She took a deep
breath. "Yes, that's me."

"Senor Maceo, he left a note for you." She pointed at the side of the refrigerator, but then changed her mind and walked the note over to Izzy.

The paper was folded in half, *I-S-O-L-D* marching across the front in a dark font. She unfolded the note.

I decided to visit Jace after all.

Seven little words but their meaning was unmistakable. He had cancelled an appointment with this "Jace" to be with her the day after their little ménage-a-quatro. Now he was cancelling their day after. He was gone and his bedroom door was locked. He addressed the note to *Isold*. Not *Izzy*, not *Love. Isold.*

A death grip on the note, she grabbed the cordless phone and went into the dining room. The chair opposite the fireplace hadn't been pushed in and she sank down onto it while she numbly punched in the numbers to his cell phone.

Voice mail.

She waited for the greeting to finish playing. Her pulse pounded in her ear as he suggested the caller leave their name and number, and then there was the blessed beep. "Maceo, please ca . . ."

The rest of her entreaty died on her lips as she glanced up to the fireplace mantel. The obsidian clock that had been in his bedroom the night before was back in its original spot. Thumbing the phone off, she pushed away from the dining room table. Her legs were shaky but she managed to make it back to the rotunda, nodding once as she passed the concerned Latina to assure the girl she was okay.

But she wasn't. Her chest had constricted at the sight of the clock where it no longer should be. It hadn't unclenched and her breathing was down to shallow pants. She'd hurt him, sneaking back to the rotunda—perhaps as badly as she was hurting now. She could forgive him, she'd been wrong in the first place. But would he forgive her?

Her chest muscles cinched tighter at the possibility that he might not. Izzy stumbled to her supply table and began mixing the colors she would need for the Gemini through a veil of tears. Picking up the brush, she shook her head and folded butt-first to the floor. She couldn't paint the twins just yet. They wouldn't fade from memory and she had something else to paint first.

Her apology.

Moving back to the table, Izzy studied the mix of colors on the palette. Some she could use, others she couldn't. She scraped the latter off and began mixing the additional colors she would need for Capricorn. That Capricorn's section of the mural would be off-plan briefly flitted across her mind, but she shrugged the thought away.

She placed her supplies on the mobile platform and rolled it over to the blank section of wall. Picking up a palette knife, she used a gritty, textured paint to cut in the outline of a soaring mountain. Capricious in its nature, Capricorn was ruled by the Seagoat—its upper half a goat, its bottom half the curving tail of the fish. She had joked once that the form made it unsuitable for traveling on land or in the water, but Maceo had wrapped his arms around her and explained. Above and below, all fell within the domain of her rule.

"I certainly do," he had whispered before burying his face in the refuge her hair provided.

Cleaning the palette knife, she took a slim-tipped brush and lightly ran it across the smudge of black paint on her palette. Dropping to her knees, she edged in the lower half of her Seagoat. Already, the colors of the tail danced in her mind—a shimmering opalized blue, darkened in places by an undercoating of Prussian blue, would make up the scales. Small highlights of liquid silver on the scales would catch the daylight that filtered through the rotunda's twelve windows.

At points, the line of black paint ran so thin as to be invisible. These areas would be below the waterline—only the hips, tail curve and part of the tail fan would be visible. Scraping more black paint onto the palette, she reloaded the brush tip and started sketching the upper body.

An actual goat's head and torso would, of course, be unacceptable, and so she drew the sensuously curving waist and breasts of a mermaid. Slender arms stretched out in supplication for the return of something lost. Finished shading the outer oval of the face, Izzy fanned the brush away from the face in wildly curving lines to represent windblown hair—black like the mysterious night side of the planet that ruled her sign.

Saturnia, a solitary ice queen, alone and melting at last.

Izzy brushed away a tear and started to outline the final section of her Seagoat. Every queen needed a crown—even the cold and lonely ones. Up from the mass of black hair, she shaped the curving crest of the headpiece. At the base of the crest, she weaved intricate vines, six in all. At the top of the crest, she drew the horns. Unlike the spiral of Ares, Capricorn's horns were slender and sharp—curving stilettos dangerous to any soul foolhardy enough to run a finger across one of the twin blades.

Sunlight reflecting off it, she would color the horns with liquid gold, except for where crimson stained their tips.

Finished with the basic outline, Izzy stepped back. She rolled her shoulders and glanced at the balcony door. The temporary drapes were closed and blocked out too much light to tell her how much time had passed since she started painting. *Hours*, she thought, and rotated her shoulders in the opposite direction.

She scratched her collarbone and then looked down. The little black dress. Well, at least it was still black—even if she could see smears from the paint. She patted at her uncombed hair. It felt every bit as unruly as Saturnia's black mane. She needed to shower and change into fresh clothes.

Oh, yeah . . . underwear would be nice.

But first, she had to put away the paint and clean her brushes.

EIGHT

HOLDING HER SANDALS IN one hand, Izzy walked barefoot along the beach. Typical of the Monterey shoreline, very little of it was all sand—just a sixty-foot expanse in the center of Maceo's water frontage. Left and right, the beach turned rocky. She walked along the rocks too—careful to avoid the jagged ones while she tried not to slip on any of the smoother rock surfaces and disturb the creatures that lived in the tide pools.

So far, she had spotted sea urchins—favorite snack for the Bay's resident otters—an anemone colony and five starfish, including one with a sixth limb. Coming to the edge of the property line, she reached another tide pool. The pool was shallow and she could see its bottom through the clear water. Placing her sandals on one of the surrounding rocks, she hunched down over the pool. The rocks were slick and she grabbed a half-shorn outcropping of one to steady herself.

She knew she wasn't supposed to look away from the ocean for very long. More rocks lined the bottom of the Bay, bigger and sharper than their cousins on shore. They made the waves unpredictable and sometimes deadly.

Watch the water, stay back from the shoreline. Everyone she knew was familiar with the warnings and they all pretty much ignored them only to brag about their close calls over margaritas at El Gaucho's while they watched the waves on the rocks from behind the safety of the restaurant's thick windows.

But a hermit crab had found its way into the pool. More than that, it seemed to have found a new shell. The tide had brought in the empty shell of a black turban snail and the crab was midway through moving into his new home. The urge to ease her hand into the water and pull out his abandoned shell had her fingertips itching. Some rules she paid strict attention to. Some other crab might come along later—so look, but don't touch.

She wrapped her free hand around her knee and tightened her grip on the rock she was steadying herself with.

Some other crab might come along.

The thought of Maceo and the three days spent without any contact with him brought Izzy to her feet. She grabbed her sandals and carefully picked her way back to the sandy area of the shoreline. The evening walk on the beach had managed to ease most of the tension from three days of marathon painting from her back and shoulders, but she could feel it flowing into her again with just the whisper of his name through her mind.

When he returned, he'd find both Gemini and Capricorn drying, each done but for a few minor highlights. Hell, he might find everything done if he was stubborn enough to stay away until her thirty days were up.

If she could finish without seeing him again. Cancer and Taurus were left—his two selves, Sun and ascendant. He hadn't given her any lessons on those two signs. Then again, perhaps the whole affair had been a lesson in the natures of Crab and Bull.

She dusted the sand from her bare feet and then put her sandals back on. She looked up the staircase that led to the house. The hope that the house wouldn't be as empty as she left it sparked small but hot. She frowned and blew a little puff of air through her nose.

Head down, she started her ascent. At the top, she crossed the patio. The interlocked marble stones that formed the patio were irregular in shape. She had been passing over them for weeks and knew that if she walked a straight line from the rough stairs to the door, she would cross through twenty-seven stones. She counted them again as she went, her hand reaching into the pocket of her capris to pull out the key to the balcony door.

She stopped a foot from the entrance. The doors were open. Relatively confident that burglars weren't in the habit of leaving such warning signs, she stepped across the threshold. Her eyes quickly scanned the room for some sign of Maceo.

Nope, just her.

She jogged down and across the lower level, circumnavigating the bed only because it was too long to jump over. Leaving the rotunda, she slowed her pace and listened for some sound to guide her to him.

Quiet, except for the beating of her heart.

Too quiet, she thought, and wondered whether she had forgotten to shut the balcony doors behind her. She shook her head. She had definitely shut and locked them—and set the alarm. He had to be back.

Reaching his bedroom door, she paused, her hand hovering over the doorknob. Should she knock? Go back to the rotunda and wait for him? More importantly, had he already been in the rotunda? Had he noticed it—her little apology? And why hadn't he waited if he had?

Biting down on her lower lip, she grabbed the doorknob and twisted. The knob turned and she checked her forward progress to keep from bursting into the room. Instead, she pushed at the door and let it swing inward under its own weight.

On the mattress and in front of the bed were new suitcases and a travel case. He'd left without packing. Another bad sign. They were layered pretty high now—those bad signs—and she wasn't confident whether she was sure-footed enough to scale them.

Turning from the bed, she scanned the dresser top. Her heart sank further in her chest. She could almost feel it resting atop the knotted pit she had once referred to as a stomach. The missing clock, she expected. She'd already seen it back on the mantel. But the little silver box that had rested on the right was gone too.

That pretty much settled it.

Izzy left the room, closed the door behind her and walked back to the rotunda. She would finish the mural, but she wouldn't be spending any more nights in the house. They'd done all the communicating they could do, apparently.

Entering the rotunda, her vision was watery with the tears she was promising to keep in check until she was safely past *Casa di Silvio's* front gate. She bumped her way around the bed to the wardrobe and began pulling out her clothes.

"What are you doing, Izzy?"

She froze, her fingers gripping the neck of a hanger. Slowly she looked up to where he was standing in front of *Saturnia*. When she didn't answer, he rephrased his question.

"You're not leaving, are you?"

Izzy sucked her bottom lip in, concentrating hard on not letting the first teardrop fall. If she answered, she wouldn't be able to stop it.

"I don't want you to leave," he said, and stepped down to the lower level. He coaxed the hanger from her tight grip and returned it to the wardrobe. He took the rest of the clothes she had pulled out and replaced them before shutting the wardrobe doors.

His gaze returned to *Saturnia* and he studied it a full minute before he said anything else. "It's really well done. I wouldn't think the woman who painted that could just walk out."

"You walked out." She forced the words through clenched teeth, dismayed by how quickly her so-called Saturn reserve had abandoned her. She felt the first tear, hot and salty, crawl along her upper lash and splash against her cheek.

"You . . . you locked the door." Another tear, another splash. She fisted her hands, her nails leaving their mark in the flesh of her palms.

"You m-moved the clock . . . a-and the little box—"

"Look at the bed pillow," he interrupted. Grabbing her by the shoulders, he turned her toward the bed. Nestled atop the pillow was the silver box.

Still holding her by the shoulders, he stepped closer until his chest brushed up against her back. "I'm sorry I moved the clock and locked the door and brought your dress back into the rotunda. I'm sorry I didn't call for three days."

He paused, and his lips traced the curve of Izzy's neck until she broke the silence with a sob that twisted up out of her throat all ragged and wet at the edges.

"It was stubborn and mean-spirited . . . but I was hurting too, love."

Love. She trembled at the word, at the fact that he would still use it to address her. She turned in his arms until she could bury her face against his chest. She knotted the front of his shirt in her hands and rubbed her cheek along the rough silk.

"Maceo," she whispered. No, that wasn't enough. Still clutching his shirt, she looked up at him. Her eyes brimmed with tears and she couldn't see him well enough to read his expression. "Maceo . . . love . . . I meant to come back."

No, that was too little, she thought, and shook her head. "I-I shouldn't have left. But I wanted to come back, to wake up next to you." She threaded her arms around his neck. "I want to wake up next to you."

He lowered his head, tasting the salt of her tears as he kissed them away. Running his fingers through her hair, he trapped her head between his hands. When he claimed her mouth, the kiss was hard and demanding. He was sucking the breath out of her, making her fall back onto the bed in a half swoon. Afraid of falling alone, she tightened her arms around his neck and pulled him down with her.

Maceo was on top of her, supporting the bulk of his weight on his elbows while his hands curled under her shoulders to hold her in place. "Three days," he moaned in between kisses to her face and neck. "Three days of not holding you, seeing you smile. Three days of not tasting your mouth or that sweet pussy."

Izzy squirmed her consent against his growing erection. She wanted to be naked and moving against him, their bodies slick from the heat they generated. She clawed at his shirt, her fingers clumsy with need. Letting go of her, Maceo pulled the shirt wide, the buttons flying across the room and pinging off the walls and floor.

He was no gentler with the thin cotton tee Izzy was wearing, quickly laying it to waste. Famished for more of her, he gnawed at the flesh of her ripe breasts while he tugged the back closures of her bra open and stripped the impediment away.

Grabbing a breast with each hand, he sucked first one and then the other nipple to a shiny, wet point. His pants and briefs were gone an instant later and he was down on his knees, tugging the capris from her hips. Seeing the thin, white gauze of her panties, he groaned and buried his mouth against the fabric. His hands shot up and he rubbed her breasts together as he squeezed their sides.

He breathed against the thin barrier of cloth, warming the cream of her cunt until she was sure steam would rise up. When she pushed her mound against his mouth, he abruptly flipped her over. He pulled the panties down, the cool air wafting in through the open balcony doors breezed along her exposed pussy and she gasped.

Maceo lifted Izzy fully onto the mattress and then pinned her stomach-down with his weight. His fingers invaded her cunt. He withdrew, spreading her juices over her labia and across the pink pucker of her ass. Clutching the bedspread, she groaned her need for more.

She felt him entering her four fingers wide. Her vision

clouded over, the little box a streak of silver as it slid off the pillow and came to a stop in front of her face. She curled her hand around it, holding it tight but not opening it.

His fingers withdrew completely and she felt his thumb dipping into her pussy. Then the wriggling quartet thrust into her again, the pad of his thumb slick and teasing the entrance to her ass.

"Take it," she moaned, knuckles whitening from her hold on the silver box.

Maceo cupped his hand, his fingers stretching the opening to her cunt while his thumb made shallow intrusions past the nervous circle of her ass. Her pussy tried to suck him in while the rest of her tried to push him out.

"Take it," she pleaded.

Threading his arm beneath her, Maceo hoisted her ass up into the air. He moved behind her, his belly flat against the mattress as he started to lick her pussy. She rocked against his mouth, increasing the friction of his tongue moving over her clit. Her torso moved in waves as he teased the hood of her clit, a small cry escaping her in the space between one wave's completion and the next one's beginning. And then her body dissolved into a series of sharp jerks as her climax unfurled.

But the tension that was knotted low in her gut didn't dissipate with her orgasm. "Take it . . . take me," she ordered him in between the deep pants that fed fresh oxygen into her trembling muscles.

Maceo slid off the bed and scooped his pants from the floor. A tube, slim and cold against the side of her calf, fell onto the mattress. She heard the crinkle of the condom and then he picked up the tube. His right index finger, slick with lubricant, invaded her nether hole. She started rocking again, the motion wiping out the thought that he may have planned to seduce her into forgiving him, into bowing before him as she was.

When he found her slick enough, Maceo moved Izzy onto her side. She was still holding the silver box in her tight grip and he eased it away from her. He opened the box and slipped something into his mouth before he drew her left hand to his lips. Her gaze stayed focused on his mouth, but he was dividing her attention with the slow circles the tip of his erection made against the ring of her ass.

His lips moved down to cover the end segment of her ring finger at the same time his cock head pushed into her. She blinked once, slowly, and felt a second slide of cock and mouth. He was only halfway in, her muscles clamping down on the thick shaft to impede any further progress.

Maceo pulled back up on her finger and she could feel something dragging against her skin. She relaxed her muscles, moaning with a new need as he buried his cock deeper inside her ass. His mouth descended to completely cover her ring finger. He held it there, sucking on it as his hips moved in shallow circles.

She started to move with him. Moaning that she wanted more, Izzy slipped her free hand between her legs and started stroking her clit. The hood was swollen and she pinched it thin, gasping as Maceo retreated to the tip of her finger, his engorged cock head threatening to breach her ass in reverse.

Her finger was bare, but she could feel something resting against its tip.

"Take it, take me," was all she could say.

Maceo plunged back into her, his lips sliding down to cover the base joint of her finger. When he reached it, he let go, revealing an immense garnet solitaire on a silver band. Wet from being inside Maceo's mouth, the gem glittered like the dark red seeds of the pomegranate. A symbol of fidelity, of forever, Persephone had swallowed the seeds as a promise to return to her dark lord after each spring spent aboveground with her mother. Was that what Maceo offered now?

She brought her hand up to her chest, nestling the ring between her breasts. Meeting the rich blue of his gaze, she mouthed the word to him. *Forever.*

He smiled at the exchanged promise, his left hand moving down her top leg. He pushed the leg up until the heel rested against her other knee. She could feel air brush against her exposed pussy and then a cold squirt of lubricant at its entrance. The tube clattered onto the floor and then she felt the warm wedge of his fingers pushing into her cunt.

Izzy drew both arms tight to her chest, crisscrossing at the wrists to hug herself as Maceo invaded both holes. A layer of perspiration formed across her forehead and upper lips. His cock buried inside her and immobile, he worked a fourth finger into her pussy with slow, rotating thrusts.

Her mouth trembled and she tightened, her body vibrating around his fingers and cock. If the last night of pleasure hadn't driven her into a coma, this level of penetration surely would.

But Maceo was only beginning to teach her the true level of possession. His thumb slid along his palm. He twisted his hand slowly in a semicircle, Izzy releasing a sharp moan each time he changed directions. When the ring of her cunt closed around his wrist, a shudder passed over her body.

He started to move inside her, the strokes gentle and in complete unison. She could feel her climax building. The sensation doubled as he closed his hand into a fist.

Too much. Not enough. More. She was sobbing into the bedspread, her cries unintelligible. But she moved with him, writhing against his fist and cock, feeling the tension in his body as he kept his muscles under tight control. His lower abdomen was pressed hard against her ass, his forearm jammed against his balls as he moved in tight circles.

Izzy froze, any ability to control her body oozing from her pores as she began to shake in orgasm. Maceo groaned, his body locked into position as she fluttered around his cock and hand. His orgasm pulsed through his shaft, the thick stalk jumping with each burst of cum.

She went limp beneath him, the muscles of her body shutting down except for the little contractions that hungered after Maceo as he slowly eased first his hand and then his cock from her exhausted body.

Maceo kissed her hip and got off the bed. Closing the balcony doors and crossing to the interior doors, he promised her he would be back in a few seconds. He returned with a warm washcloth. Rolling Izzy onto her back, he bent down and kissed the top swell of her mound. He passed the washcloth over her pubic hair, his thumb pushing between her labia to stroke her clit with the wet cloth. Satisfied that Izzy's clit was clean, he moved the cloth lower, his lips taking over the tender care of her sensitive button as little aftershocks of ecstasy moved through her. He washed the exterior of her pussy, his tongue dipping into her center while he wiped the cloth down her perineum and lower to erase the last of the lubricant from her skin.

Tossing the washcloth to the side, he moved back up the bed. A low, satisfied sound gurgled in the back of Izzy's throat. It was somewhere between a dove's cooing and the purr of a sleeping cat.

She was still making it when he woke the next morning to find her sleeping in his arms.

EPILOGUE

A SMALL CROWD OF sixty guests were gathered at *Casa di Silvio*. Some came purely to see the completed mural, others to congratulate host and hostess on their engagement. Izzy drifted through the crowd, letting Maceo charm the guests while her anxious ears strained to hear what people thought about the mural. When she reached the two sections that she simply thought of as *Maceo*, she stopped.

"I guess the sex was anything *but* vanilla."

Izzy felt the soft dig of Milly's chin on her shoulder and turned her head. She brushed her lips across her sister's cheek. "Do you like the sections?"

Milly let out a small, contemplative snort. Her gaze flicked in the direction of Saturnia's section of the wall. "I hate that he made you feel like that."

"More like my stupidity made me feel like that," Izzy said. "Though he definitely played a part in it."

Looking briefly at the seven signs that had offered Izzy the least trouble, Milly rolled her shoulders. "Some are very high-concept . . . a little more liberated than your usual structure, but still what I would have expected."

A conspiratorial grin spread across Milly's face as she gestured at the remaining four signs. "On those nights"— the smile widened— "I think you were pretty thoroughly fucked, dear sister."

The grin was infectious and Izzy tried to stop it from spreading to her with the straight-faced response that she could neither admit nor deny the allegation.

Facing the images of Maceo, Milly rested her head against Izzy's shoulder and sighed. "I want to be inspired like that."

The sections framing the balcony door held the same masculine figure. On the left, he looked south to the mountains, the terraced cliffs rich with vegetation. The man's black hair was tied back at the neck and he was bare but for a pair of doeskin pants. Eyes baked blue by the sun were focused on the day's task. He pushed a plow, his head and back bent at an obstinate angle. He wore a harness around his chest and neck, but it was clear the yoke was there to let him better possess the plow and the land beneath.

To the right, he looked north to a storm-capped ocean. Here, the black hair was loose and wild and he was completely unclothed. The blue-gray of the surrounding tempest swirled in his gaze. One hand he held between chest and stomach, the other reached out as if to embrace the cresting wave that threatened to wash over him.

Izzy slipped her arm around Milly's waist and brushed her lips against Milly's ear. "You will."

They stood like that for a few seconds until Maceo was behind them and calling Izzy back to the present.

"Love, someone I'd like you to meet."

The two women turned together, Izzy's eyes lingering over Maceo's beloved face before she looked at the guest he was presenting. She tried to place him, recognition eluding her until she felt Milly stiffen beside her.

"Jason Covington," Izzy said, and extended her hand.

"Please, call me *Jace*," he said, and covered her small hand with his much larger ones.

Izzy risked a questioning glance in Maceo's direction and he gave a slight nod, confirming that this was the Jace he had met with when he had disappeared for three days. She felt her own body tensing, wondering how she was going to convince Milly she had no prior knowledge that Maceo was acquainted with the playboy from the restaurant who had seemed intent on staring Milly down.

Jace gave Milly a stiff nod. "Miss Kirsch."

When Milly didn't respond, Maceo filled the silence. "Milly's helping Izzy plan the wedding—one of her great talents." He clapped his hands together. "Oh, and organizing the showings at Izzy's gallery."

Jace swallowed his response and said nothing.

"From what I hear, you should see about trying to charm her away from Goulden's for your new venture."

Izzy's gaze widened at Maceo's suggestion. She tried to discreetly motion to him to drop the discussion but her attempt came out as a frantic slice of her hand through the air. Backpedaling, she pasted a smile on her face and looked at Jace. "You're starting a new venture?"

"Some, uh, bed-and-breakfasts along the coast," he answered.

"I didn't think *that* was legal outside a few counties in Nevada," Milly said. She gave a sharp half smile and turned back to study the twin contemplations of Bull and Crab.

Jace looked like he had just been sucker punched in the gut— or lower. He gave a stiff bow and then turned on his heels and headed for the buffet tables in the great room.

Leaning close to Maceo, Izzy whispered in his ear, fingers crossed that Milly wouldn't hear her. "They kind of know each other."

She pulled back, confused by Maceo's expression. Tugging him by the arm, she pulled him farther out of earshot from Milly. "Why are you smiling?"

"Milly, she's eight and a half months younger than you, yes?"

With Milly's blessing, Izzy had revealed to Maceo how their father had been married to their mothers at the same time—his frequent trips between Phoenix and Los Angeles providing him with two daughters less than a year apart.

Izzy nodded, her expression drifting from confused to worried. When he closed his eyes and let his head fall back, thumbs tapping against the first two fingers of each hand, she shook him by the shoulder. "No!"

He looked at her, his eyes soulful and stubborn at the same time. *Dammit,* Izzy cursed internally. Those eyes and that smile were going to be the death of her willpower. "I said *no,*" she repeated.

"Umm . . . actually, it was *No!*" He pulled Izzy close and held her with his arms around her waist and his hands tapping lightly against her bottom as he finished calculating. "A Libra then. And in Los Angeles instead of Phoenix, right?"

Izzy shook her head. "Uh-uh. You're not getting any information out of me."

"Have to," he said. His lips grazed her ear as he tried to tease the truth from her. "I've already done Jace's chart."

"Irrelevant," Izzy shot back. "This is my sister we're talking about."

"I did his chart," Maceo pressed, "and told him he'd meet his soul mate here tonight."

Izzy pulled back until her astonished green gaze could meet the persistent blue of his. "They—they've already met."

Maceo drew Izzy back to him, the embrace growing more sensuous as they pitted their wills against each another. "This is astrology, not semantics, love," he whispered into her ear. Bringing his hand up to cradle her head, he stilled her building protest.

"And the stars tell me—your sister is that soul mate."

SINDERELLA

Jan Springer

ONE

ELLA'S HEART RACED AS she lay bound and naked on the gynecologist's examination table. A fine sheen of perspiration laced her skin. Her hips undulated as Roarke fucked her with the dual vibrator. Sucking sounds of her soaked pussy clutching the sex toy just about drove her mad. Her well-lubed ass burned with pleasure-pain every time he thrust into her and the erotic way the stimulator slid softly over her aching clitoris had her pulling against her bound legs and wrists as she tried to escape the incredible sexual tension.

The rhythmic motions made her body hum, pulse, ache for release.

He'd kept her on the edge of a climax for so long she could barely think straight.

"I've wanted to do this to you since the first day I met you, Ella." His deep voice smoothed over her flushed skin like a jolt of lightning.

"You want more, Ella?"

Excitement flared like a firecracker. Her body trembled.

She could barely see him through the sexual haze. Could hardly see his sparkling, lust-filled green eyes or the sexy smile he reserved only for her.

Oh, God!

She wanted his long, thick cock inside her, not the freaking vibrator!

"I want you," she pleaded hoarsely, and thrashed her head back and forth. She needed to come so bad. Needed release or she would simply go mad with desire.

"Please, Roarke, please make love to me. Please fuck me," she whimpered.

"And so you shall have me, Ella," he said hoarsely. His face twisted with sexual hunger. "You shall have my big cock deep inside your tight little pussy—"

"Good morning, sorry I'm late," Dr. Roarke Stephenson's deep, masculine voice slammed into Dr. Ella Cinder's fantasy like a sensual punch, making her suck in her breath and spill her coffee onto the elaborate oak conference table.

"Christ, Ella! You're such a damn loser!" Her stepmother's harsh whisper made her flinch and Ella quickly threw a pile of napkins over the puddle of steaming coffee.

Her face flamed as her two stepsisters, Drs. Wanda and Manda Cinder elbowed each other gleefully and chuckled snidely beside her.

Bitches! Ella thought as she pushed against the bridge of her old black-framed glasses in order to keep them from falling off her nose while she wiped at the steaming coffee. From the corner of her eye she spied the man of her frequent sexual fantasies stroll into the room.

He scowled at her stepmother, obviously overhearing her

rude remark, but thankfully, he said nothing. Roarke was still relatively new and she didn't want him getting into trouble on her account.

When he passed by, his delicious male scent slammed into her with such a wicked force her senses spiraled into sexual awareness mode.

Oh, God! He always looked so damned sexy. He wore the traditional white lab coat fully opened, revealing a light green shirt that stretched across his big chest as well as a pair of tight jeans that cradled his awesomely huge bulge. With shoulder-length black hair pulled back in a tight ponytail and a shadowy stubble covering his strong jaw, he looked more like a dangerous bad boy than a prestigious gynecologist.

He sat down beside her and she noted his lust-sparkling gaze slide over her in one hot wave making her entire body tighten with need.

Her self-control, or at least what was left of it, crumbled as visions of her most recent fantasy invaded her thoughts again. Their naked bodies fused. The scent of their sex hanging heavy in the air. His long, thick cock pushing deep inside her wet, hungry vagina.

Her pussy creamed in reaction.

Oh, God! She had to stop fantasizing about the sexy doctor. She had a bad habit of daydreaming about him whenever she felt overworked and tired . . . which was pretty much all the time. Overworked because she accepted twice the number of patients than any other doctor in the hospital did at the same wage they got, and tired because of her deliciously naughty nighttime activities. Activities that made her fantasize about Roarke day and night.

Was it any wonder whenever he came near her she felt so nervous and flustered she became all thumbs?

The last thing she wanted to do was to appear incompetent in front of her fellow gynecologists. Especially when she needed them for the occasional problem cases she snuck into the consultation pile, just like the one she'd boldly plopped onto the pile today. She didn't want her patient to suffer any longer, and had decided to bite the bullet and seek the second signature required as per Cinder policy for giving medication without awaiting the lab results to confirm her suspicions.

"You really should cut down on all that daydreaming, Ella." Her anorexic stepsister Manda rolled her eyes with disgust. Then she scrunched her thin lips in an unattractive grimace as she looked at the pile of donuts set on a crystal plate in the middle of the conference table.

"It's not her daydreaming. The klutz simply drinks too much coffee," her other stepsister Wanda chuckled as she heaved her overweight frame out of her chair and picked up her fourth chocolate-dipped donut.

Ella sighed wearily as their comments needled into her heart. By now she should be immune to their rudeness. Yet she wasn't. Compliments of her oversensitive nature, she supposed.

What in the world had she done to deserve such a horrid stepfamily anyway?

"Doctors, please. Let's not show our immaturity so early in the morning," Roarke grumbled as he poured some coffee and grabbed a donut. To Ella's surprise he winked at her.

Oh sweet mercy! Roarke winked at her, and she was gushing back at him like a silly schoolgirl.

"Oh for crying out loud, Ella. Hurry up and clean the mess so we can get on with today's caseload. We're already ten minutes behind schedule," her stepmother huffed. Disgust flashed on her wrinkled face and her three chins wobbled as she also grabbed herself a donut.

Ella bit back a sharp retort. She wished she could just tell them where to stick their donuts and their snide remarks. One of these days she would do just that. Not today though. Today she needed their help.

"So tell me about this latest problem case you're working on? This girl named China Smith," Roarke suddenly asked. She hadn't even noticed he'd started reading the file of her problem case.

Ella stopped wiping the table. Ignoring the irritated looks of her stepsisters and stepmother, she relished the familiar pounding of adrenaline that roared through her system. This time it wasn't the usual sexual energy she felt whenever she thought of Roarke, but the energy of living on the edge with these complicated pregnancy cases she had a tendency of taking on.

"Her symptoms include a rash, a stiff neck, blood in her mouth, seizures, to name a few," Ella replied in a rush, hoping her stepfamily wouldn't interfere just yet with their embarrassing protests. "I've done the appropriate tests to rule out stomach cancer, sepsis, meningitis, checked for intracranial bleeding—"

"What do you know about her personal life?" he asked softly. His gaze held hers and Ella took yet another deep breath to steady her nerves. Was that concern in Roarke's eyes? Or was he deliberately prodding her for more information so her stepfamily could gloat when they shot her down. No, he wouldn't intentionally hurt her.

Although there was nothing she could put her finger on, she sensed there was a gentle side to this confident man. A side he kept well hidden. Up until now he'd seemed to fit in at the hospital quite nicely, thinking only in dollars and cents and taking in wealthy clients who would benefit the hospital. Perfect Cinder material, her stepmother had cooed after they'd interviewed him several months ago. Perfect husband material, her stepsisters had whispered.

Ella had been smitten with him too. Wishing and dreaming that she would one day have this handsome, confident, rich doctor for her very own. Unfortunately her dreams and wishes had died a cruel death when she'd seen the photograph of him and his fiancée in his office shortly after he'd been hired.

Over the months he'd appeared quite the professional with her. Those heated looks she caught him throwing her way were probably just her imagination, but they'd ignited erotic fantasies that just kept on coming.

"She's thirteen," Ella admitted. "About four months pregnant, a prostitute, no prenatal care and she desperately wants to keep the baby."

Her anxiety mounted as the others mumbled their disgust. Thankfully she managed to keep her attention focused on Roarke, who merely nodded and kept reading.

A moment later he cocked an eyebrow as he shuffled through yet another report she'd put in the pregnant girl's file. "Her blood looks like it's been whipped through a mixer. Her pregnancy could have thrown her hormones totally out of control. Have you checked for TTP?"

TTP or Thrombotic Thrombocytopenic Purpura. It was a rare

condition that she'd only considered when the other lab results had come back clean. TTP could be deadly to both the baby and mother as it turned a pregnant woman's body against her and caused a host of problems from seemingly innocent rashes to awful seizures.

"I'm waiting on those test results now." She wanted to ask him for the required signature right then but, despite her impatience, she figured it was best to wait until he'd read the entire file on the off chance she'd missed something.

Apprehension mounted as he said nothing and shifted through more of the contents of the folder.

Ella inhaled slowly, trying to keep a tight grip on her frustration about her young, sick patient. She'd found the pregnant girl huddled on her assigned parking spot in the elaborate Cinder hospital's underground parking lot yesterday morning. How she'd gotten past security, Ella had no idea, but the girl's dark brown eyes had pleaded for her help. She'd said she'd heard of Ella's sympathetic nature and about Cinder's specialized hospital through a mutual friend. Had told Ella she sensed there was something terribly wrong with her pregnancy. Had begged for her to save her baby. A moment later the girl had gone into convulsions right then and there.

"I don't know why you two are even bothering to discuss her case," Manda snapped as she licked chocolate icing from her fingers. "As you said the slut is homeless and a prostitute. She's scandalous for our hospital. If anyone gets wind of her being here, it could ruin our reputation."

"Her pimp probably holds her purse strings," her other stepsister chimed in. "He won't pay to fix her up. He'll simply get another hooker to take her place."

"She's simply a waste of our time," her stepmother cooed. "Let's please move onto the next case."

The familiar burst of anger erupted inside Ella at their cavalier attitude toward a young woman's life. But she kept her mouth shut and her emotions of disgust and anger well hidden. She'd learned early in life that arguing with her stepfamily was unproductive.

"Let's work like the team we're supposed to be, shall we? Isn't that one of the reasons I was hired for? To shape us all into a team?" Roarke said abruptly. Without waiting for an answer he continued, "This young girl is good promo for Cinder Hospital."

Was that a tinge of anger she detected in his voice? Was it aimed at her? Or the rude, unprofessional behavior of the others?

"How is a homeless, pregnant prostitute good for us?" her stepmother broke in. Her perfectly arched tattooed eyebrows rose in curiosity at Roarke's promo comment.

"We can leak word to the medical press. Tell them that due to the quick thinking of Cinder's hospital staff, a pregnant woman's rare condition was quickly treated and her life was saved. It will give Cinder free promo in the headlines. Other hospitals and doctors will seek us out with their problem pregnancy cases."

"Yeah and those cases won't be able to pay just like this one," Wanda grumbled.

"That's not the point," Roarke said rather coolly.

Internally Ella cheered him on as he settled casually back against his seat and threw her stepsister a disarming smile. "Our clients will realize we're sympathetic toward the less fortunate. It'll make us appear more . . . human."

Ouch!

Her stepmother and stepsisters all frowned. It was obvious they didn't like what Roarke was saying. They only took on cases from rich, snobby people who could pay their exorbitant professional fees. Due to the increase in rates, just to subsidize their high living now that her stepfamily had finally drained her father's estate, business for Cinder Gynecological Hospital had taken a downward turn.

"I think what Roarke also means," Ella came to his rescue, taking advantage of the thread he'd created, "is that we can also leak word to the general public via the newspapers. I know a couple of reporters," she lied. "I can release word we saved the life of a very young pregnant girl. It will garner sympathy in a lot of mothers' eyes. Mothers who have daughters of their own. Mothers who will remember us when their daughters get pregnant and run into medical problems. We'll be discreet about what hits the newspapers. We'll feed them only the appropriate information about a problem case that was quickly solved due to the quick thinking of the Cinder Team. TTP is rare. Most hospitals don't even test for it until they rule out a cause for each symptom as it appears. Those tests can be torturous on the patient. We'll mention we're private. That will eliminate the needy and low-income cases." Of course she'd forget to mention the private part. As far as she was concerned, she would accept any patient who had a complication in her pregnancy, poor or rich. Payments could be worked out afterward. "We'll make sure this case hits the medical journals also. As Roarke mentioned, other non-private hospitals will refer their pregnancy problem cases to us especially if they are overcrowded, hence more business for us. I'm sure with Cinder agreeing to pay for the girl's hospital stay and her medication, it's a small cost for all the future business she'll be bringing in."

"Exactly." Roarke slammed the file onto the table and stood. "Now let's get our asses in gear. I don't want to wait for the test results to come in. Let's get her on the meds before it's too late. Ella, she's your client. You tell her what's happening."

"I'll tell her."

"I can see you've already got the requisition form signed. I'll sign it too as your backup and get it over to the nurses' station. They can start administering right away," he said.

Ella nodded, suddenly feeling a burden lift off her. It felt good having someone else on her side for a change. Very good. However, now wasn't the time to relish in her relief. She had a patient to see.

"Just one moment!" her stepmother snapped as Ella stood. "You stay right there, Ella. Mandy you call an ambulance to get Ella's slut out of here. We cannot go against protocol and administer drugs to someone like that without the proper lab results. We could be sued if Ella is wrong."

"Then they'll have to sue me too," Roarke snapped with apparent irritation.

Ella broke in. "According to Cinder protocol, if two doctors decide it is in the best interest of the patient to administer drugs without having the lab results yet, all that is needed is a second signature. I have that signature from Dr. Stephenson. You wouldn't want to go against our own protocol would you, Stepmother?"

Ella didn't wait for her answer. Instead she forced herself not to smile at the furious looks plastered across her Stepmother and stepsisters' faces as she followed Roarke out the door.

• • •

Later that day Roarke swore like a son of a bitch when he hopped into his car and maneuvered out of Cinder's parking lot. As the months passed it became increasingly difficult to remember why he'd taken on this job with the prestigious Cinder Hospital. Lately he'd had to constantly remind himself that the fantastic pay he received from this establishment would keep his dream alive. A dream it seemed he'd been working his ass off for much too long.

Today's case of China had really hit home. Too bad he'd had yesterday off or he would have been able to help the girl earlier. Ella was an excellent doctor. Unfortunately, she'd never had the support she needed from her step-broads and understandably kept her Good Samaritan cases well hidden. This case had been a close call. Too close. If Ella had waited for the test results, the baby and mother could have been irreparably harmed. Or died.

He'd been stunned to say the least when he'd found the homeless girl's file sitting right up at the top of today's consultation pile. Either Ella was finally getting herself some balls and standing up for herself and her patients, or she'd just been desperate in this case.

"Fuck!" He slammed his fists against the steering wheel, feeling the gut-wrenching frustration turning his belly into a queasy knot. Why the hell hadn't she called him at home about this case?

Hell! He knew the answer to that. Days off at Cinder were "do not disturb the doctor's day off." No on calls and no midnight surgeries. Just shitty nine-to-five shifts. But that's one of the things that had attracted him to this hospital in the first place. Fantastic pay and evenings free to help take care of his girls.

By day he gave breast and pelvic exams to rich, horny women who winked and flirted with him as they placed their legs into stirrups and acted as if having a metal probe slip into their vaginas was akin to him fucking them.

Unfortunately for him, the only pussy he wanted to fuck belonged to sweet, klutzy Ella.

Her shyness and refusal to stand up for herself irritated him and attracted him at the same time. Overall she seemed a gentle woman, but on days like today she proved she had streaks of boldness. To further his irritation, she continued to drown her innocent-looking baby blue eyes behind sexy black-rimmed glasses that simply made his hormones go haywire every time he saw them.

Roarke frowned. Maybe he had a glasses fetish or something? No, it couldn't be that. Every time he saw her, he became transfixed by her compelling beauty. The lack of makeup allowed her skin tone to glow and her natural beauty to shine. Her cheeks always seemed flushed, and although her hair was a mousy brown and short and spiky, sometimes windblown, it gave him the impression she'd just tumbled out of bed after a night of mind-blowing sex with some lucky guy.

He'd done some discreet investigating and discovered from the staff as well as some patients that Ella didn't seem to date and kept mostly to herself.

Too bad he'd decided she was off-limits due to the fact she was a part owner of the hospital. Although she never acted like she was the daughter of the man who'd started the private hospital, he'd decided long ago in his career it was safest to never mix business with pleasure. Or he'd be pursuing Ella with a passion.

There was nothing more he wanted than to have her naked and bound. His engorged cock driving shrieks of delight from her flushed body.

Roarke blew out a tense breath. Right now he couldn't think about sexy Ella or he'd end up masturbating right there in the car. He needed to keep his focus on why he'd taken this job and why he'd told everyone at work the big white lie that he had a fiancée.

Truth was, he rarely had the time to date. Speaking of time, he glanced at his watch.

Shit!

If he didn't get home, shower and change, he'd be late for the private adult play of Sinderella showing at his colleague Merck's house. The man was an asshole but he was also an old coworker who knew a lot of important people in the medical profession. Burning bridges with Merck was not an option if he intended to continue climbing up the ladder. Merck was a bit of a ladies' man so he wasn't surprised when the older man had mentioned he was hosting an adult play in his home tonight. Roarke had been invited on several previous occasions but he'd always been busy. Tonight however, he'd decided it was time to cut loose. Merck had also said the play would blow Roarke's mind.

Right then he needed a damn good distraction before his own mind exploded with the anger he felt toward the Cinder bitches' casual attitude regarding the less fortunate as well as their mistreatment of Ella. Usually he kept his annoyance well hidden. If he didn't, he'd surely get fired when he told his employers exactly what he thought about their rudeness. The three of them acted so fucking immature that sometimes he simply wanted to tell them to drop dead or to shove their jobs up where the sun doesn't shine.

But every time he saw Ella he had the totally opposite reaction. He wanted to take her into his arms, kiss her and do so many naughty things to her. Naughty things that would make her blush up a storm.

Today he couldn't help but allow her to see a bit of his soft side, and damned if it hadn't given her a boost. He'd felt quite smug at having her follow him out instead of staying behind as her stepmother had ordered.

Ironic that he was going to see this private Sinderella play. Kind of reminded him of Ella and her mean stepmother and nasty stepsisters.

Gripping the steering wheel tighter, he pressed harder on the gas pedal.

Since before meeting Ella he'd never had any trouble unwinding with some no-holds-barred casual sex with his women friends. Now however, the only person he wanted to have sex with was his klutzy coworker.

Since that was out of the question, he'd just have to force himself to relax tonight. To forget the young, pregnant prostitute who'd reminded him so much of his own young mother and to shove out of his mind the sexy, shy doctor who quite literally had him by the balls.

TWO

ELLA STOOD AT THE back door of Merck Manor, a dark brooding castle-like building nestled on seven acres of lush fields in upstate New York. She stifled a sob before shoving yet another tissue beneath the silver mask she wore for her secret performances as Sinderella.

Call her sexually twisted or perhaps she was just shy, but the mask allowed her to participate in many naughty adult scenes.

Sinderella. Her invention. Her naughty secret. Her creative release from reality.

Performing always calmed her down. It was the only time she felt alive and free and separate from her stressful life. Of course keeping her face hidden behind a mask helped. If the people she performed in front of knew her true identity, she'd never be able to do the naughty things she did in front of them. It was because of the luscious sex acts she and her masked troupe performed in the privacy of other people's homes that made Sinderella such a wild success.

If ever there were a night she needed to escape the pressures of her day job, tonight was the night. After seeing China's quick recovery due to the meds Roarke had cosigned, she'd been bawling like a baby. She did that when one of her really sick patients started to get better. She couldn't help being emotional. Had always been that way especially because of her innate ability of putting herself in each of her patient's shoes.

This time the tissue came away damp instead of soaked. Well, at least she was improving.

Running a hand through the shoulder-length, luscious blond curls of the wig she wore, she looked down at herself and admired the skintight black outfit peeking out from her open spring jacket. The sexy clothing hugged her every sensual curve and allowed a generous amount of skin to show. The halter top gave quite a revealing view of her creamy breasts and the thong that barely covered her pussy would allow her audience to view her naked ass.

To keep herself in shape for her secret performances, she worked out for a couple of hours every morning in the privacy of her apartment. Aerobics, weight bearing exercises, the treadmill, rowing machine and daily jogging at a nearby park. She did all of it to keep her abs perfectly toned and her body perfectly curvy. Not to mention the exercise helped to wake her up from her naughty, late-night activities.

Excitement began to push away her tears and she rapped on the back door.

She had to wait only a few seconds and the door swung open. Caprice, the motherly woman who Ella had hired to play her fairy godmother in the play, stood there worrying her lower lip.

Uh-oh, when Caprice bit her lower lip it meant trouble. She wasn't wrong.

"Dammit, Sin. Where the hell have you been? The audience is here and they're getting nervous. We were supposed to open fifteen minutes ago," she whispered as she quickly ushered Ella in the back door and down the dimly lit hall of Merck Mansion.

"And Prince Charming never showed either," she added.

"Shit!" Trouble. Big-time.

This just wasn't her day, was it? First she'd had to ask for help with her case and now her freaking Prince Charming had dumped her.

"The next time you hear from him tell him he's fired. We'll start looking for another prince first thing in the morning."

Caprice nodded.

They slid into the room where the rest of the small group had gathered in their colorful, sexy outfits. The instant they saw Ella they stopped talking and waited eagerly for further instructions from her.

God, she loved being the boss. The power made her feel strong and confident—something she never felt in the medical world where her stepsisters and stepmother always managed to make her feel like a clumsy idiot.

"The performance is still on," Ella reassured the small group as she slipped off her jacket and shoes and put on her black dance slippers.

"I've already mentioned to Merck what the problem is, he said he'd be more than happy to play the prince," the petite, white-haired elderly woman who played Prince Charming's mother said innocently.

I'm sure he did.

Merck had a crush on her. Well, maybe a crush was too gentle a word. He wanted her in his bed and that's the last place she ever wanted to be.

"I'll scan the crowd for a prince before any decisions are made." At least that way she'd have some control over what happened tonight. In order for the play to work she needed someone she was halfway attracted to.

Someone like Roarke.

Just thinking about him made her pussy clench wickedly and cream with liquid heat.

Oh yeah, Roarke would be her perfect Prince Charming. But now was not the time to start fantasizing.

Ella clapped her hands. "Okay everyone. Don't worry. We'll find a prince. As always, let's give them hell tonight!"

The group cheered.

"You guys are the best," Ella complimented her smiling troupe.

She nodded to Caprice who quickly tied the traditional peasant kerchief over Ella's wig and smudged her cheeks lightly with black soot to give the effect of a woman who spent most of her time cleaning. Then she led Ella from the room. A moment later she stood outside the door of the room they'd be performing in.

The first act she'd be alone doing a sensual dance while cleaning out the fireplace. She'd also be singing one of the songs she'd learned by heart when she'd been a kid and watched various Cinderella plays over and over again. Of course, she'd made her own adjustments to the tunes, turning it into an adult play her group performed secretly for private audiences. Ella's take of the money went anonymously toward several local charities.

Tonight wasn't the first night she'd have to pick a man from the audience to play her prince. For some reason the part of

Prince Charming was the one most often recast . . . usually because after the show the prince wanted the play to continue . . . in the bedroom. She had no patience for such unprofessionalism. She considered Sinderella a tasteful, professional, adult spin-off of Cinderella from which, according to the rumors, she'd heard it had been originally invented for adults long before it had been reinvented for children.

Her Sinderella version was a serious, lucrative business and there was no time to play to a man's ego or his aroused cock after the show. It was up to him and not her to get himself relief.

Gosh, she still couldn't believe she did this erotic stuff. If her stepmother and stepsisters found out about her secret life, they'd die right on the spot.

Ella smiled. Wouldn't that be a lovely thing to happen? To see their shocked expressions if they ever discovered their loser, klutzy Ella wasn't as much of a loser or as clumsy as they always teased her about being.

Music drifted from the room. It was her cue.

Swallowing back a last blast of stage fright, she forced herself to glide into the dimly lit room. As she appeared, shocked gasps rang out. A maddening applause quickly followed. The warm welcome washed a sizzling rush through her almost nude body and she couldn't help but be pleased at the way her troupe had decorated the performance room.

Ordinarily Merck used it as his library. On presentation nights, it became Sinderella's living room. Pine beams laced the white stuccoed ceiling and a cheerful fire crackled inside the fieldstone fireplace. Pulled in front of the hearth sat a lone New York ladderback chair. It would come in very handy in just a few moments.

Grabbing her feather duster with the dildo-shaped handle from the fireplace hearth, she began to dust the furniture and sang her sad tale to the audience of mostly men.

She was Sinderella. Lost in a world of servitude. Her father had married a nasty woman who had two awful daughters. He'd died and her stepfamily had made her their servant. Their slave, who cleaned the chimneys and dusted the house while she fantasized about being rescued from her dismal life.

The song always gripped her heart. It was a song of fantasies. Fantasies of who she wanted to be. Of pretending she was a beautiful princess and had fallen in love with a well-hung prince who would cherish her and make love to her every day—it made her feel sorry because she knew in reality romance would never happen to her. She was thirty and had never been on a date. Why start now? Sinderella was her sex life and she enjoyed it immensely, even if it wasn't normal behavior for a woman.

While she performed, dancing about with her feather duster, she scanned the excited faces of the numerous male members in her search for a Prince Charming. No one captured her interest tonight.

Frustration began to claw at her belly at the thought of giving in to Merck and allowing him to be her prince. Merck enjoyed tormenting her by dropping hints that if she wanted him to continue to throw private showings for Sinderella, she would have to sleep with him.

He was a millionaire heart surgeon and by far Sinderella's greatest sponsor. She needed to consider his threat and either do as he asked or tell him to shove his request right up his ass.

She leaned heavily to the latter.

Denying Merck would put a dent into the pocketbook of the charities she anonymously donated her share of the Sinderella performances to, but she did have her principles.

Suddenly from the corner of her eye she noticed a door opening at the other end of the room.

A latecomer.

Her breath caught as she spied the silhouette standing in the open doorway. The play of light and shadow hit his face in just the right way, illuminating his profile. Blunt cheekbones, straight nose and sharp angles that made her heart kick-start.

Roarke?

She almost faltered in her song but managed to keep on track, her pulses picking up speed as he hunched into the shadows. He moved with the confidence of a man on the prowl. Just like Roarke.

Oh, God! It couldn't be him, could it?

She noted the extra-wide shoulders, his tall figure. The dark hair pulled back off his face as if he wore a ponytail . . .

Just like Roarke.

Her body tightened with awareness. Carnal sensations bombarded her most intimate parts. She could literally feel her nipples elongate. Her breasts wanted to be touched, to be cupped, to be held. Her pussy sizzled to life and she ached to be filled by this newcomer's cock.

She almost faltered again as the wicked assault heated her with exquisite want. Almost dropped her feather duster as she slid onto the chair they'd set beside the fireplace just for her.

Angling herself so the newcomer would have the best view, she artfully spread her legs wide, capturing his full attention.

Even in the darkness she felt his hot stare upon her flesh as she teasingly guided the dildo-shaped handle of her feather duster up along her thighs, getting closer and closer to her thong.

She'd known right from the beginning when she'd first conceived the idea for this show that her sexual prowess became heightened when people watched her doing intimate things to herself. Without her face being hidden though, she would never have the nerve to be so bold. Would have been much too embarrassed as to what she was doing in front of all these eager patrons.

She continued to sing about her fantasies of a well-hung man coming to her rescue while her free hand tugged at the string holding her thong in place.

The thin garment fell away. Warm air breathed against her pulsing flesh, revealing to all her nude pussy.

Women gasped and men leaned forward in their seats to get a closer look. Sinderella held the newcomer's fierce gaze.

Using the tip of the dildo, she split her pulsing pussy lips and gently rubbed her engorged clitoris. Within seconds she felt the familiar stirrings of arousal and couldn't help the moan from escaping her mouth as she dipped inside her entrance, stretching her vagina as she collected the juices quickly accumulating.

Tension mounted inside her as she slid the now lubed dildo over and over her aching clitoris. Her thighs tightened. She forced herself to keep her legs apart, giving the stranger a prelude of things to come should he accept her offer to be her Prince Charming tonight.

Her breaths grew quicker. Her breasts strained against the tight halter.

With her free hand nestled over a clothed breast she pinched her nipple, gasping at the pleasure-burn.

She continued to rub her sensitive, wet clit. Need grabbed ahold of her cunt. Her body began to ache. Involuntarily her hips arched and gyrated, the fierce arousal rising quickly now.

This act was only one of the erotic sights that made her play famous. She never faked an orgasm during this scene. She knew the tender parts of her body well. Loved touching herself. Arousing herself in the privacy of her own bedroom as well as in front of her captive audience. Tonight especially she enjoyed fucking herself in front of this dark stranger who looked too familiar.

The newcomer, unlike the other men who leaned forward in their chairs, remained seated in a leisurely, relaxed pose. She sensed he was fully enjoying what she was doing to herself. Could almost imagine his scorching grin. A grin that would look just like Roarke's.

Her breathing stalled. At the thought of this stranger actually being Roarke, the man she'd been fantasizing about for so long, she moved the dildo quicker against her swollen clit, dipping harder into her vagina gathering more of her juices.

Her body sizzled, ached to be touched, to be held by this newcomer. She blew out a breath and almost faltered.

She'd tell Caprice to seek him out when she finished this scene. To ask him if he'd mind being her Prince Charming tonight.

Clenching her teeth, she bit back yet another moan. Her breath halted as the beautiful sensations whipped through her. She shuddered.

Plunging the dildo faster and faster in and out of her pussy, she keened and hissed as the inferno spread. Grinding her hips against the dildo, she finally allowed herself to lose control.

Just before she closed her eyes to welcome her orgasm, she took immense delight when the stranger shifted uneasily in his chair and leaned just a wee bit closer.

Oh yes! Come closer. Come closer.

Ella closed her eyes and groaned out her hot release.

Roarke couldn't keep his eyes off the luscious, curvy blonde. She'd been dancing erotically when he'd arrived, not to mention barely clothed. The carnal sight caught him totally off guard. He'd stood in the doorway transfixed by her beauty. Totally in lust as he'd watched her every movement sensually orchestrated, her voice so soft and familiar it slid over his flesh like a seductive lover's song.

Everything about her called to him. Made his cock shoot into alert mode. Her full, kissable lips reminded him of Ella's. Her long, smooth, feminine legs begged to clasp around his hips. And he found himself wanting to buck his engorged cock in and out of her slit until she cried out in pleasure.

Beneath her skintight halter he easily made out the two lusciously curved mounds that pushed against the slinky, black lattice cloth. His hands itched to cup her breasts. To feel their weight. His fingers ached to pinch what he could tell were unusually large nipples.

When she'd sat on the chair and spread her legs, her fiery gaze had captured his. He'd been amused at the feather duster turning into a dildo. But when the thong gave way to a deliciously nude pussy, her inner thighs glistening with wetness, her labia plump and her clit red and engorged, Roarke's cock had hardened and lengthened like a thick piece of steel.

His reaction surprised him. Lately he'd only been reacting this violently whenever he got near Ella. From what he could make out about this woman, she did look similar to his klutzy colleague. Maybe that's why he was so captivated with this woman.

He almost laughed out loud at that thought.

Ella and Sinderella were total opposites, but there was something attractive about this woman, just as there was something attractive about Ella.

However Ella was off-limits. This woman wasn't. He focused his attention on Sinderella.

Every inch of her oozed sexuality. Every soft curve delighted his imagination. Her luscious clit looked engorged and ruby red. Ready for his lips to suck and taste and tease.

His mouth watered at the delicious thought.

She was aroused.

Big-time.

"So? What do you think about Sinderella?" Merck nudged him out of his hot trance. For a moment Roarke wanted to tell his colleague to fuck off so he could enjoy the show. But it wouldn't do to antagonize Merck. He'd have the information Roarke would need about this mysterious woman.

"Who is she? I'd like to meet her after the show." No use beating around the bush.

"That's the beauty of it. No one knows her true identity. The entire troupe performs with masks and they only accept cash in payment so there's no paper trail. They all leave in separate cars and, from what I've heard, most of the actors don't know her real identity. Maybe you'll get lucky."

Damned right he'd get lucky, Roarke thought as he settled back against his seat to enjoy the show. He couldn't wait to find out more about this mystery woman who hid her face behind that mask. Most of all he needed to find out why she sounded so damned familiar.

Ella's pulses blasted heat through her veins as she awaited her next scene. She'd sent Caprice to do her bidding and wondered if the newcomer sitting in the shadows would accept her offer of being her Prince Charming for the evening. She'd only had to do this on a couple of other occasions and her picks had always been eager, charming and quick learners, yet their cocks had been a little on the small size. For her, size did matter. It just seemed to make the show that much more erotic.

Gosh, she hoped this guy was well-hung.

The rustle of clothing grabbed her attention and Caprice entered the back room where Ella had sequestered herself to mentally prepare for the next scene. It would be her first meeting with the prince.

But who would it be? The sexy newcomer? Or Merck?

"He's agreed."

Yes!

"You've told him everything required of him?"

"He knows what to do. I've got him out back getting into a costume."

Double yes!

"He's quite a hunk. You picked very well, Sin," Caprice complimented as she popped out a compact from nowhere and applied lipstick. "I know he's a lot younger than me, but I think I'm going to have to see if I can't get my hands on him tonight after the performance."

Over my dead body. The thought popped into Ella's head without warning. The intensity of her need to have this stranger all to herself frightened her.

Oh dear. Not good. She couldn't afford to follow these lusty feelings. She needed to keep her mind on the performance, not on the man.

"Sin, ready in five," another performer said as he popped his head inside the room. It was the father of the prince.

She nodded to the man.

Excitement flared as she headed to the door. And to meet her Prince Charming.

THREE

ROARKE SWALLOWED AGAINST THE sudden bout of nervousness as he awaited his cue to enter.

He'd been decked out in some unbelievably tight pair of leotard shorts that really enhanced his package.

He'd been stunned when a woman had asked to speak to him privately. She'd whisked him out of the performance room and inquired if he'd mind being Prince Charming to Sinderella.

Hell, he hadn't even thought it over. Had simply reacted and said yes he'd love to. When she'd given him the directions of what would be expected from him during his first scene, it had made his cock hard as stone. So hard he now ached like a son of a bitch. Yet he wasn't really sure he could go through with this. He'd never acted in front of an audience.

Actually that wasn't true. He'd done many gyno procedures on sedated women in front of a viewing audience of students. This could be similar . . . unfortunately he hadn't been required to take off his clothes, among other things.

Roarke swallowed the tightness in his throat and took a few deep breaths to dispel his nervousness.

Concentrate! Concentrate man!

From the door he peeked into the room to see what was happening.

At the moment Sinderella was being chastised by her stepsisters and stepmother for slacking off on her cleaning duties. The pout on her pretty lips slammed into his stomach like a rocket. Those gorgeous lips reminded him so much of Ella. He shook his head at his craziness.

Not possible. Ella would never have the nerve to do what Sinderella had just done. Masturbating in front of a crowd of onlookers took guts. Ella was too shy. Too sweet and innocent.

Most likely she'd be curled up tonight on her couch with her head in a medical book sipping coffee. He found himself chuckling at that thought. Found himself realizing he wouldn't mind cuddling on a couch with her, kissing her ruby-red lips.

Shit! Why did he keep thinking about Ella when he had this luscious woman right in the next room?

"You're not allowed to peek. Come away from there." It was Caprice, her hand curled around his shoulder, and she was pulling him away from the door.

"Sorry," he muttered. "Just trying to get rid of some of that stage fright."

"Don't worry. Sinderella will be quite pleased with you." Her interested gaze dropped down to parts south. "She picked well."

"She picked?"

Shit! He sounded like an excited schoolboy.

Caprice nodded. "She seemed quite flustered when she asked me to seek you out."

Really? This was damn good news. He'd thought he'd been selected from the audience at random. Now that he knew Sinderella was just as interested in him as he was in her, it made things a little more interesting and a lot more intense.

"Have you memorized what you're supposed to do?"

Roarke nodded. Oh yes, and he'd be surprising Sinderella with a few tricks of his own. By the time he was finished with her, she'd be begging to know his identity and she'd be very eager to rip off that sexy silver mask of hers so they could get to know each other a hell of a lot better after the show.

Ella swallowed at her suddenly tight throat as the traditional trumpet blew announcing the arrival of the prince. This next scene entailed Sinderella's first meeting with his royal highness . . . the prince had been to far away lands searching for a wife but had come back empty-handed. Now he was on his way home and had run out of water and was very thirsty.

As he entered the room, his face concealed by a sparkling blue mask, Ella's pulses began to pound in wicked anticipation.

God! He was built! He wore nothing but skintight shorts that perfectly outlined his huge cock and swollen balls.

Ella licked her lips. Very nice! Very nice, indeed.

"Hello! My lovely wench," the prince said as he neared her. His deep, masculine voice sent shock waves coursing up her spine.

God! It had to be Roarke!

Hot eyes peered back at her through the slits in the mask. Excitement flared and her body heated with fierce awareness as he read the handful of lines Caprice had given him to remember.

"I'm very thirsty," he said. "May I draw some water from your well?"

Oh dear! If this was Roarke . . .

"I'm sorry, my Prince, but the well is dry."

She could hear his breath quicken, could feel her throat grow dry as he drew closer, as she awaited his next words.

His gaze locked with hers. Although she could barely see his eyes in the darkness of the mask, the sensuality of his look seared into her like a rocket. So intimate she almost forgot about the audience watching them.

"Then you wouldn't mind if I quench my thirst upon your lusty body?"

"I . . . I don't know. I should seek permission from my family, but they are not at home," she replied.

"I'm too thirsty to wait. Would you have my death upon your head?"

"No, I could not. I must submit to you, my Prince."

Readying herself to sit on the chair, she gasped as his hands seared into the naked flesh of her waist. Masculine heat hugged her as he pulled her into a tight embrace.

What the hell? This wasn't part of the performance.

"First a kiss from your sweet lips for a parched man," he said softly.

Oh boy, a kiss was not in the play.

She could feel the coiled tension in his body. The soft press of his chest against her breasts. The rock-hard cock branding her lower belly.

Her cunt quivered, whether out of fear of his massive size or out of excitement, she wasn't sure. He gripped her waist tighter, as if sensing her confusion.

Then his head was lowering and the breath in her lungs stalled.

For a moment she thought of turning her head away. Of regaining some measure of control, but the instant his warm, firm lips touched hers, her body became lost in a swirl of lusty tensions.

She could barely think as his tongue speared into her mouth.

Possession.

Desperation.

Desire.

Eagerness. She sensed it all in his heated kiss.

His mouth burned into hers as he explored. His tongue smoothed over her teeth, mated with her tongue. The brand of his hands slid down her body, cupping her naked ass cheeks. The push of his thick bulge against her lower belly grew harder. The intimate gesture made her vagina clench with primal demand. She found herself melting against his hard contours. Boldly pressing herself into his erection.

He groaned. It was a sensual sound. One like she'd never heard before.

She shivered. Fire raged through her veins. She could barely draw in a breath when he abruptly broke the intoxicating kiss.

She couldn't resist him as he led her to the chair by the fireplace and made her sit. She watched as he got down on one knee between her widespread legs. The wicked burn of his fingers over her knees had her grabbing the edge of the chair just to keep herself steady.

With a quick tug, her thong left her body.

"I'm so thirsty . . . you will not deny me a drink from your well." His voice sounded strangled, aroused.

How could she resist? She couldn't even speak. Couldn't move. Her body felt so tight with anticipation. Her breaths came in such harsh gasps.

"Your pussy is as red as wine," he said, the tip of his tongue peeked out from his luscious mouth. The sight mesmerized her. Sent her pulses careening.

He leaned his head between her legs, his hot breath blazing against her pussy.

"Oh, God," she found herself whispering, her performance lines totally forgotten as she noted his black hair tied back in a ponytail low on his neck.

It had to be Roarke!

She could never have imagined in any of her fantasies, the anticipation, the sweet torture gathering inside her at the sight of Roarke going down on her. Since he was a newcomer without experience in acting, Caprice had instructed him to simply place his mouth over her pussy, allowing her to fake the orgasm. But the strong, moist tongue that licked between her pulsing labia made her just about come out of her chair. She couldn't help but cry out at the fire of his touch and the erotic bristle of his stubble rasping against her tender flesh.

Sweet mercy! Roarke knew how to orally pleasure a woman.

For the first time in her life she allowed herself to simply feel.

And it felt damn good as he sucked a plump labia into his mouth. The heat of his lips branded her. His teeth nibbled gently on her flesh. Fire raged. He seduced her other labia in the same way. Then slid his tongue over and over her clit until her fists turned into tight knots and her lower belly clenched erotically.

When his tongue dove into her slit, she simply came apart. Blades of pleasure zipped through her and she barely heard the strangled cry ripped from her throat as Roarke's tongue plunged in and out of her like a miniature cock. Shudders ran rampant.

Tossing her head back, her lips parted to allow her pants to escape.

His tongue continued the erotic thrust. His nose acted like a clit stimulator, pressing, smoothing, until pleasure spiraled and her cream gushed down her channel.

Slurps quickly followed as he drank greedily from her.

Erotic sensations continued to tear through her, and when he finished, she felt weak from the climax.

"Thank you for quenching my thirst, oh beautiful wench."

Her pussy still fluttered in the glorious aftermath and she found it hard to open her eyes at the sound of his voice. When she did, he was licking her cum off his lips. His chin and nose shone with her juices.

He remained on one knee and she trembled in awe at the way his chest muscles rippled as he released her legs.

"You taste so sweet, like wine. What is your name, lass?"

The soft caress of his words almost had her telling him her real name. She caught herself at the last moment.

"Sinderella, my Prince."

"Sinder . . . ella." Her name rolled off his tongue in two syllables. The Ella part more pronounced.

Her pulses faltered in a sudden bout of fear. Did he know her true identity? But how could he? She always borrowed a friend's car to come to the performances so no one could trace her. Always removed any jewelry from her body that would give her identity away. Unless he'd recognized her voice? Surely if he had, he would have said something.

No, she was just grasping at straws. He had no idea who she really was.

He stood.

"Alas, my thirst has been quenched as it has never been quenched before. I shall never forget your hospitality or you."

He bowed and then he was gone. Leaving her staring after him. Wanting him. Needing him.

The audience clapped. It was a roar unlike any she'd ever heard before and it sent tingles of happiness slithering up her spine. Obviously they'd enjoyed the performance just as much as she'd enjoyed what Roarke had done to her. The applause faded.

She trembled when she heard the laughter of her approaching stepfamily. It was her cue to continue straight into the next scene. A small scene with her two stepsisters and evil stepmother complaining how tired they were after a day of shopping.

It took every ounce to gather her wits to continue on track with the play. She'd never found it so difficult to concentrate on her lines. Fire laced her cunt. Sticky dampness clung to her inner thighs as she quickly retrieved her thong and tied it back into place.

She wanted to go after Roarke. Wanted to grab him. Push him up against the wall and just fuck him. She blew out a tense breath.

God! She'd never had such a fierce urge to be fucked. To fuck.

She wanted more of those delicious licks he'd given her. At the same time, her mind whirled in disbelief.

Had she really been mouth-fucked by Roarke? Or had she just fantasized it was him and actually given his face to the newcomer?

Passion pounded through her as she suddenly remembered the other delights in store compliments of her Prince Charming.

"Fuck! You lucky dog, Roarke. I've been trying forever to get inside her pussy. How did the bitch taste?" Merck was laughing and slapping congratulations on Roarke's back as Roarke changed into yet another pair of skintight attire. This time he would wear nothing but a thong.

Being practically naked in front of people who knew him made him a bit nervous, but Merck's crude comment about Sinderella sliced deep into his gut and he resisted the urge to take a swing at the man.

"You'll never know, will you?" Roarke growled.

Merck backed up a step, obviously picking up on his hostility. "Take it easy, man. She's just a slut."

Roarke saw red.

Before he knew what happened, he'd grabbed Merck by his shirt collar and pushed him up against a nearby wall. The sharp sound of a whoosh as the wind left Merck's lungs and the way he blinked back at him—totally stunned—made Roarke regain his senses. However the red-hot anger remained.

"You're a fucking asshole," Roarke hissed, and let go of Merck. "She's not a slut. She's an actress doing her job."

"And it seems her pussy cream has drugged you, my friend."
Merck chuckled as he straightened his tie. "Maybe I'll have to get
myself a little taste too."

Before he could tell Merck to back off, the bastard had already slipped away.

Clutching his hands into fists, Roarke fought the anger. He
was being ridiculous. The woman in the play was just an actress.
She was used to having a man's mouth on her pussy. It was part of
the act. Caprice had instructed him that because he wasn't
trained, he would only have to place his mouth over Sinderella's
cunt and she would simply fake the rest. However, when he'd
gotten between her legs, he'd been enticed by her overpowering
scent of arousal. He'd simply had to taste her, pleasure her, fuck
her with his tongue.

Roarke closed his eyes and stifled a moan. She'd tasted so fine.
Addictive like a fruity, expensive ice wine. The intense way her
vaginal muscles had eagerly clenched around his tongue . . . well,
he knew she'd been pleased with the oral sex he'd given to her.

No faking orgasms tonight, Sinderella. Not if he continued to
get his way, which by the way her shoulders had tensed up as
he'd leaned closer, led him to believe she wasn't used to not being
in control.

When he'd pulled her against him, he'd sensed her fear, her
indecision.

She'd fit perfectly against him. Soft flesh in all the right
places. Her curves melting against his hard planes. She was even
the same height as Ella.

Not to mention how innocently she'd kissed. As if she were
inexperienced.

Roarke's eyes snapped open at the thought.

Jesus.

Could Sinderella be more innocent than she let on?

"Here's the new dress for the Prince's Ball as promised," Caprice cooed proudly as she entered the back room where Ella had sequestered herself, the harsh, crinkling sound of plastic following her inside. "And before I present it to you, I have to say you did a fabulous performance with the prince. He really brought out the best acting in your career. You really looked like you were climaxing." She wiggled her eyebrows and laid the unwrapped dress on a nearby chair.

"I was climaxing," Ella admitted, still trying to settle her nerves over what had just taken place with Roarke and what would be coming during her next meeting with him.

Caprice's mouth opened in shock. "No way, are you serious?"

Ella nodded.

"Oh, my God! I specifically told him what to do, and going down on you was not in my instructions."

"Obviously he has problems following the rules."

"Obviously. And what was with the kiss? You've never allowed a prince to kiss you before . . . at least not until the last scene."

"I couldn't stop him." Hadn't really wanted to.

"Like hell. You ever hear of slapping his face?" Caprice snapped. "I cannot believe he would take advantage of you like that in front of an audience. I've always told you I do not like it when you pick right from an audience. It's too risky. We should have cancelled tonight's performance. I'm going to have a chat with that man and tell him we've got rules." Caprice started for the door.

"No, don't. I've got my own revenge plans for him."

"Ella. We're professionals. We've got a pristine reputation. We can't afford to screw it with games."

Ella smiled. "Don't worry, Mom," she said using Caprice's nickname affectionately given to her by the troupe. "I'll stay on track with the show. There won't be any surprises." Except for Roarke. A surprise he'll truly enjoy.

"Now get rid of your frown and let's take a look at that sexy new dress you made for me."

"Just remember, my sweet Sinderella, miracles are happening every day. All you have to do is believe in the magic. Believe in the magic of miracles and a miracle will come true for you," her fairy godmother cooed as she and Ella stood in the middle of Sinderella's living room. Her stepsisters and stepmother had already left for the Prince's Ball, leaving Sinderella crying and desolate that she was prohibited to go because she had her cleaning duties to attend to.

She'd wanted so badly to see the prince again. Wanted so badly to have his mouth on her pussy again.

"But I do believe in the magic of miracles, Fairy Godmother."

Sweet mercy! She really did believe in miracles tonight. Especially now that she'd had the pleasure of kissing the man of her fantasies. Of having his head between her legs, licking and sucking on her cunt, making her experience the best orgasm she'd ever experienced in her life.

"Then close your eyes, Sinderella. Close your eyes and believe in the magic of miracles."

"But I cannot attend wearing these rags, Fairy Godmother."

"Believe it and it will happen."

She closed her eyes and knew the cinematic smoke would gush through the performance room.

"Hurry, hurry," Caprice said. Ella's eyes popped open, and it took only a quick tug on her halter and thong and she stood naked in the smoke. Lifting her arms, she allowed Caprice to slide the slinky dress over her. It fit like a glove.

Personally she'd always wished for a fairy godmother. Someone sweet and nurturing like her motherly friend who would help her garnish her self-esteem and self-confidence. Someone who would grant her wishes and make all her dreams come true, someone who would banish her insecurities around men she felt sexually attracted to . . . men like Roarke.

She'd never had sex with a man without her mask. In a way she was a relationship virgin. Always avoiding men because she didn't really know how to act around them. Didn't possess the self-confidence or self-esteem to be bold enough to go after Roarke, no matter how much she craved to.

She knew she shouldn't, but she'd always blamed her father for her troubles. For him being such a damn fool in picking the wrong woman for himself and for her, thus ruining her childhood. She'd been only five when her beautiful mom had died in childbirth. Her baby sister had died a day after, leaving Ella without a mother or a sibling. Her father became so obsessed with his private hospital that she rarely saw him anymore. At that point her craving for his attention grew and her interest in becoming a gynecologist just as he was took root.

She still remembered the amused way her father had laughed at her when she'd told him in her naïve five-year-old, defiant stance that she wanted to skip school for the rest of her life so she could go to work with him and learn everything about his doctoring trade.

His laughter at her newfound dream had stung. Had ripped a hole in her soul. He'd merely patted her on the head like she was an amusing dog and ushered her off to school with the nanny he'd hired. A year later he'd married a gynecologist who worked at the hospital, saddling Ella with two stepsisters. They were horrid creatures, already in their early teens. They ignored her and studied hard so they could go to medical school and be doctors themselves. They garnered all the attention from her father and new stepmother, leaving her totally alone and frustrated.

In turn, Ella threw herself into her fantasy world. Studying ballet, taking singing lessons and doing anything that would keep her mind occupied at her growing insecurities that she would never be the doctor she wanted to be.

One year later her father died of a massive heart attack, leaving her an unloved stepchild who was shipped off to an all-girls private school so fast it had literally made her head spin. Over the years in the school she'd continued her dance lessons, singing lessons and even taken acting classes.

When she graduated, her stepmother presented her with the trust fund her father had set up with the provision Ella study gynecology and become a doctor so she could carry on with the rest of the *family* in the family business.

In the end, she had succeeded in what she'd wanted to do

with her life. She had become a doctor. Unfortunately all her studying and seclusion in her fantasy world hadn't prepared her for interacting with the opposite sex. Hence her creation of Sinderella, which enabled her to hide behind a mask as she dabbled in sex with strange men. Men who seemed to fall in love with the fictional Sinderella, but not really with *her*. Well, maybe if she'd given them the chance they would have loved her, but she'd been unable to remove her mask to get intimate with them.

"And now, sweet, sexy Sinderella, you will go to the ball," her fairy godmother's voice made her snap from her thoughts. "Just remember you must leave the ball before midnight for then the beautiful, sexy clothing will vanish and you will return to the rags you had before."

The audience clapped their appreciation as Sinderella was ushered from the room to await the next scene with her prince.

Roarke blew out a tight breath as he heard the audience clapping and whistling in appreciation.

Shit! They really seemed to be enjoying themselves.

He wished he could be out there in the audience seeing what that sexy woman was up to. But he'd only be squirming impatiently in his chair. Craving her, needing to be inside her, wanting to know exactly what kind of a woman would be bold enough to masturbate in front of a live audience as well as allow a complete stranger to go down on her with thirty or so people watching them.

His cock pulsed violently against his thong and he almost groaned out loud at what would transpire between them at the ball.

"It's time," Caprice said as she and the rest of the troupe, all decked out in sexy, sultry party clothes, moved like one well-oiled machine toward the door.

He was impressed he had to admit as he followed them out into the hallway straining his neck in order to catch a glimpse of his sultry, sexy Sinderella.

To his disappointment she was nowhere to be found. A sliver of frustration nibbled at him. It made him wonder if the real Prince Charming had felt this same kind of frustration when he'd gone about town placing glass slippers on women's feet, hoping to find the woman who had eluded him at the ball.

Oh shit, get this crap out of your brain, man. It's just fantasy.

Short of ripping the mask from her face, he might never find out the woman's true identity. At least that's what he'd learned from the group of actors who, after working with her for a couple of years, still didn't know the identity of their boss. They'd also explained about what had happened to the other princes who'd fallen for the elusive Sinderella. One by one they'd become frustrated with not being able to find out who she was and had quit.

He wouldn't quit that easily.

Before the night was out, he would have her silver mask in his hands or, at the very least, have a way of finding out her true identity. Of that, he was certain. No sane man would put up with what had transpired between the two of them in front of the audience tonight and not want more from her.

FOUR

ELLA TWISTED HER FINGERS into anxious knots as she waited outside the door to where the play was taking place. Cripes! She wanted so badly to get a look at her prince. Wanted to push open the door. To run inside and tell him she was Ella. That she wanted him to fall in love with her and *not* with Sinderella.

Caprice seemed to sense her need and kept her figure smack-dab in her way, preventing her from so much as taking a peek through the door at the prince who by then must have danced with Sinderella's two evil sisters. One anorexic. The other extremely overweight.

When Sinderella had been looking to hire the sisters, she'd made sure they reminded her of her own stepsisters. It gave her a morbid satisfaction during the performances when she ended up with the prince and not them. Perhaps this was her immature way of acting out against her own stepfamily.

Whatever the reason, she'd never been so nervous about performing in her life as she was tonight. Come to think of it, ever since she'd caught sight of Roarke's shadowy figure she'd been on the sexual edge of hell.

"I've been told your prince is just as eager to get together again with you as you are with him."

Oh dear. Now she was even more nervous.

Mom smiled softly. "Do you by any chance know him?"

"Good God! Why in the world would you ask that?"

"Because I've never seen you like this before. Your cheeks are so flushed and you're trembling. Not to mention the way you seduced that dildo duster and kept your eyes glued in his direction when you orgasmed—it was as if you were making love to him and not the audience. You should know that's a no-no, Sin. Work the audience. That's always been our number one rule."

"Sorry, I'll do better." God! She couldn't believe she was actually apologizing to her employee.

"Sweetheart, I know you will. I just thought I should mention it."

"I'm glad you did, Mom."

She needed to concentrate. Needed to make this a fantastic performance. Merck was a very rich man and he had deep pockets. The friends he brought here also had deep pockets. They paid handsomely to see the private production.

The sound of a trumpet announcing her arrival snapped her to reality. It was her cue to enter.

For a split second she hesitated.

Dare she go in there? She could screw this up because of her nervousness performing with Roarke.

"Go, go, go," Mom whispered.

Ella nodded and took a deep breath. Renewed gasps of approval zipped through the air as she entered the room dressed in the beautiful, sultry, skintight dress. Of course while she'd been out of sight, there had been a couple of surprises added, but her audience and Roarke would discover it soon enough.

The loudest gasp came from Prince Charming who stood in the corner in front of the king and queen, his parents.

The intense way he watched her made her breath ram right up into her lungs. If looks could undress her, then this man was doing it.

For the first time since she'd started Sinderella, she wanted her mask to be smaller . . . to be gone.

His mask gone.

As she approached Roarke, he simply stood there and stared at her. His intense gaze caressed her skin. Made her feel hot all over.

She wore the sexiest, clingiest, tightest white spandex mid-hip-length dress. The material shimmered with the wet look and hugged her every curve to perfection. The front had an adjustable lace-up cord that revealed her belly button and could reveal as little or as much of her breasts as she wanted.

In anticipation of tonight, she'd left the strings so loose that her prince would have little trouble getting easy access to her.

She shivered beneath his hot stare and the room grew deathly quiet as he moved toward her. His steps were long, confident. It made her heart race with excitement.

His cock seemed so much bigger now. The swollen outline nestled between two perfectly shaped spheres fired her blood. Velvety muscles laced his chest and a sexy shadow of black stubble caressed his cheeks. This time he wore a sparkling white mask, the color contrasting wonderfully with the thick black hair he now wore loosely over his shoulders.

He was a devastatingly handsome man. A man she wanted in her bed with his hard, long cock plunging in and out of her in uncontrollable thrusts.

At those thoughts she could feel her breath coming faster, harder. Could hear his breath getting louder, raspier, as he held out his hand. Such a wonderfully large hand. A hand meant for caressing her skin, for touching her breasts and a whole bunch of naughty things.

"Shall we dance?" he asked in a low voice that melted over her.

She nodded. Placing her fingers against his warm palm, she immediately sensed the erotic tingles of awareness zip through her. He pulled her close, pressed his body intimately against hers. Pushed that wonderful bulge tightly against her lower abdomen.

Her pussy reacted immediately. Grew hot and wet. Her vaginal muscles clamped around empty air.

She found herself moaning out loud.

Oh, God!

"Have we by chance met before? You seem familiar to me, my Princess," he asked, saying the lines that were expected from him. She sensed he wasn't acting. He was serious.

"Anything is possible, my Prince," she replied.

He smiled and she noticed immediately he wasn't the best of dancers when he stepped on her toes.

Music filtered through the room. They danced to a slow waltz, gazing into each other's eyes as if there weren't thirty people watching them.

And for Ella they were alone.

He moved against her in a sensual rhythm. One hand at her waist, his fingers branding through her clothing. His other hand remained intimately intertwined with her fingers.

His cock burned against her, making her blood pump strong and fast. She found herself answering his rhythm by softly grinding against him, slowly swaying her hips. He inhaled sharply. She noticed his jaw clenched.

Her mind reeled with happiness. He was just as turned-on as she was.

They remained silent as they danced, but she could feel his hot gaze beaming through the mask, burrowing into her skin like a blast from a furnace. When the music finally came to an end, she was breathing so hard and so fast in anticipation of what would come next she actually felt a bit faint.

"Who are you?" He whispered the words so softly she wasn't even sure he'd said them.

Suddenly his head lowered. She trembled and held her breath, thinking he was going to kiss her, instead his warm lips nibbled along the side column of her neck midway between her ear and her shoulder. The erotic touches sent ripples of shivers tingling up her back making her body tighten with exquisite need, and she couldn't stop the soft whimper that escaped her mouth.

He stayed there at her neck, his demanding lips nibbling at her tender flesh. Sucking gently at first, then harder until a sweet burst of pain from his sharp teeth made her whimper again. He calmed the fire he'd created with long, wet strokes of his tongue until her flesh throbbed wonderfully before he pulled slowly away.

Then he spoke, his voice a low, tortured whisper so only the two of them could hear. "I would make love to you right here and now, up against the wall, but I want our first time to be alone."

Her body tightened against his words.

The lights dimmed setting the next scene.

"You're a very beautiful woman. Very desirable," Prince Charming said louder this time so the audience could hear.

"I find you quite irresistible, my Princess."

"And I you," she replied, her heart now beating against her chest like a battering ram.

Oh boy, did she ever want him!

She trembled as he reached for the string holding her corset dress in place. It only took one pull and the strings loosened, allowing him to slide the material over her shoulders, allowing her breasts to spill free in front of him.

And in front of the audience.

She heard the soft inhalations from some of the men. The excited whispers of women when they noticed she wore nipple rings with thumb-sized sparkling glass slippers attached.

Prince Charming was breathing hard. His Adam's apple moved wildly as he swallowed.

"Exquisite breasts," he said hoarsely.

She'd had her nipples pierced a couple of years ago. It allowed her to dress her breasts in some unique ways for her show. By the way Roarke sounded, he certainly appreciated how she'd decorated herself.

He licked his lips and Ella followed the movement of his rosy tongue. Sexual hunger roared through her. She'd never been turned-on so hot and so fast by the sight of a man's tongue.

She held her breath as his head lowered toward her right breast.

She moaned out loud at the whispering impact of his wet tongue teasing the tip of her pierced nipple. Gasped as he placed his lips over her entire pink nipple, including the ring with the dangling glass slipper.

He sucked. Hard.

Lightning streaks seared a line from her breast straight into her pussy.

More! She wanted more!

Automatically her legs parted. Oh boy, did she ever want his mouth down there too.

Her urgency made her moan. Made her want him to rebel against the story line and simply take her pussy with his cock.

Sharp teeth nipped at the tip of her aching bud. Pleasure-pain sliced through her breast. Sensitive nerve endings shimmered as his fingers cupped her other breast, squeezing, kneading, massaging, making her flesh swell with arousal.

At the same time he continued to savage her nipple. His fierce licks, sharp nips and long pulls made her moan louder.

When he had finished tending both her breasts she felt drugged. Drugged with pleasure-pain. It left her so hot and achy she just wanted his cock buried deep inside her. Even with all these people watching.

Then his earlier words whispered at the back of her mind.

I want our first time to be alone.

She didn't think she could wait that long.

When he drew away, she reached out to him. She wanted to touch him. To make sure he was real. Make sure he was actually Roarke and not just wishful thinking or another fantasy.

Her fingers hungrily explored the raspy stubble on his cheeks and chin. The smooth curvature of his moist lips. The strong, corded column of his neck.

Her hands splayed over his velvety chest muscles. When her fingernails scraped the tips of his nipples, she heard him groan in response.

Ella smiled.

Payback is a bitch, Roarke. But a very nice bitch. Now it was her turn to get even.

Ella's hands trailed over his hot, tight abdomen. Hard muscles quivered beneath her fingertips. Quivered with anticipation. With need.

She slipped downward to his waist, to where the white thong held his erection hostage. She pulled the material and it fell away.

She heard herself gasp in surprise. Heard the females in the audience gasp in appreciation. Some of the men swore softly, enviously.

Fierce need consumed her at the juicy sight. Roarke was naked. Powerfully naked.

Nestled amid a spattering of dark, curly hair, surrounded by a couple of perfectly shaped, swollen testicles, his cock looked like stone—hard and curved upward against his abdomen.

Her cunt contracted wickedly. He must be at least ten inches long, maybe even three inches thick.

Prime male. Her fantasy man come to life.

Only better.

"Do I please you, my Princess?"

She nodded, her lines totally forgotten. She couldn't take her gaze from the spectacular sight. Roarke was bigger than she'd ever imagined.

She licked her lips. Felt her naked breasts swell, ache. Her pussy creamed. She could feel the warm stickiness flowing down her inner thighs.

"I take it my Princess is at a loss for words."

The audience chuckled, broke her trance.

"Oh yes, my Prince. Oh yes, your size does please me!"

"I've never felt this way about a woman before."

"And I have never felt this way about a man."

"You have made me so horny, my beauty. Pleasure me, my Princess."

He stroked his straining arousal, and his cock twitched like a live wire.

Ella shuddered with longing. Her body hungered for him. She wanted his huge cock buried deep inside of her.

"I will pleasure you, my Prince. I will show you that I am worthy of your intentions."

He made a move to retrieve one of the flavored condoms kept on a nearby chair for such occasions, but she grabbed his wrist, stopping him.

"No, my Prince."

She heard the soft whispers signal uneasiness through the audience.

Perhaps they thought she would deny the prince, or perhaps they were shocked at her break in protocol. Sinderella always practiced safe oral sex with the prince wearing a condom, but this time . . . this time it was Roarke. This time she would make an exception.

"I want no barriers between us tonight, my Prince," she said loud enough for the audience to hear.

His lips tightened. Was it in arousal? Or in disapproval.

"I will trust you. If you will trust me," she whispered softly so only the two of them could hear.

"I'm clean," he whispered back. "And I trust you."

Warmth spread through her at his words and she smiled. Dropping to her knees in front of him, she eagerly opened her mouth and he guided his swollen cock head toward her face. She wrapped one hand around the pulsing base, his flesh felt like lightning-hot, silk-encased steel against her fingers and palm.

Looking up, she saw the controlled set of his jaws, but he couldn't hide the rapid rise and fall of his naked chest. His hard flesh slid between her lips and her tongue immediately dove against the tiny slit in his bulging head. She tasted the salty pre-cum of his arousal. Swirled her tongue around his impressive flesh, savoring his masculine heat, feeling the pulsing veins straining against his rigid cock.

With her other hand she gripped his firm hip, steadying herself. She could hear his harsh breaths split the air. Felt the carefully restrained thrust of his hips as he moved against her. She began to suck his cock. Her mouth a tight suction as he slid in and out, going deeper with his every delicious thrust. She moved her hand farther up the hard shaft to the point where she could safely take some of his length.

Rubbing her tongue along the sensitive bottom of his cock, she took great pleasure in hearing his groans. The erotic sounds sifted through her, warming her pussy, making her cream over and over.

Taking her time with Roarke, she teased his shaft by gently biting down, allowing her teeth to scrape along his tender flesh as he plunged in and out of her mouth.

His groans grew louder, wilder.

His hands speared through her wig, holding her head captive. His fingers tightened against her scalp and she knew he was dangerously close to losing control.

She backed off, relishing his moans of protest.

Oh yes, she had Roarke right where she wanted him—at her mercy.

Her tongue cradled his cock, welcomed him in. But her teeth, ah yes . . . her teeth were just about bringing him to his knees. His cock jerked and pulsed in what she perceived as him experiencing pleasure-pain.

Once again she increased the pressure of her teeth against the frantic plunges. Enjoyed the untamed groans.

She loved the feel of his cock sliding in and out of her mouth. The velvety skin. The rock-hard flesh. The powerful taste of man and musk.

She sucked harder. He thrust his hips harder.

"I'm coming," he suddenly gasped.

In the past, the prince would spew into his condom and then throw it into the nearby flickering fireplace. With the change in protocol, Roarke probably felt unsure of what to do.

Digging fingers harder into his hip, she pulled him closer. If that didn't give him an indication of what she wanted, she then tightened her lips around his shaft and she sucked with all her might.

"Oh, God!" he ground out as his thrusts came quicker. His cock grew tense. Jerked.

And then she savored what she'd worked so hard to get. Loved the thick jets of his warm semen as he came inside her mouth.

Ella swallowed every drop.

When he was spent, he slumped onto the nearby chair. Crystal beads of perspiration dampened his chest. His eyes were scrunched tightly. His lips parted from his harsh gasps.

Ella smiled despite the arousal roaring through her.

Sitting down wasn't a part of the show, but in this case he'd be excused.

"Did I please you, my Prince?" Her voice shook and his eyes blinked open. A knowing grin flittered across his delicious mouth.

"I have fallen in love with you, my Princess."

"And I with you, my Prince."

The clang of the clock striking midnight made Ella groan her frustration.

Oh, God! Not now. The sound was her cue to run from the ball.

"I must leave," she said, and she stood.

"But you've only just gotten here, my love."

My love. That wasn't part of the script.

In the background the strike of the midnight bell continued to clang.

Oh damn! She didn't want to leave. She wanted to stay there with Roarke. Enjoy more of this fantasy play.

Unfortunately if she didn't go at the strike of midnight, it would ruin the show. She had an audience watching them. An audience she'd totally forgotten in her haste to have Roarke's delicious cock.

Ella headed for the door. Her legs felt weak, her pussy sopping wet and, to her horror, she almost forgot to drop the nipple ring with the glass slipper onto the floor.

• • •

"What in the world happened out there? Are you insane? We always practice safe sex! I can't believe what you've done!" Caprice hissed as she and a couple of the troupe ushered her to the nearby dressing room.

"Slight deviation from the plan," she answered truthfully. But she wanted more of the deviation. She could feel the sticky wetness of her arousal wetting her inner legs. Could feel her engorged clit throbbing in desire, her pussy aching to be fulfilled.

A roar of applause, whistles and shouts followed.

"That's the scene ending. He must have found the nipple ring. Why did you do the oral sex without a condom? God, please tell me you had a good reason, sweetheart. Please tell me you haven't lost your mind?"

"Mom, rest assured I do know what I am doing. Please trust me," Ella reassured the frantic woman.

"Okay, okay. I trust you. I do. I really do. I know you do things for a reason."

"Did the audience seem to be okay with it?" She'd been so greedy in not thinking about their reaction. Most of them were from the medical profession. Doctors, nurses and others she'd seen at medical conferences. They would not be pleased.

"I hadn't realized. I was too busy watching the two of you." Shoot!

"Okay. Spread it around that we know each other. That we trust each other." Her admission of the truth was her only source of damage control. Her only way to show she had been a responsible adult tonight. She truly did trust Roarke. Instincts told her he would never put her in any kind of danger, sexual or otherwise.

"I knew it! You two have a sexual energy that permeates the room. You looked absolutely smashing together and you act so naturally with each other," Caprice cooed. "You obviously enjoyed him. We should hire him."

"No. He can't be my prince."

"Surely we can—"

"I said no!" Ella found herself snapping as reality reared its ugly head. She couldn't chance Roarke finding out about her secret life. He could not know she was Sinderella. If he found out, then her life would be too distracting at work. Hell, with her frequent fantasies about him, it was already too distracting at work. Surely with tonight's experience popping into her mind whenever she saw him, her klutziness around him was bound to worsen.

Oh, God! What was she going to do?

She caught Caprice frowning at her.

"I'm sorry for snapping at you, Caprice. I didn't mean to."

"Well, you're the boss, sweetie," her fairy godmother said calmly, embracing Ella in a hug she really needed. "You've never steered us wrong before. If you don't want him for your Prince Charming, I'll tell the rest of the troupe before they get too excited. I'll drop word to the audience you are intimately involved and trust each other."

"Okay," Ella nodded.

Caprice let her go and smiled warmly, knowingly. "Are you sure you don't want him?"

"I'm sure." Liar!

"Okay, get yourself ready for the next scene."

With a soft rustle of clothing, Caprice left the dressing room.

But I want him to be my prince. I want him to be mine, Ella thought.
All mine.

Closing her eyes, she concentrated really hard and whispered
to herself, "I believe in the magic of miracles. I truly believe.
Roarke will someday become my Prince Charming in every way."

Roarke was still savoring the sweet, erotic way Sinderella's tight
little mouth had wrapped so perfectly around his penis when a
sharp rap at the door cued him to get his ass in gear for the final
scene.

He'd never seen a more erotic sight than having this gorgeous
woman drop down on her knees in front of him. He'd been told
what would transpire. Had been told to ejaculate into a condom
and throw it into the fireplace, but when he'd tried to follow the
rules, Sinderella had turned the tables on him.

No condom. Her grip had tightened. The sensual way her
mouth had worked his cock made him her prisoner. At her mercy.

He'd never known a woman to go down on him so eagerly. So
unconditionally. Sweet, sexy Sinderella. The woman of his
dreams. His woman in every way.

Or she would be . . . when the time was right.

FIVE

"I HAVE FOUND YOU. I have found the love of my life."
Ella held her breath as nude from the waist up,
Roarke's warm, slightly trembling fingers brushed
against her naked breast as he quickly inserted the missing nipple
ring with the sparkling glass slipper.

"We will be together. Forever," he said softly, and she accepted
the prince's warm hand. His fingers clasped intimately with hers
and he squeezed gently when they both bowed, indicating the
performance was completed.

The applause was deafening. The audience stood and Sinderella held her breath at the sight.

A standing ovation.

Oh my gosh! She felt so exhilarated. So unbelievably happy.

When Roarke raised her arm and pointed at her, the audience
went wild.

Have mercy! They really liked her. She felt herself gush like a
schoolgirl.

In return, she raised Roarke's arm. The audience went equally
wild.

Oh dear.

As was tradition her troupe surrounded the prince and princess and ushered them safely from the performance room.

A warm blanket was thrown around Sinderella's shoulders and Caprice quickly ushered her into another room away from the troupe.

"Merck wants to see you," Caprice said. Worry etched her voice. "And he sounds serious. Before you tell him where to take his disgusting offer, make sure he pays you first."

Ella had confided in Caprice about Merck's sexual insinuations and Caprice had been chilly with the man ever since, insisting they never perform there again. But Ella had insisted they continue to accept Merck and his generosity for as long as they could.

"I'll handle him, don't worry," Ella reassured her friend as Caprice helped her into a gorgeous red velvet dress that made Ella look both professional and sexy at the same time.

"Sweetie, I always worry about you. You're just like one of my daughters to me and I don't like it when a dirty old man makes unclean advances toward you. So please promise me you'll be very careful with him tonight. I didn't like the smile he had on his face or the way his fingers were groping inside his pants while he watched you and that stranger performing."

"That's why we're here, Caprice. To make our audience horny."

Ella winked as she slipped on a pair of red high heels and headed for the door.

Caprice grabbed Ella by the elbow stopping her short.

"Sin, you're not taking me seriously."

Geez, she'd never seen her friend act this way before.

"Okay, I promise. I will be careful. Really." She patted the woman's hand and Caprice reluctantly let go of her.

"Thanks for worrying about me," Ella soothed. "I'll make sure I get the money before I kick his ass."

"Maybe I should come with you?"

Caprice's frostiness toward Merck wouldn't help the situation. "No you stay here and wait with the crew. I'll be back soon."

Even though she'd reassured Caprice she'd be fine, uneasiness swooped around Ella as she walked down the deserted hallway to his personal office where she usually collected the cash from Merck.

The wooden oak door stood wide open and she readjusted her mask before knocking and entering. She found Merck dressed in a dark gray smoking jacket and matching pants, standing at the far side of the rectangle-shaped room looking out the night-darkened window and puffing on a stinky cigar.

Overhead a crystal chandelier sparkled splashes of bright light against the sultry red walls, tanned leather sofa and the giant, sleek mahogany office desk.

"Ah, beautiful Sinderella. Please come in. Come in." The gray-haired man of seventy smiled and waved her in.

"I hope you were pleased with tonight's performance," Ella said as she took a few steps inside, trying hard to appear confident and strong despite the bulge pressing at the older man's pants when he strolled toward her.

"Please, have a seat. I'll pour you a drink. How about a sherry? I've just had it imported from Jerez in Spain especially for you."

"I'd be pleased to have a glass, Merck." But she'd rather stand. Despite her uneasiness, she came farther into the room. It was tradition that they share a drink before talking business. Asking for the money due her performers was always the worst part of being boss. But the members of her crew depended on her to get what was rightfully theirs and, until now, she'd never failed them.

Ella watched as he poured the drinks, scrutinizing his every move to make sure he didn't slip any type of date-rape drug into her drink. Call her paranoid, but in her line of business, she knew it was better to be paranoid than sorry.

"Sinderella, I must say your show was exceptionally well done tonight." He handed her the drink in an exquisitely long-stemmed wineglass. She waited until he took a few sips.

"I'm glad to hear you and the audience enjoyed yourselves. We aim to please."

She took a taste of the fruity drink and sweetness exploded against her taste buds.

"Exquisite sherry, Merck. You have exceptional taste."

Merck grinned. Instincts and experience told her it wasn't a genuine smile and tendrils of fear curled through her confidence.

She'd learned in their relationship that flattery got more help from Merck.

"How did you enjoy the new Prince Charming?" The question caught her totally off guard. "I was sure you'd pick me, Sinderella."

He'd moved closer. Way too close for comfort.

"I . . ." How did she tell a seventy-year-old man that she didn't pick him because she just wasn't impressed with him? And if she wasn't impressed, then the audience wouldn't be either.

"I apologize if someone gave you the idea you would be picked, Merck."

Blue cigar smoke twirled from his cigar and stung her eyes. She resisted the urge to move away from him, opting not to show him how uncomfortable she was getting. "But I'm the one who makes the final decisions."

He pouted. "I volunteered long before my friend Roarke did."

Oh for Pete's sake! He sounded as if he were a spoiled child.

"I've decided I want to be your Prince Charming tonight, Sinderella." He reached for her arm, but she managed to step away just in time.

"I'm sorry, Merck. But the performance for tonight is over. I am here to collect our payment."

"And what if I told you I'm not paying until you allow me to fuck you."

"I'd say you'd be insulting the group of Sinderella and we'd have to withhold any further performances until payment is rendered," she said firmly.

Gosh, why couldn't she be this bold with her stepmother and stepsisters? Because she was hiding behind the mask, that's why. Life was always easier when she pretended to be someone else.

His lips twisted with apparent contempt. "Well, then. How's about a little kiss. Your performance with Roarke has gotten me so horny. You let him kiss you. I want to kiss you too."

"Kisses are out of the question, Merck. As I said—"

She cried out in surprise as Merck suddenly lunged and grabbed her by the arm, yanking her against his body. For an old guy he sure was strong!

"What the hell is the matter with you?" She tried to jerk away, but his grip tightened. His eyes seemed glazed and not at all normal. It looked as if he were in some kind of a trance.

She swallowed frantically at the panic climbing into her throat and shivered in revulsion as he rubbed his engorged erection against her thigh.

"I knew you'd like that cock, teasing, little slut," he growled. She grimaced at his acrid cigar smelling breath.

"Let go of me!"

God! She couldn't believe this was happening. Couldn't believe how paralyzed she suddenly felt. She should be kicking him, struggling, but she could barely breathe.

"Merck, please. I'm tired. Just—"

"Oh but, no, I've just begun," he snarled.

Suddenly he pushed her. Hard. Ella gasped as she found herself sailing so easily backward, landing on the couch with a soft bounce. Before she could react, he'd dropped on top of her, pinning her beneath him, his heavy weight knocking the breath clear out of her lungs.

Oh, my God! She couldn't even scream for help, let alone gasp for air. Terror unlike anything she'd ever experienced swooped around her.

"Oh, sweet Sinderella. I want to put my cock into your tight pussy. I want to fuck your brains out."

Get off me! Her mind screamed. She could barely breathe. The bastard felt like a cement block on top of her. His erection burned into her lower belly and she felt totally helpless as she lay trapped beneath him. He'd even trapped her arms or she would have been scratching frantically at his eyes, his face, anything to get him off of her.

"A kiss. Just as you gave Roarke. And then I want to suck on those big nipples and your juicy pussy just like Roarke did. Nice and sweet, I bet."

Her eyes widened with disgust.

"Oh yeah, Roarke was bragging when I talked to him in the dressing room. He told me how I should taste your sweet lips and how the cream from your cunt drugged him. How good he felt with your mouth wrapped around his cock. How he wanted the both of us to get to know you better after the performance."

No way! There was no way Roarke would ever say something like that!

Merck's face drew closer.

"You'd like that wouldn't you, Sinderella? Having two Prince Charmings fucking you?"

His obscene breath seeped into her lungs.

Oh, God! Please someone help me!

She could feel his grubby hand trailing up her inner thigh. Nausea rippled through her belly.

"Let me see how wet you are for Prince Charming, sweet Sinderella. It'll be over fast. You've made me so horny. I'll just stick my cock into your cunt."

"Get the fuck off her, Merck, or I will kill you!"

Merck's body stiffened at the sound of Roarke's harsh voice and Ella said a silent *thank you* for her prince coming to her rescue.

"Oh, my God!" Caprice whispered, her voice laced with the same horror Ella was experiencing.

When the man didn't move fast enough off her, she watched in stunned admiration as Roarke's long fingers gripped Merck's shoulders and he literally picked the man up and stood him on his feet.

"Pay the women what you owe them and leave her the fuck alone!"

"Hey, come on. It's not like she's your girlfriend." Merck laughed uneasily as he brushed at his clothing.

The muscles in Roarke's jaws twitched angrily but he said nothing. He merely stared at Merck in disgust.

"Fine." Merck's hand slipped into a side pocket of his smoking jacket and pulled out a sizeable envelope. "It's all there."

"It better be." Roarke snapped the envelope away. "Now get out of my face before I do something you'll be sorry about . . . if you're lucky to wake up."

"Fuck you, Roarke," Merck grumbled, and then stomped off.

"Sweetie, are you all right?" Caprice was suddenly sitting on the sofa beside her, enveloping Ella in her embrace. "Thank God, Roarke came with me. I told you Merck was up to no good."

"I'm okay, really," Ella whispered, quite thankful for Caprice's strong arms holding her tight.

"Caprice," Roarke said gently. "I think you'd better get the money to the troupe and tell them to leave. There won't be any more performances here."

Caprice nodded and pulled away. Her friend looked totally defiant and ready to fight if Ella didn't agree. "He's right. We can't come here again. Not after what's happened."

"Please don't tell the others," Ella whispered, feeling shame heat her cheeks as Roarke frowned at her in the background. She avoided his gaze. Did he think because of the way she dressed and the way she acted in Sinderella that he had the right to gossip to Merck?

Oh damn! Now she really didn't want him to find out her true identity. He'd think she was a whore.

"You've done nothing wrong," Caprice reassured, and smiled warmly. "You have nothing to be ashamed of."

But she did feel ashamed. A man had literally thrown himself all over her without her heeding the warning signs. She'd been stupid to come in there alone.

"Let's please just forget this happened, okay?" She tried to smile at both of them, but her lips just kind of wobbled.

"Okay. I'll go give everyone their share," she whispered, and let Ella go from her embrace.

"Thank you. I'll stay here for a few moments."

Caprice nodded. She looked at Roarke, and then nodded as if to say to herself Ella would be safe with him.

"Are you sure you're all right?" Roarke asked after Caprice left the room. The softness with which he spoke brought tears to Ella's eyes and she suddenly realized the full impact of what had almost happened. She could have been raped by Merck!

"I . . . I'm fine," she said as he sat down on the couch beside her, a severe frown on his face. His body warmth wrapped snugly around her, making her feel just a little bit safe and secure.

"You're shivering."

"Just adrenaline. I'm sure it'll go away in a few minutes. I do have to say thank you," she found herself saying. "I know what you must be thinking. How it looked. I mean I've never seen him act quite that way. He's insinuated things and I've told him I'm not interested, but I never thought . . ."

"No man should force himself on a woman. If there hadn't been witnesses, he'd be dead now."

Ella blinked at the fierceness in his words.

"I'm sorry. He must be drunk . . . I didn't mean to break up your friendship—"

"Christ, woman! He's no friend. And don't make excuses for him! Do you always accept blame for other people's stupidity?" He inhaled and shoved a hand through his luscious-looking black hair.

Oh boy, he was really pissed off. Even when he was mad he looked sexy.

"I'm sorry. I shouldn't have yelled at you. He's a disgrace to mankind. I'm glad I've seen his true colors. Although, I'd rather it have been under different circumstances."

"Spoken like a true gentleman." She found herself smiling.

"Or a true prince. Which leads me to why I was looking for you."

His green eyes glittered fiercely as he held out his hand. She spied the nipple ring with the pretty glass slipper nestled in the palm of his hand.

"You dropped it again after the performance. I thought you'd be needing it."

"Thank you." When she picked it up, her fingertips blazed as she touched his flesh.

"Would you like me to see you to your car?"

"No, I'm fine."

He nodded and an uneasy silence stretched between them.

"I should go now," she said. Yes, she should leave before she told him something she shouldn't. Despite her need to go, she couldn't move. "I guess I should personally thank you for agreeing to be my Prince Charming tonight."

Back off, Ella. Dangerous territory. Get out now while you still have a chance, her mind warned.

Her breath halted in her lungs as he suddenly reached up and caressed the bite he'd given her earlier. His intimate touch created sparkles of warmth. In all the excitement she'd forgotten about the mark. Realized she'd have to find a way to cover it up tomorrow at work so he wouldn't see it.

"I apologize if I went too far. I just couldn't resist you."

Ella swallowed. "I . . . I've never had better," she admitted truthfully.

"I know you're upset about Merck. Maybe I should take you back to my place until you've calmed down."

Oh, God, how she'd love to go back to his place.

"No, I'm sorry. I'm sort of interested in someone." *You idiot! Tell him you're interested in him! Tell him he's everything you've ever dreamed of. Everything you've ever fantasized about. Only better.*

"Sort of interested? Meaning?"

"He's engaged."

"But he's not married. Maybe you would still have a chance with him if you told him your true feelings? I am assuming he doesn't know?"

"No," she admitted, wondering how in the world they'd gotten onto this subject.

"You should tell him. He may feel the same way about you. Maybe he's very attracted to you. You're a beautiful woman."

Oh my gosh. Roarke thinks I'm beautiful? Or does he think Sinderella is beautiful?

"Without the mask, I'm different," she admitted.

"With or without the mask, you're still attractive. You still taste the same. Talk the same. Act the same. Sexy. Beautiful."

Warmth scuttled over her cheeks.

"You're blushing."

"I'm sorry."

"No, don't be. It's very sexy."

Blushing is sexy? Her breathing went shallow.

His intense gaze held her captive. "Does this guy you're interested in know that you do this Sinderella show?"

"I've never told him."

"Why not?"

God! Was he persistent or what?

"Because he might not understand?"

"Hmm. How do you know unless you tell him?"

"It's too big of a chance to take. If I tell him, then he'll know what I do. If he doesn't understand . . ." If he didn't understand, he'd laugh at her. He'd think of her as being a big fool. She'd be devastated. For Roarke not to know might be easier for both of them.

His hand came up and a thumb caressed one corner of her mouth, making her heart pick up speed and her insides quiver with need.

"Is he the jealous type?"

She'd never really thought about that. Was Roarke the jealous type? Would he consider her a slut for having oral sex with strange men? All her fantasies had been about him loving her. Sinderella hadn't been in the picture. Maybe because she had been fantasizing and not really considering reality. That's why she'd never seriously thought about it.

"I don't know if he is," she answered truthfully.

"Why not tell me why you sing and dance and perform in such a luscious story? Then I could tell you from a man's perspective if he might have a problem with it."

Here was her chance to find out exactly what Roarke would think about her. It was an opportunity she might never have again.

"There is one main reason why I perform."

In answer he quirked an eyebrow. The sight made her belly flutter. He looked so sexy when he did that.

"Being?"

She didn't know why she hesitated. But she did. It wasn't as if she had anything to lose. She actually felt quite comfortable speaking to Roarke with her face hidden. It seemed as if he were suddenly a good friend, a confidant. Hell! He really had no idea he was talking to his klutzy coworker.

"I feel free when I perform," she admitted. "During my formative years I put all my time into working toward a career. It left me with no social skills with men and so now I hide behind my mask." There she'd said it. She'd bared her heart for him and it hadn't even hurt.

"I see." Was that disappointment in his voice? "I'd say the whole thing lies on the premise if this man you're interested in is a jealous type or not. If he is the jealous type, then he would have a very hard time with it, especially if he knew other men were sexually satisfying you and he was at home waiting in the wings so to speak. That wouldn't go over too well."

Shit! How could she find out if Roarke was the jealous type? She could come straight out and ask him. Couldn't she?

"If he's not the jealous type," he continued, "then your relationship probably wouldn't work out. It means he doesn't care enough or love you enough."

"Oh." Now she was more confused than ever.

"But if the man were me . . ."

Ella's breath halted in her lungs as she anxiously awaited his answer.

"But he isn't me so you wouldn't need my opinion on the matter."

Her hopes deflated.

"You said you had a main reason. That means you have other reasons?"

"Well, actually, yes. A very important reason. The money I make I donate anonymously to some local charities for young girls and women."

His eyes widened for a split second and he looked as if he might be surprised at her answer, but then he smiled easily.

"I'd say that's a noble and understandable cause that your man would certainly understand."

Suddenly Caprice's voice echoed down the hall. She was coming back to see how Ella was doing.

"I really have to go."

"So you wish to remain a mystery to me?"

God! Of course, she didn't want to remain a mystery to him. Especially after what he'd just said about understanding why she wished to keep her identity a secret.

But she had no choice. She didn't want to break his engagement. Whatever gave her the idea that she could? She'd seen his fiancée's picture. She was beautiful. Voluptuous. A looker. And his fiancée didn't have the Sinderella skeleton in her closet like Ella did.

"Ella, come on, honey. I'll walk you to the car." Caprice stood in the doorway.

Before he could say anything else, she headed for the door. She half expected him to follow as she left with Caprice.

He didn't.

Disappointment rocked her, and by the time her friend had her safely tucked inside the car and waved goodbye to her, Ella allowed the tears to burst free.

God! She'd really made a mess of her life, hadn't she?

Tonight she'd had oral sex with the man of her fantasies, had almost gotten raped by that bastard Merck and now she was letting her Prince Charming go. She was simply no good for his career. That is if he truly had wanted her and not Sinderella as he'd said.

Roarke listened to the grandfather clock in the hallway ring the twelve bells.

Midnight.

For real this time.

Frustration grabbed at him. Instincts told him he should follow her home and confront her.

Fuck! Why had he allowed her to go so easily? Because Merck's house wasn't the place to tell her how much he wanted her.

He'd wait. But not for long.

He turned to leave when a shimmer on the floor caught his eye.

Sinderella's nipple ring with the glass slipper. She must have dropped it again on her way out.

Roarke frowned and picked up the delicate item.

Now he understood how Prince Charming must have felt when the real Cinderella had left the Prince's ball.

Shitty. Real fucking shitty.

SIX

HEN SHE'D FIRST COME to work at Cinder her stepfamily had stuck her in an office in the doldrums of the hospital. They thought she'd be intimidated at being told there hadn't been any more office space in the mainstream area of the hospital her father had created. Instead, they'd accommodated her with a spot in the basement. In an empty room.

She hadn't been put off. Not in the least.

She craved solitude and her cozy office allowed her the quiet she needed to do her paperwork quickly and efficiently. Of course, the way she'd decorated it had helped. She'd done it in one weekend. Had painted the back brick wall in a soft yellow and done the rest of her office in a cheerful wallpaper that made it look like an artist had dumped red, green and yellow paint everywhere.

Of course, her stepmother had been horrified, but Ella had forced herself to take a stand. Had refused to submit to having a painter come in and drown her artistic endeavor with puke green paint as everyone else's office had been decorated in.

As if she could call a bile green color as being decorative. She'd further mutinied by purchasing a gorgeous desk with steel legs topped with a thick sheet of clear glass. It housed her bright red designer computer. She'd also lugged into the colorful mix her comfy yet tattered ergonomic computer chair. Sleek white miniblinds hung on the wired glass window of her office door, ensuring her privacy.

Lining the wide hallway just outside her door, she kept her huge floor-to-ceiling filing cabinet with her patients' files.

Speaking of patients, she'd just been given China Smith's lab results and was in the process of scrutinizing it when Roarke's soft voice zipped through the air making her breath still in her chest.

"Why don't you turn that frown upside down?"

Her head snapped up and she watched, transfixed by those gorgeously wide shoulders, as he strolled into her office and stopped in front of her glass desk.

The muscles in her lower belly clenched wickedly as his masculine scent swept around her, capturing her, making her tremble with fierce need.

"I just looked in on China. She's doing exceptionally well. She can be released soon," he said.

It was late in the day and he had that sexy stubble of beard growing. God! It made him look so much like a bad boy!

Ella cleared her suddenly dry throat.

"I know. I've just been looking at her latest test results. She and the baby are going to make it."

"And the reason for your frown is?"

"She's homeless unless she returns to her pimp, which she is considering. I'm racking my brains trying to get her some help. If

I can get her deemed as an adult and get her welfare, she can find an apartment—"

"There are other options."

"If you're talking about sending her back to her family, that's totally out of the question. She ran away in the first place because her stepfather was sexually abusing her."

Now it was Roarke's turn to frown. "We can get her into foster care."

"Won't happen. I already mentioned it, and she doesn't trust adults."

"She trusted you . . ."

"Only because she heard about me through a good friend, or she wouldn't have come here. She trusts no one in any type of authority. Her stepfather is a cop . . . she's afraid if she does trust any adult in authority, the same thing will happen to her again."

"And being a prostitute is different?" he snapped. His eyes blazed with a sudden burst of anger that rattled Ella.

"Her pimp is fifteen," she explained.

Roarke swore softly.

She wasn't normally a person who pried into other people's business, but the look of anguish flaring across Roarke's face made her bold.

"Sounds to me like China's story has hit a nerve. You care to tell me about it?"

"You want to tell me why you're wearing a silk scarf around your neck?"

She froze at his question.

"The scarf makes you look quite sexy," he continued. "But personally, I prefer to see your neck bare."

She found herself searching his green eyes. The hurt was still there, but it sparkled amid other emotions.

Lust. Desire. Sexual need.

"Do you always use changing the subject as a self-defense mechanism?" she whispered, suddenly understanding Roarke the man. He wasn't as complicated as she'd thought. There was another side to him just as she'd suspected.

"You're a quick study, aren't you?" he grumbled, but she noted the sweet pull of amusement tipping his lips.

"Only when you show me your tender side," she admitted. She found herself answering his smile and felt her old glasses move down the bridge of her nose as they always seemed to do lately. Quickly she pressed the metal frame against the bridge of her nose and caught him watching her. Suddenly she could barely breathe.

"You look really sexy when you do that, Ella."

"I do?"

His comment totally caught her off guard.

"Very sexy."

Oh dear.

He smiled. "I can get China into a home for unwed mothers. I have pull there. I run it."

"Oh? You run it?"

He didn't strike her as the type of a man who'd actually do something like that. Obviously she had a lot to learn about him.

"You sound surprised that I actually have a heart."

His eyes appeared to have darkened as he looked at her.

"Um . . ." Gosh she didn't know what to say.

He turned and headed back for the door again. For a moment

she thought she'd offended him by not saying anything and now he was leaving, but he didn't go.

He stared at the closed door for a moment and said softly, "You really should get a lock for the door."

Her heart thundered at the sound of his thick voice. He turned around and she instantly recognized *that* look. The searing look that made her face flame.

He wanted her.

As he came toward her, she felt nervous. Boy, did she feel nervous!

His big size made the room seem awfully small.

"Wouldn't want us to get interrupted."

Her eyes widened at his statement.

Sweet shit! He wouldn't try anything in her office, would he? Her pussy tightened at that thought.

"I guess I should tell you the truth about why I accepted this position at Cinder."

Ella blinked in confusion. One minute he acted sexy as sin, the next minute he was in confession mode.

"I know your father left you as a co-owner, but I don't feel disloyal telling you that I took this job strictly for the money and I don't really give two shits about the rich snobs who Cinder targets."

"You don't?"

"No, and I'm pretty sure you don't either."

He slipped his lab coat off and let it fall to the floor. He began to unbutton his shirt.

Oh my goodness!

"I need the money for a home I help run with my mother. The

state only gives us a certain amount and we have a tendency of using it up before the end of the allocated period. The government doesn't seem to realize how much prenatal care girls really need when they are pregnant. So I took this job to help finance my dream."

"Which is?"

He shrugged out of his shirt. She couldn't seem to keep her eyes off his naked chest. Couldn't forget the feel of the hard bunch of chest muscles she'd touched last night.

"A soft place for teenage mothers to fall is our dream. A soft place my mother didn't have forty years ago when she was at the age of fourteen raped by a neighbor. Scandal forced her onto the streets."

"You were a product of rape?"

"No, my brother was. When she was on the streets, a pimp got his clutches into her. He forced her to give him up after he was born. She's never been able to find him. He brainwashed her, stole her self-esteem and used her for almost five years before she ran off with a john of hers. They got married and I'm one of two kids they had. My mom was one of the lucky ones."

Ella swallowed. "I'm so sorry about what happened to her when she was young."

"Don't be."

His fingers were now unbuttoning the stud at the waist of his jeans.

Oh dear!

"My mother always says bad things happen for a reason. You just have to search for the positive side and use it to your advantage. If things hadn't happened the way they did, then my mother wouldn't have told me her stories and I wouldn't have this passion to help unwed mothers. My girls wouldn't have A Soft Place To Fall."

"That's the charity—" She cut herself off. She'd been about to tell him that's one of the charities she donated her Sinderella money to.

The sound of his zipper made her return her attention to his waist. His jeans were now open, riding low on his hips, exposing a tight pair of black underwear and a delicious arrow of crisp, black curls.

Ella blew out a tense breath.

"But don't let those she-devil stepsisters or stepmother know, they just might have a heart attack that their colleague might actually have a life outside of Cinder, unlike themselves."

He stood very close to her now.

"I'm good at keeping secrets," she found herself whispering.

"I know you are."

His hand was at her neck, untying the knot on her scarf. Before she could even simulate thoughts in her mind to find some form of protest, her neck was bare.

Roarke's eyes blazed. "Just as I suspected. Sinderella, I presume." He stroked a lone finger along her sore hickey, the brand he'd left on her neck last night.

His breathing seemed rough now. Uneven.

Her heart pounded. Roarke knew her secret!

"How did you know? When did you start to suspect?"

"You had me the instant I first heard you singing. Deep down, somewhere inside me, I knew it was you, but I just couldn't believe sensuous Sinderella was the same as sexy-as-sin Ella, the woman I've been craving to fuck since the first day I saw you."

Ella's cheeks flushed with heat.

"What about your fiancée?"

"Actually she's my younger sister who lives overseas. We had pictures done the last time she came for a visit. I used one of them."

Holy! He was unattached. There was nothing keeping her from pursuing him. The idea seemed overwhelming. Almost too good to be true.

"You didn't name any names last night when you mentioned the charities you donate to, but I'm assuming you are the anonymous donor for A Soft Place To Fall."

"I am," she confessed.

"My girls appreciate your help. We'd be hurting without your generosity, Ella."

His fierce gaze never left her face as his finger moved lazily up her flushed check to caress her chin. She trembled at his soft touch.

"I can think of one hell of a good way to thank you for donating to our cause."

"I don't expect any thanks. I do it because I enjoy giving."

"And I enjoy receiving."

Sparks of hunger speared through her as he leaned down and his lips slid hungrily against hers. She couldn't even think to hesitate when he yanked her to her feet beside him.

His mouth remained erotically fused with hers, his tongue dueled with hers.

Hunger gnawed deep inside her empty cunt. His hard body pressed against hers, firing her arousal.

He broke the kiss. His eyes blazed as his fingers quickly opened her blouse. Her breasts were swelling against her bra. Cool air washed over her suddenly bare shoulders as he pulled the blouse off. His hot fingers curled beneath the elastic of her pants, his touch searing her skin, making her cry out at its intensity. With a quick, desperate tug, he had her pants down around her ankles. Then her thong underwear joined them.

He jerked both of them and her shoes off her feet.

She cried out as he lifted her and slammed her bare ass upon her cool, glass table. Reaching around her, he unclasped her bra and whipped it aside. They were both breathing roughly, the sounds shooting through her office like bullets. She could feel the slick juices escape her vagina, probably smearing her tabletop.

He spread her legs wide. Stepped between them. The sight of his heavily muscled chest just about made her come on the spot. His eyes were wild. So wild.

She watched as he slipped his jeans and underwear down over his hips releasing his cock.

Thick and long, the huge bald head flushed an angry purple. Her nipples hardened at the sight, her pussy creamed more.

"You're so fucking beautiful, Ella." His voice sounded strangled, heavy. His eyes glittered with lust. "I want you so fucking bad. I can't wait any longer. I've held myself back for so long. Pretending not to care just because I didn't want to mix business with pleasure. Too many months of fantasizing."

She fought for breath at his admission. He'd wanted her just as badly as she wanted him?

Oh yes! There was a God!

"I want to bind you. Whip you. Fuck you a hundred different ways. I want you to be my fantasy girl, Ella. Every day, every night."

Ella couldn't stop herself from moaning as she remembered her own fantasy scenes with the same themes.

"Last night when I saw Merck touching you against your will, I wanted to kill him. I don't want another man near you. I am the jealous type. I care too much about you to let another day go by without showing you how I've felt about you all this time. I want to be your man and your Prince Charming in your future Sinderella productions."

Her pussy spasmed as he stroked the long length of his cock. Her body heated with longing.

"You haven't officially been interviewed for the position of my Prince Charming," she teased.

"Then we'll do an interview now. You can let me know later if I passed. Lie back on the desk."

His unexpected order made her blink in confusion. This was happening way too fast. She could barely get her mind around the fact that she sat naked on her office desk in front of Roarke without her mask and his fierce, hungry gaze was zeroed in right between her legs.

"Trust me, sweet Sin."

She loved his nickname for her and did as he asked, lying backward on the table, the smooth, cool glass caressing her ass and back.

She yelped as his hot hands sidled around her ankles and he hoisted her legs up, spreading them as he placed them over his rock-hard shoulders.

"Play with your breasts," he ordered.

As he watched her, she did as he said. Her heart pounded out of control as she looked down at her two mounds and touched her sensitive nipples. She didn't wear her nipple rings today because her nipples were still so sensitive from Roarke's attentions last night.

The instant she pinched the tips, pleasure flared.

"Keep playing with yourself," he demanded.

She did. She watched her breasts swell and her nipples turn hard and rosy beneath his fierce stare and her intimate touches. She cried out as an unexpected finger smoothed over her clit, unleashing the carnal cravings lusting inside her. It took him only seconds and he had her on fire, her pussy soaked and aching to be filled, and her breaths reduced to cries.

With a growl he thrust inside her.

Deep. Hard. Intense.

Ella exploded. *Oh God! This feels too fucking good to be real!*

Erotic pleasure tore through her as Roarke's thick, powerful cock plunged in and out of her, making her breasts bounce wildly beneath her hands. Suctioning sounds split the air. The scent of her sex filled her nostrils.

"Oh yes! Roarke, fuck me! Fuck me harder!" she gasped, and kept pinching and tugging her sore nipples, tossing her head to and fro, thoroughly enjoying the carnal spasms making her tremble.

Suddenly from the corner of her eye she detected movement. Realized the office door had opened. Someone was standing there! Her stepmother! And her two evil stepsisters!

"Oh, God!" she cried out, stunned at the increasing arousal screaming through her at knowing the bitches were watching Roarke fuck her.

Another climax gripped her. Lust, raw and carnal roared through her. She closed her eyes and drowned in the pleasure that Roarke's wickedly delicious cock gave so freely. His finger continued to massage her ultrasensitive clit and he just kept pumping into her.

Hard and fierce just as she'd asked. Oh yes! Beautiful!

"Get the fuck out of here!" she heard Roarke growl at them. But he didn't miss a beat as he continued to pleasure her.

"This is shocking behavior!" her stepmother stuttered.

"What Ella and I do in the privacy of her own office is none of your fucking business. Get the fuck out! Now! And knock next time."

The slamming of the door barely registered as Roarke continued with his deliciously hard thrusts. Her pussy continued to spasm. Her body lost in a storm of pleasure.

"First thing we do is get a lock on that door," he ground out. His hips pumped faster, his cock roared in and out, driving Ella to more carnal sensations.

"I want you to be the woman of my fantasies, Ella, and I want to be the man in yours."

"You already are my fantasy man," she admitted.

He grinned that incredible sexy grin she loved, and when she started coming down from her third fantastic orgasmic high, she felt Roarke's hot jets of sperm filling her.

EPILOGUE

Several weeks later . . .

*A*T THE SOUND OF the door to the examination room opening and closing softly, Ella bit down on the ball gag in her mouth with wicked anticipation. Oh God! Roarke was here!

Roarke, who'd turned out to be a more fierce lover than even her wildest fantasy. After the day her stepmother and stepsisters had caught Roarke making love to her in her office, Ella had gloated at their envious looks.

He'd invited her to move in with him and they'd been practically and literally inseparable ever since. From that time on, she'd also learned that having people watching her have sex was only one of her many sexual fetishes. She enjoyed being whipped, craved being taken by Roarke compliments of the doggie style and loved having her nipples clamped.

By day they continued to work at Cinder Hospital catering to the rich and snobby, yet slowly implementing new rules using her part ownership in the hospital to loosen restrictions so Ella could care for low-income and homeless pregnant girls and women who needed them the most.

Some evenings she helped Roarke and his charming mother at A Soft Place To Fall. His father worked there also. He was a tall, older version of Roarke, extremely jovial and fun to be around. His mother was sweet and so affectionate that she felt safe and loved by the older woman who Ella believed would have been an ideal mother for herself.

A few nights a month she also continued being Sinderella with a disguised Roarke as her Prince Charming. Despite Merck not being involved any longer, the carnal act had expanded quickly based on word-of-mouth alone. They always closed to a standing ovation.

When Roarke got her alone, he continued to surprise her with a variety of delightful pleasures such as tonight when he'd brought her to one of the examination rooms at the hospital that contained a rigged-up gyno table where he'd instructed her in what to do to ready herself for him.

"All ready for your examination, Ella?" His deep voice ripped her back to the present and her pussy spasmed with excitement. She swallowed at the rustle of clothing being removed and blew out a shaky breath through her nose at the sound of his bare feet padding closer to her.

Her cheeks warmed as he suddenly stood beside the gyno table where he'd instructed her to strap her feet into the cool, silver stirrups and to lash restraints over and under her breasts securing her.

She inhaled a quivering breath as Roarke's hand smoothed over her wrist, bringing it to her side. The snap of Velcro quickly followed and she automatically pulled against her bond. Nothing budged. He did the same with her other wrist, binding her. Making her his captive. Putting her at his total mercy.

Oh boy.

"You okay?"

Ella nodded. Bondage was something she'd always wanted to try. Now she had the chance.

I trust you, her mind whispered. Her body tingled at the warmth flooding through her. She was lusciously naked and ready for Roarke's intimate exam.

"Let's start with your breasts."

She couldn't help but whimper around the gag as he looked at her full mounds. Her nipples responded immediately to his hungry gaze, blushing a beautiful burgundy color as they hardened into knots.

"Very nice. I can see your breasts are in great condition."

Did she detect huskiness in his otherwise confident voice? For a moment he left her view, and when he came back he held a small whip in his hand.

Oh sweet mercy!

Her pussy contracted. Creamed in anticipation.

"You ready?"

She nodded. Braced herself.

The whishing sound of the whip sailed through the air. Pain snapped into her left nipple. She jerked in reaction. Watched her tip turn red with anger. Her tummy clenched. Her pussy grew warm.

Pulsed.

More lashes. This time on her breasts. Blistering heat mixed with pain. She bucked against her restraints with every lash.

Bright red stripes interlaced her globes. By the time he finished with her breasts they burned and her pussy was creaming up a storm.

"Are you horny, Ella?" His strangled question made her avert from his lusty gaze. Heat fused her face. Her body tightened with exquisite need.

"No answer? Hmm, I guess I'll have to examine your pussy."

Ella's thighs tightened with need as Roarke moved to the foot of the table. Her legs were spread wide. Her feet held captive by stirrups and her heart pumped madly at the anticipation in his green eyes when he noticed the wide base of the butt plug in her ass.

"Very nice, Ella," he complimented.

She bit against the ball gag as his hands glided softly along her inner thighs toward her pussy and her plugged anus.

A single finger smoothed over her clit, bringing instant pleasure.

"You're so fucking responsive, Ella," he groaned. She knew he loved the way she reacted so quickly to his touch. Knew it meant she craved him just as much as he yearned for her.

His finger dipped into her vagina, smoothing back and forth, massaging her G-spot until she shivered and whimpered beneath his sensual touches.

The pleasure built swiftly and she twisted against her restraints.

Please! Fuck me! Her mind screamed. God! She loved Roarke so much. Loved the things he did to her body, the sexy way he made her feel.

"Let's get rid of that butt plug so I can fuck your tight little ass, shall we?"

She nodded eagerly, her mind screaming at him to hurry. She'd always wanted to experience anal penetration, but hadn't had the nerve to ask. When he'd broached the subject several weeks ago, she readily agreed. She'd worn the various sizes of plugs. Allowing them to stretch her, to fill her, prepare her for him.

The last one, the huge one was just about as big as his cock and now lay buried inside her rear end.

"Before I fuck your tight little ass, I've got a present for you."

Her eyes widened as he produced a large, black glass wand. It looked to be about ten glorious inches long with a straight shaft at least two inches wide with one half-inch smooth swirls and dots webbed along the entire length. And the stylized, round glass head looked so wonderfully huge.

"I had it made just for you, sweet Sin. I call it the pleasure rod."

Heat spread through her as he dipped the glass wand between her legs. While he massaged her clit with the round head, she groaned at the pleasure the rod created.

A moment later she felt the sex toy pushing into her. Stretching her. Making her moan as the smooth ridges and dots caressed her insides.

He began to thrust it in and out of her. She arched her hips, silently demanding more pleasure. Wanting harder thrusts.

"You are insatiable, Ella. I love that about you. I love everything about you," Roarke groaned.

And then the glass wand stopped, and through her sexual

haze, she heard the slurpy sounds of Roarke dipping his fingers into the jar of lubricant she'd noticed earlier on the nearby table when she'd first entered the exam room. She whimpered her excitement as he liberally applied the lube to his cock. Smearing every glorious inch of his thick, pulsing, rigid piece of flesh.

She found herself flushing as he leaned forward, felt the butt plug move. Strange sensations she rather liked gripped her anus as he slowly pulled the object from her body.

His breathing had quickened. Her heart raced with anticipation. She groaned around the ball gag as a generously lubed finger thrust inside her ass, pressing past her now loosened sphincter muscle. Despite his finger feeling so small compared to the huge plug, incredible sensations wrapped around her as he moved in an erotically slow exploration. He groaned. "I can't wait to fuck your sweet little ass."

The glass wand was on the move again, slipping across her engorged clit with a delightfully hard rub.

Sweet pleasure flared in her pussy.

"Your virgin ass isn't going to be that way for much longer, Sexy Sin."

Roarke slipped another generously lubed finger into her anus making her moan at the foreign intrusion of two hot, slippery fingers widening her. Invading her.

He slipped the glass wand into her tight cunt. The large ball stretching her. Filling her soaked pussy.

In no time flat he had her moaning at a gentle yet insistent rhythm of both her channels being gloriously filled. Her thighs clenched tightly. Her body hummed.

Oh wow! It felt unbelievable.

"I can tell by your wide eyes, you are pleased."

Pleased was an understatement! She bit down on the ball gag as a third lubed finger thrust into her tender ass.

Oh God! His fingers were stretching her ass so incredibly full. The glass wand slurped in and out of her snug cunt making Ella moan beneath the dual thrusts.

Perspiration dotted her skin. Her harsh breaths came fast and tortured.

"And now, Sweet Sin, brace yourself."

She whimpered as he withdrew his fingers with a slurp and guided his angry-looking, stiff cock closer to her splayed-out body. When the hot, lubricated cock head pushed against her sphincter, she couldn't help but cry against the gag in wonder at the odd sensation.

Keeping the glass rod impaled inside her soaked cunt, he pushed his long, thick cock into her ass. Immediately his face became an image of tortured pleasure. And he'd barely penetrated her.

"Oh yes, Ella. Your ass is so tight."

He pushed into her ass farther. She felt her eyes widen in wonder at the sudden burst of pleasure-pain.

He'd warned her about it. Warned her to simply keep herself relaxed and breathe into it. And that's exactly what she did. She focused on the pleasure-pain while he kept his hungry gaze glued to her face, to her eyes, watching her carefully.

She knew he searched for her safe signal of three rapid eye blinks for him to stop if she felt she couldn't endure it. But she didn't want him to stop. The exquisite intermingling of pleasure mixed with sweet pain had her craving for more.

His thick cock filled her ass—her muscles eagerly gripped his hard, hot length. Her thighs clenched as his hard cock burrowed deeper.

Sweet mercy but he was long! She could feel every hard, delicious inch of his rigid flesh buried deep inside her.

He kept the wand on the move. His thrusts becoming quicker, fiercer. The smooth glass ridges seared into her vagina, making her forget exactly how big an intruder his cock felt as he impaled her ass.

Without warning he pulled his cock out and speared back into her again. She whimpered at the brilliant onslaught. The dual thrusts became faster. Erotic sensations flared. Her body tightened, flared with wicked pleasure.

She closed her eyes and breathed into the glowing eroticism as it exploded all around her.

Sweet carnal sensations.

She convulsed beneath his hard thrusts. Exquisite spasms tore through her. She could barely assimilate what was happening.

"Beautiful, Sin! Just fucking beautiful!" Roarke's pleased voice ground out so far away.

As he came inside her, she simply allowed herself to float into the erotic bliss all the while her mind kept repeating over and over again, *Oh yes, Fairy Godmother, I believe.*

I believe in the magic of miracles because my miracle came true.